APPALOOSA
RISING
OR
THE LEGEND
OF THE COWBOY
BUDDHA

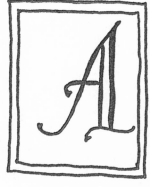

APPALOOSA RISING OR THE LEGEND OF THE COWBOY BUDDHA

by Gino Sky

Doubleday & Company, Inc.
Garden City, New York
1980

All of the characters
in this book are fictitious

Parts of this book
have been published in *Jonquil Rose,*
Five Trees Press, San Francisco, 1976;
Northwest America, Boise, Idaho, 1979;
Penthouse magazine, New York, 1980.

Library of Congress Cataloging in Publication Data
Sky, Gino.
Appaloosa Rising.

I. Title.
PZ4.S619737Ap [PS3569.K9]
ISBN: 0-385-15386-4 Trade
0-385-15387-2 Paperbound
Library of Congress Catalog Card Number 79–7810

This book is dedicated to my two
daughters, Roan Krishna and Appaloosa
Shoni, my most favorite of sidekicks;
to my grandmother, the old Cedar Woman
with blue eyes, who taught me how to
throw my scars and calluses into a lasso
of visions; to Rosalie Sorrels, whose
music and friendship have given me the
inspiration to waltz along the banks of
the rampaging river; to Elia Haworth,
who rode point on a wild herd of Cowboy
Buddha dreams as she helped me discover
the Himalayan pass from Tibet to Cheyenne;
to my Sweetheart of the West, who rides
the Appaloosa spirit within the songs
of the Six-gun Owl; and to all of my
good friends who have lived with me at
the Cowboy Buddha Hotel—this book is for
you and the mountains forever.

CONTENTS

1	Jus' One More Cowboy	11
2	The Complete Trombone History of Mankind	21
3	The Cool Earth Loves You	31
4	The First Light of Sunday	55
5	Save the Last Dance for Me	65
6	A Weaver of Light	93
7	The Floating Rose	115
8	Black Rose of the Yin	155
9	The Fat Mystic's Film Festival	167
10	Sun Trine the Gods	189
11	The Wild Tibetan Yonder	243

APPALOOSA
RISING
OR
THE LEGEND
OF THE COWBOY
BUDDHA

Jus' One More Cowboy

I'm jus' one more cowboy
sometimes high, sometimes low

Al Jacobs

It was Saturday evening, and the first day of summer. Jonquil Rose had been working at the Sleeping Beauty Ranch all day getting ready to move five hundred head of cattle up to the summer range. He was tired, damn near wore out, and ready for a good time at the bar. But first he was going home to have a steaming hot bath, a steak three feet thick and blood rare, a massage by his lovely one-quarter Apache wife, Infinity Cactus, and a good quiet smoke. And maybe, if he could round up the money, a bottle of Dickel's Sour Mash Whisky Number 12 to take the edges off all those saddle sores.

As soon as he walked through the door he knew something was wrong. The cabin, built by his grandfather back in 1888, was empty. His five-hundred-dollar saddle with an eagle on the horn was gone. His Winchester was missing, along with one of his finest possessions: a photograph of himself. The top money winner of the Bone, Idaho, Stampede standing next to the queen, Roselita Pocatello. The deer, elk, and bearskin rugs were gone. The drawers were open and empty, and the ironing board that had been standing forever in the corner had collapsed. Infinity's clothes, hair dryer, and three boxes of curlers were gone . . . and she was too.

"My God," he said to the sound of one confused cowboy, "I've been robbed and I need a drink."

The first thing he did was go over to the old icebox that antique dealers would give ten porcelain thunder mugs and two Chippendales for, hoping to find some whisky left over from last night's party. He opened it up and looked in. It was empty too, except for an unopened bottle of sour mash whisky and one lonely note. Jonquil opened the bottle, threw down twelve gulps in one swallow, and then he sat down on the pine floor and read the note.

> Dear Jonquil Rose . . . Jus' One More Cowboy. I have just run away with a baby-blue-eyed hippy mountain climber from Los Angeles. I know you'll never be able to understand, but if you'll drink this bottle of whisky the hangover in your head will be greater than the pain in your heart. I sold your saddle, rugs, and your antique Winchester for two one-way tickets to Nepal. Please don't try to find us, but then I know you're so insensitive you don't even know where Nepal is. I still love you, and I hope we can be friends someday. But right now, I've got to explore my own destiny. Just remember,

I'm a person too, you goddam, arrogant, cowpoke bull-shitter. I sincerely hope your balls get caught on the barbed wire of life!!!

Love and hugs,

Infinity Cactus

P.S. Everything is Everything

Jonquil finished the rest of the whisky in one more long, slow swallow, and then he tried to stand up. It took him three tries, and a helluva lot of swearing, and then he broke every handmade pine chair in the cabin. His grandfather, Toofast Goodnight, was probably cheering him on. (Once, Jonquil's grandma tried to run away with a train engineer from Boise, and Grandpa shot that wife-snatcher right between his heart and holy ghost just as he was helping Grandma onto the train.) After breaking all of the furniture in the cabin, he still didn't feel any better, so he tucked his shirt into his Levi's, straightened his collar, punched the dents out of his Stetson, and walked out the door in a strange spiral to his 1955 Jimmy maroon pickup with four on the floor and compound low, rear tires as fat as tree stumps, and an electric winch on the front bumper that one time at the circus had pulled twelve elephants into a big mud bog during a tug of war. He loved that pickup almost as much as he loved his Appaloosa, Mariposa Lily. He reached under the front seat and pulled out his six-gun and holster, and with a gunslinger's smirk popped the wheel, spun it seven times, and slammed it home. Then he jumped into his 1955 Jimmy maroon pickup and headed for town.

Except for Cutbank, Montana, the town of Stanley is the loneliest, coldest town in the U.S. of A. But on Saturday nights it's the hottest spot for six hundred square miles. Three bars, and three Country and Western bands playing like there was no tomorrow, the day after, or any other night but Saturday night.

The town of Stanley is six thousand feet high right in the middle of a large basin surrounded by the Boulder, White Cloud, and Sawtooth mountains—the headwaters of the Salmon River. In the winter you need a rope, a dog team, and a sled to find the outhouse, and in the summer the grass and flowers will bury a short horse and rider in ten seconds flat. Big fat clouds float around looking like the Quaker on the Quaker Oats box. The streets are unpaved, and when a drunken cowboy named Jonquil Rose, Jus' One More Cowboy, comes booming into town in high gear at sixty miles an hour, even the tourists get dusty.

Jonquil slid sideways into the hitching post of the Quick Draw Saloon, stopped on a pile of road apples, and jumped out. He threw his sweat-whipped hat into the air and before it hit the ground he had five holes through it. The sixth bullet had shot down the only neon sign in town, which had been put up on V-D Day, 1945.

"Who in the hell wants a fight?" he yelled to the twenty people standing on the wooden sidewalk. He twirled his six-gun and dropped it into the holster. "Fuck-off ya sonsahbitches! B'fore the night's over I'm gunna have me a hippy mountain climber's ass nailed to the outhouse wall. And, if I can't git me a hippy mountain climber I'll git me a nice fat tourist with yellow shorts. Drinks on the house!" he yelled to the town as he walked into the bar.

His two closest sidekicks, Johnny Donner and Slug Hornet, made a bet between themselves that they would have Jonquil passed out and sleeping like a newborn calf by midnight. On Saturday nights they usually took a hit of acid and polished off a bottle of Dickel's Sour Mash Whisky waiting for sunrise. But tonight, they knew they had to be on their toes with Jonquil Rose waving that pistol under every stranger's nose asking them if they were a hippy mountain climber from Los Angeles. So they only took some El-S-Dee, and made a cowboy pact to stay alert and sober until Jonquil was tucked away dreaming of rodeo queens and beautiful buckarinas.

They were also the sheriff and deputy so it didn't do the tourists one goddam bit of good to complain to the law.

"Listen here, you two-bit gravel eater, that buckaroo in there is the sweetest, finest high-rollin' roper and bareback rider in the goddam state. And we ain't gonna do a thing about trying to stop him from nailing a tourist or a mountain climber to the shithouse wall. That cowboy in there has a hurt, a deep hurt, and he needs to burn it out, kick ass and explode. Now, if you want to be some self-righteous broomtail, go in there and try and take that six-popper away from him. But, if you get yer balls shot off, don't come crawlin' back to us askin' for a Band-Aid or a reefund. Now git the hell out of here!" They kicked the tourist with the yellow shorts in the ass and walked into the bar.

"Can you believe, can you ever imagine that my whoa-man, my sweet lovin' brown-eyed one-quarter Apache squaw, would run off to Knee . . . whatever that fuckin' place is with a son-of-a-bitchin' applegrabber? Hell and goddam! I knew she was a person, but I didn't know she wanted to explore her own destiny. I always thought she was 'fraid of the dark. She never wanted to go to the outhouse alone . . . 'fraid the bears would git her. Oh, shit 'n' shinola!" Jonquil turned the bottle upside down and let the whisky run down his face and all over the floor. "Ah . . . stick that right into yer Toni Lamas, you bastards!" he grumbled to the mirror.

"Well, I bet he wears those funny-fuckin' square-toed boots that look so weird only a mother could love," Johnny Donner mumbled into the top of Jonquil's hat. Jonquil spun around and executed a quicker-than-the-eye-quick-draw and stuck the barrel of his forty-four into the guts of Johnny Donner. "Listen here, ya meat-eatin' high-roller, jus' because you got yer high school deeploma don't mean ya can tell me what to do! Now drink this whisky made from the sweetest mash in Tennessee and from the tears of the Cowboy Buddha and shut up! I promise I ain't gunna do too much damage to yer town tonight . . . I'm jus' gunna have some fun cuz somebody's gunna pay." Jonquil pulled the brim of his shot-up Stetson down low with the gun sight and looked out from under the shadow. "Any mountain climbers lurkin' 'round?"

Johnny slapped Jonquil on the back and ordered another bottle. He was rolling with the acid, and all he saw were halos and auras, visions of women smiling high in the sky with sourdough biscuits for clouds. "Sheeeet," he said to Slug Hornet, "it's gunna be one of those good nights once again."

The moon was full. Those high Buddha clouds were hanging around being soft and warm. It was almost midnight and Jonquil Rose was still sloshing down the whisky with one sidekick on each flank to answer all questions, help soothe the sorrow, and keep his six-gun from nailing a toe or a tourist.

That night Jonquil was the best show in town, and the house was packed. The word had gone out that a drunken cowboy was out to shoot up the town, and the Winnebagos were bumper to bumper trying to find the action. Jonquil knew, even with all the pain in his heart, that this evening of his twenty-ninth year could be his finest hour. He had hunted the grizzly in Montana and was treed for two days and nights in a bull pine. He had hunted the moose in Canada and returned with three pet squirrels and a bobcat. He had parachuted into enemy territory in Vietnam, landing right in the middle of an opium den where he spent the next three years. He had won and lost as much as any man will ever win or lose: his pride, his dignity, and now his woman. He had two things left that he loved as much as he loved his two sidekicks: his 1955 Jimmy maroon pickup with four on the floor and compound low, and his Appaloosa, Mariposa Lily.

There is no whisky strong enough to kill pain forever, just one night at a time. And sometimes only dynamite is the answer to deaden. The brain keeps grinding its gears and it doesn't matter if it's Sour Mash Whisky Number 12 or 88 once the gun is loaded, somebody's going to die. Ask any killer.

"Oh boy," Jonquil said as Johnny and Slug Hornet tightened the noose around him so he wouldn't fall over backward. "You buckaroos act like yer up to no good. I'm gittin' out of here. I'm gunna git me a mountain climber or my name ain't Jonquil Rose . . . Jus' One More Cowboy." He started for the door and everyone in the bar stood up. Three young ladies dressed in turn-of-the-century pale blue fainted; two werewolves left town; and the blackjack dealer slid under the table with the bartender's wife.

Jonquil hit the batwing doors and spun them right off their hinges, knocking them out into the dirt streets. The moon was as big as his own mother's birthday laugh, and the streets were suddenly empty. He walked up and down the road shouting, laughing, and crying at the same time. He wanted revenge. He wanted a miracle to happen, and he wanted to change the sorrow and the pain. The guides in his body, the spirits of ancestors, were telling him that the only solution was the ultimate—to take his passion as far as he had the courage to go.

Jonquil began his soliloquy: "Come on out here, ya broomtailed, back-shootin' claim jumper! I'll cut ya down so fast you'll think these bullets were made from God's own gunsmith. Git yer ass out here and you'll see one hunnerd and sixtee-five pounds of nuts, guts, and speed blow ya right off this planet. Ya might be able to climb a mountain, but by sweet mother-lovin' Cowboy Buddha I can rope it, blow it up, and eat it with my pancakes, and use you fer a toothpick. Ah . . . fuck it! Ya ain't worth the sweat from my Idaho balls." He suddenly whipped out his six-gun and yelled as loud as any man can ever yell. "Infinity, Infinity Cactus, ya bitch! Ya beautiful goddam one-quarter Apache Whoaman . . . I love ya. Can ya hear that Infinity? I love ya! I don't care if ya chain smoke, wear curlers to bed, or hate to buck hay. I love ya! You can be anything ya want to be, but fer God's sake . . . be here! I love ya, Infinity . . . I love ya."

And then, he cut loose with his long-barreled six-gun and slammed five shots right into the laughing face of the moon. He spun around, dropped to one knee, and with the aim as deadly as the Falcon's third eye he fired the last bullet into the motor of his 1955 Jimmy maroon pickup with four on the floor and compound low, and passed out right in the middle of his hometown, Stanley Basin, Idaho.

The Complete Trombone History of Mankind

Sooner or later, every buckaroo and buckarina who is a member of the Church of the Last Chance Cowboys must stand up in front of all the other members and perform, do his or her thing, no matter whether he or she has a thing or not. It doesn't make any difference if you are shy, suffering from a chronic speech impediment, a hunchback with prickly heat, a drunkard, or a dirty no-good spit-baller, eventually the Higher-ups will get you on stage and make you find an act. Yodel, cry, talk about how God saved your spinach from the earwigs, the alfalfa from the varmints, or just stand pigeon-toed and run the zipper of your fly up and down in Country Swing time . . . sooner or later, you must do something.

One hummer of a Wild West afternoon, Buddy Sunday's girl friend was struck by lightning while walking home from the rodeo. As soon as she was released from the hospital she had to stand up in front of her church members and tell them how she had been saved by God from being burned and fried like a skinny ass'd shoestring potato. And what had really saved her was a yellow plastic beanie with a red propeller that turned in the wind. The lightning melted the beanie right down into her hair and couldn't go any further. Her parents had to fix her up with a wig, false eyebrows and eyelashes, and gobs of make-up so she could stand up on Sunday morning to bear her testimony to God, Jesus, and the Phantom Rider of the West . . . the Holy Ghost.

Then, there was the time Buckarina Chute told how her husband had been run over by a freight train just south of Blackfoot. And where his secret Last Chance Chaps covered his body there wasn't a scratch on him. He was dead, but by sweet lovin' Jesus, his body had been saved from mutilation by his amazing overalls.

Everyone had a miracle. Even Buddy's friends got up and told strange stories that he knew weren't true, but he figured they had as much right to pull the bull rope as anyone else. He slowly began to realize that all you had to do to make a story become a miracle was to tell it in church laced with pipe organ music, light shining through stained glass, two women crying, a sinner on his knees, and beautiful flowers hanging in wicker baskets. And then, all dreams, visions, and good ol' bullshit became the Golden Voice of Truth. If you told the same story in a good ol' cowboy bar, you'd get thrown out on your ass in ten seconds flat. Buddy knew that someday he would have to get up there and do something, but he had no idea what he could do. He was sixteen years old, and searching for his miracle.

One week before Easter, Buddy had the strange feeling

that his theatrical virginity was going to collide head-on with destiny. He had stalled them off long enough, and the Higher-ups were running out of Truth to feed their anxious herd. That morning, Buck Higher, the bishop, found Buddy making out in the sacrament room with the sinner's daughter when he should have been gettin' the sourdough bread and Texas wine ready for the sacrament.

"Buddy, when ya goin' ta do sumthin' fur us?" he said, eying the girl.

Guilt! That was Buddy's downfall, and he fell right into the bishop's box canyon trap. His eyes were burning doughnuts through Buddy's Holy Ghost as he was patting the ass of the sinner's daughter.

"I can't do nothin'. I stutter 'n' stammer when I git in front of people, I've never had a vision, I can't read very well, and I can't even play the pedal steel. Maybe I could go out there and show 'em how to bulldog a heathen in four seconds flat . . . how 'bout that?"

As Buddy was showing the bishop how he was going to bulldog a heathen his new girl friend took off and for a lot of strange reasons she immediately joined the Reformed Church of the Last Chance Cowboys. Buck was gettin' angry, and his eyes looked like a summer storm had moved in. There was a tornado in one eye, and a hurricane in the other. No one turns down the bishop.

"I heerd you'd been takin' trumbone lessons."

"Oh, sheeeet, who told ya that?"

"Never mind! Next Sunday I want ya up there givin' us a trumbone solo."

"But I can't," Buddy said, "I don't know nothin' 'cept the scales." He suddenly felt his heart trying to sunfish right out of his mouth.

The bishop raised his body into a full ten feet of authority and power, and Buddy saw in his eyes all of the cowboys who had ever ridden the six cattle trails of Texas. He saw the stampedes, Indian bushwacks, quicksand, and rustlers, and he heard the voice of God telling the cowboys to get their dreams across the rampaging rivers. And then, he saw the bishop's tongue become the bullwhip of the Cattle Empire.

"Larn sumthin'! Pray, and perhaps God will hep ya!" And Buck Higher spurred himself out of the room so fast Buddy felt like a small, simple, and lonely pilgrim standing alone on a tall mountain after the deluge.

Buddy's trombone teacher cracked up when he told him what had happened. He said it was impossible for Buddy to learn anything that quickly and refused to help him.

All during the week Buddy tried to learn "Jesus Was the Trail Boss for God," but he couldn't hit any of the high notes, and very few of the lows. So on Saturday night he got down on his knees, and he prayed his ass off hoping for a divine revelation. And just before he finished he snuck in a little P.S. to the Cowboy Buddha . . . his secret God hero.

The next morning all of the flowers were a peacock of arrogance on this day of the triple header: Sunday, Easter, and the first day of spring. Buddy went down into the basement of the church and prepared for his debut. He shined up his old pawnshop trombone as best as he could, and he even tried to pound out a few dents with the heels of his new cowboy boots. And then, he took a gallon of bubble soap and poured it into the bell of his old trombone.

The group singing was over, and he knew he was next. He went upstairs and waited behind the altar until the bishop called his name.

"And now, Buddy Sunday will surprise us with a trumbone solo."

Buddy's knees were shaking so much the bell in the steeple began to sing, but somehow he got out in front of the congregation. He found his mother in the audience so he could get some strength by looking at her beautiful face. He even tried to say something about his search for the miracle, but his words came out sounding like a braying gargoyle. So he put his trombone up to his lips, and he closed his eyes. He said a short, air mail, special-delivery prayer to his superhero, the Cowboy Buddha, and then he blew out one of the finest bubbles in the History of the West. At first, there was a long-held silence as if a real miracle had actually happened, and then he heard a few laughs and giggles, and he opened his eyes just in time to see his mother cover up her head with her new spring coat. He saw his amazing bubble floating in the air with the first-day-of-spring-Easter sun diving right through the middle. The people stopped squirming in their seats, they stopped picking their noses and hitting their kids with songbooks, and they raised their eyes to the heavens of the church, and inside that first bubble was the sweet, smiling face of Jesus in Vista-vision Color and Quadraphonic Sound.

The next bubble he blew came out looking like a watermelon. It tumbled around until it found its own circle, and then it started for the sun. The Twelve Apostles were inside washing the feet of Jesus in the Pecos River. He was dressed in batwing chaps, a "Baron-of-the-Plains" Ten-X Beaver, a Chinese silk shirt, and a neckerchief made from the hem of God's gossamer robe. Buddy blew out another and Jesus was dancing the Road-apple Fandango on top of a Brahma bull at the national rodeo finals in Oklahoma City. The next came out multicolored and side-ordered with angel smoke and Jesus was wearing an Easter egg jump suit at the All-gay Rodeo in Winnemucca. There were two bedroom scenes that no one had ever read about in the Bible, and then a complete, full-blown orgy came rumbling right out the bell of Buddy's trombone and he knew he was in for real trouble. He tried to knock it down with the slide of the trombone but it got away and took off for an open window high in the roof of the church. A few Mayan gods in full ceremonial dress snuck out in turquoise blue bubbles and proceeded to show all of the gringos how to sacrifice three nude, virgin rodeo queens to the Great Brahma Rodeo God. And then, for some strange reason known only to the Cowboy Buddha, Satchel Paige and Mary Queen of Scots came running nude through a field of pink daisies.

Buddy's church members were beginning to yell at him. They were trying to knock down the bubbles with songbooks, hats, and purses, but their shots were falling way too short. Buddy knew he had to leave, but before he split he gave them one more super bubble that was produced and directed as the complete, unexpurgated life of cowboy kind. That was it! It was like the great and famous sonic fart in church, and it blew them right out of their saddles. They started throwing songbooks and silver buckles at him, and then he got hit by a pint bottle of Dickel's Sour Mash Whisky Number 12. So he blew them an encore and it was the Cowboy Buddha riding a Brahma bull right out the third eye of God.

He grabbed his magic trombone, and he ran for his life right up the guts of the church and out the gilded doors. His mother had fainted, but he knew deep down inside his young cowboy heart he couldn't stop. He had to leave home sometime.

The bishop was calling for the sheriff as Buddy cleared the front steps and headed for the highway. He stopped the first semi leaving town and jumped in. The driver was going to Cheyenne and Buddy was too. The bubbles had finally escaped, and they were catching the wind currents and floating all over town. The complete, trombone picture show of mankind, and by God, they were going to Cheyenne too.

The Cool Earth
Loves You

(Back in the Olden Days When
God Was Still Male)

Virginia Spring was the cheerleader of the Great Dream Team, and Ranger Rose was the basketball star of Idaho High. They had been front porch stargazers, hand-holders, and spirit-lovers from their first recess in the third grade. She was rich and he was poor, and their love for each other was as constant as geological time. It looked as if only the great magic of the Sky Conductor would ever interfere with this amazing union of love. However, in the middle of their senior year when they were being inundated by awards, prizes, grants, and scholarships, she became pregnant. The amazing truth of this slight-of-hips was that she had never made love with Ranger or anyone else. Virginia and Ranger had done their share of "messin' aroun'" deep inside the haystacks, and they had even gone so far as to stand bare-breasted for the bus depot photomat, which churned out four titty-to-titty snaps, but they had never gone for the Big One. She was a true and devoted member of the Church of the Last Chance Cowboys and therefore she was saving herself for a real silver and leather marriage at the Last Chance Cowboys' Temple of Fame. And Ranger was much too innocent and naïve to know where his magic wand was supposed to be waved. Nevertheless, despite all of those western assets and advantages, Virginia was knocked-up.

After her second month of Period-absentia, Virginia was convinced that God, the Celloist of Sunsets and Sunrises, had some virgin birth scheme lurking up the sleeves of his gossamer robes, and her destiny was being controlled by the power and the glory . . . Amen.

Virginia valued her virginity more than anything else. Her pom-poms, riding trophies, Arabians, palominos, and Ranger Rose came second in the showdown to her cherished fruit that was tucked so far away inside the mysteries of her beautiful seventeen-year-old body. Therefore, she felt very confident about explaining to her parents that God had been her lover and she was carrying his child. She decided that the best way to announce the news to her parents was to do it as a cheer using her finest pom-poms made from the feathers of fifteen rare birds, dyed red and blue. Her parents, conservative and humorless, were eating their evening meal when Virginia came running down the stairs wearing a halo, wings, and long flowing scarves. She jumped upon the dining room table, and in a low, religious crouch, and with her pom-poms singing in the air, she began her Grand Apologia Cheer:

> Zinga-zinga hurrah hip hup,
> Our ever-loving God has knocked me up.

Oh heavens no, is this really true?
But I'm still a virgin through and through.

Another savior is coming to earth,
And I'm the woman of this Idaho birth.

Zing zing, booma booma booma,
The kid could be born in this very rooma.

Virginia jumped off the table in a double back flip just as her mother passed out and her father was running for his secret stash of Idaho vodka spiked with buffalo grass. Needless to say, her parents did not believe her, and as soon as her pregnancy was confirmed by their family physician she was taken par avion to Mexico. Her magnificent flights into the fantasies of immaculate conception lasted only five days. As soon as she had recovered from the abortion she was back in school getting straight A's and leading the basketball team in cheers and songs to the state championship play-offs.

The blame for this amazing Believe-it-or-not was naturally dumped on Ranger. He wasn't so lucky in escaping the penalties for supposedly trespassing into the cherry gardens of virginal temples. He got IT at the final game of the state championship. With five seconds to go in the game, his team was behind by one point. Ranger stole the ball and streaked down the court for a simple lay-up. As he laid the ball with great care and gentleness onto the backboard his momentum carried him past the boards and he fell into a big sack of chloroformed prime goose down. He was immediately whisked outside and stuffed into the trunk of a Rolls-Royce pickup. The next thing he knew he was walking around a frozen lake near the Canadian border. The only clothing he had on was a pair of three-sizes-too-big cowboy boots and a World War II sheep-lined aviator's coat. A note was pinned to the sleeve.

Dear Ranger Weed (you ain't no rose no more),

Consider yourself legally in exhile. I would suggest that you never try and return to Idaho, or anywhere close. Great repercussions will occur! Your mother will be taken care of . . . she even cried at the ceremony we held for you. You might be a great basketball player, but you sure are a wild shooter with your pistole. You're very lucky you still have it.

The Brethren of the Church of the
Last Chance Cowboys

P.S. Follow the North Star to the end of the trail or else. . . .

Did Ranger make the basket? What about his future with all of the scholarships? Virginia, his true and only love? His mother? And besides all of those questions with no answers it was ten degrees below zero. Ranger started walking through the snow until he found a guard station. The ranger almost shot him when he peeked through the window, but he finally let Ranger inside. Ranger sat by the wood-burning stove and told him his story, but he could tell that his words were falling on very unimaginative ears. The guardian of the forest kept his forty-four Magnum at quick-draw the whole time.

Naturally, the only thing Ranger wanted to do was go back home and demand a hearing; and he wanted desperately to find out where the sperm came from. He knew that Virginia was still a virgin, but he could not understand the strange pregnancy. After many days of thinking about the source of the sperm he could only come up with one solid solution: One night before a game a player from the opposite team had sneaked into the gym for a little midnight practice or trickery. To prove his bugling manhood he had whacked off, hoping to shoot his wad through the magic hoop. This protean chowder of DNA razzahmahtazz landed right where Virginia did her cheers—ready to spring into action at the whiff of the scented target. Virginia, in all of her virginal innocence, had picked IT up on the floor when she was doing one of her fancy splits: jumping high into the air and coming down feather-like with her You-know-what gently kissing the hardwood, and IT (once again) was upstream like a fighting trout.

That was Ranger's one and only theory, except for a haunting and persistent vision of the Cowboy Buddha calling for Virginia to meet him at the waterfall with green eyes. It had been rumored that many of the children in the valley came from his voice, which rode the shores of the women's minds like the Japanese current carrying the lotus of spring. His name would create smiles from every woman—a laughter of yin. Even Syringa, Ranger's mother, danced in lilacs and roses, humming the movement of wheat at the very fragrance of his mind. The Cowboy Buddha . . . could it be? Naw. . . .

There Ranger was, a star lost in the wilderness—trapped into the silence of nonexistence. He knew if he returned to his home he would have his balls chopped off and sent to the Republican Party as a campaign contribution. Handcuffed, he snowshoed out of the mountains of Montana to begin his many years of exile.

After he had finally cleared himself with the Honchos of Authority, Ranger boomed around Montana, Washington, and Wyoming working as a miner, logger, dishwasher, fry cook (the I Ching cast on the short order plate with french fries), pickup truck cowboy, janitor, and fifteen or twenty other jobs that were as boring and deadly as the dreaded Russian icicle torture. A guaranteed brain rotter. Instant mush and welfare skim milk. Horse pucky to all of the short and long handles of ass-breaking labor for The Company. Ranger remained a mystery to everyone he met. Even to himself he couldn't get the handle on who he was—whether he was real, a dream, or someone else's fantasy. The only thing that kept him holding on to any connection to his past was his daily concerts about Virginia. But he could only go so far and then the stage was empty. Where was she? He kept thinking about her strange fascination for the Church of the Last Chance Cowboy and how she had always told him she would be a virgin forever, or until Jesus took her away into the heavens of sexual glory as the apostles were doing cheers and singing Roundup Songs in Happy-go-lucky, hand-clappin', boot stompin' fandango time.

Seven years drifted by. One summer, Ranger was given a job working on a dude ranch in the Grand Tetons. It was a soft job and all he had to do was take the tourists horseback riding, care for the horses, muck the stables, and buck hay. By this time, after all of those years of being in exile in Shit-kicker's Land, all he wanted to do was sit on a horse, stare at the mountains, and wonder if Everything was really Everything.

One day, right after he had been thrown by a pernicious applejack mare with volcano eyes, chewed out by his boss, and beaten over the head by an angry tourist who had been locked in the outhouse for two days, he read on the toilet wall in Jackson Hole, "The Cool Earth Loves You!" The hippies were replacing the Bible bangers with their new sayings for salvation and truth. It did, however, make him think once again about his destiny in this strange hieroglyphic spin.

That same evening, when he was riding the whisky-spirit of an Appaloosa vision, his boss told him that he had just sold four horses, and he wanted Ranger to trailer them over to West Yellowstone. It was a lousy time to go into the park because of the Tourist Hordes, but Ranger needed the extra money to help pay for the many drinks that rode him through the night.

He rose before daylight and loaded the horses. There were two Morgan mares, a Roan gelding, and a magnificent, but very onery Arab stallion. The stud-at-large, yup, almost kicked all of the shit out of the trailer before Ranger finally got him loaded. Just as the sun was coming up across the Wind Rivers onto the Tetons, Ranger was rolling north drinking coffee and Dickel, singing in a major key. He was high, and for the moment, feeling real good, because he loved having the chance to be alone and watch the sunrise on the mountains. It was all too powerful for personal sorrow, and he knew at that moment he was as close to the Magnificent as he would ever be.

Ranger was eleven-in-the-morning drunk when he arrived at the stables in West Yellowstone. He pulled his old snow-and-rain-stained Stetson down low over his eyes, and yanked his cuffs over his boots. He released his silver buckle two notches and eased himself gently out of the cab so he wouldn't disturb his water table. He spied a beautiful stand of spruce and lodgepole pines on the far side of the stables, and the trees looked like the ideal location to unload half of Wyoming's water supply. He began to roll his six-foot-three-inch western sculptured frame toward the trees hoping to look sober and stay-pressed just in case any of the hotshots were watching. Halfway there, at the moment when time was the ultimate between a wild-ass'd dash or a major accident, Ranger looked into the riding ring to see a woman dressed in a sky-blue outfit riding a palomino. His mind was working very hard trying to make sense from what his eyes were telling him. Because what he saw was his true and only love . . . beautiful Virginia Spring.

He closed his eyes and said a poker game prayer to all of the gods who control the mysteries of life, but he had to cut it down short because his bladder was beginning to signal a major breakdown of the valves. He quickly tried to say something to her, but he could only start high-tailing it for the trees.

Seven cups of Dickel and coffee later he buttoned his fly and ran back to the ring. There she was! He wasn't having a drunken-bum's vision. He slowed down from a hundred-yard sprint as his eyes came into focus on the real-life being of Virginia. She was as lovely as ever. He could almost see a halo of blues and greens pulsating above her head, with cupids dancing and robins singing. But he stopped dead in his worn-down tracks when he realized how down-'n'-out shabby he looked. He was wild and shaggy, and she was slim, graceful, and dignified. He had no money, house, or horses, and she was so fine. He had never been in Who's Who, and she had been all the way to Katmandu. His Stetson was covered with horseshit and beer, and there was a big pee stain on his Levi's. But nevertheless, there are some things that are more biological than appearances, and true love rides high on the list.

"Virginia, Virginia Spring," he forced out a name. "Remember me . . . it's . . . Ranger . . . Ranger Rose."

How many years can you watch flashing through someone's eyes as she searches for one infinite thread of recognition or feeling? Ranger saw nothing but question marks in her deep green eyes flecked with gold. He took off his hat and rolled it into a small wad, placing it over his heart. He tried to stand like he did when they played the National Anthem. He was afraid that she would not be able to see through all of the many forest fires and quicksands living on his face. Could she look through the evolution of errors and see the hero? Ranger Rose . . . All-American Forever.

She opened her mouth, and the moisture on her lips flashed and danced in iridescence and rose. She looked at him as perhaps a prima ballerina might look at a car muffler. And then she finally saw through all of the layers of sorrow, hard work, and defeat, and she saw her Ranger, the ballet kid of the basketball, who shot rainbows instead of baskets.

"Ranger, Ranger . . . oh, I thought you were dead." She didn't move. Was this a resurrection? Had he returned?

Sometimes it takes several lifetimes for a rebirth, and one hell of a lot longer for a major league reincarnation. But Ranger had to do all of them quickly to convince her that he was really the true Ranger of the hardwoods, the magician of the helixical spin. He told her about their first kiss in the third grade, and the time they played God and the Virgin Mary in the Christmas pageant. He told her that she was ambidextrous, which was the reason for her great pom-pom artistry. He was down on his knees speaking with the gift of tongues, telling her in all of the poetics of the sacred language how much he still loved her. And then, she came in closer as a magician might approach the last remaining meta-physician—moving so curiously—floating on every step. She made one fast move and unsnapped his cowboy shirt to find his birthmark—a star-shaped mole just above his right breast.

She moved as a snow egret into emerald-pooled waters to find his mouth. She closed her eyes, Ranger closed his —they kissed. And the dumbshit cowpoke turned into a prince and a magician as he came tap dancing out of his body, flying to the top of a triple sun shining in the sky.

"Ranger, guess what?"

"What?" He didn't dare move.

"I still have my Good House Keeping seal."

"What?" He broke away from her.

"I'm . . . I'm still a virgin."

"Really?"

"Yes. . . ."

"Guess what?"

"What?"

"Me too. . . ." and he let out a giant whoop and a yell that cut through the mountains like a bolt of miracle lightning through heathens. They sat down on the wild mountain grass and tried to bring the past from out of the darkness. They laughed and cried, holding on to each other, touching each other's hair, eyes, and lips. She told him in the order of importance that she was still a devout buckarina sister in the Church of the Last Chance Cowboys, lawyer, airplane pilot, and that she owned a horse ranch in Hawaii, and a cattle ranch in Montana. Ranger didn't have much to say about his past because it had been one long out-of-focus trickster's rodeo. But he gave her as many flowers as he could find and wove them into her hair as the past came back to him so vividly and deadly. He had been opposed in life by Quick-fingered Fate, and she had been living as if God (her Porsche mechanic who also plays a wonderful pedal steel) was her personal escort.

The morning quickly pole-vaulted itself into the early afternoon. Virginia had to meet a client who was flying in from Kashmir, and Ranger had to finish taking care of the horses. They promised to meet at nine that evening at her cabin on Hebgen Lake. As they left their eyes danced long slow waltzes into each other's score cards.

Ranger was damn scared, and he didn't know what to do. All of the many guides in his body were telling him so many different things: leave and go back to Jackson Hole; ride a horse into the disappearing sunset (bleeding right off the page); spend the night with the buffalo; or just go with her and make it happen. Seven years ago it had been so easy for him to do the right thing. Now, there were no events in his life to use as inflatable ego supports. He had seven years of being the sound of one cowboy crying, and he didn't know who he was. He had become passive and that is not what a young, six-foot-three, good-looking hero is supposed to be. He probably would have knocked-up the first woman who asked him, but no one did, and he couldn't ask. It's a strange place to be in—accepting life as it arrives at the front door. It's only sought by a few who have decided to bail out of the battle for a place in the hidden forest. But Ranger hadn't arrived at that place, and he needed to find his own spirit —his own shadow before he could begin. He needed this one night to free himself from the exile of carnival mirrors.

An evening in August. There were so many great forces working in the universe to produce this one night. Ranger could feel the power moving through his body. All of the birds in his inner forest had for this night stopped singing; the trees in the forest were calm, and all of the waterfalls were moving in slow motion over the cliffs. A beautiful piano sonata was being played . . . pianissimo.

He was moving quietly through space as arrow into darkness. He only had to appear in the sunlight to be discovered. The resurrection was beginning.

At nine o'clock it was time to begin. Ranger had bathed in the Madison River, drying his body with wild flowers and peppermint. He was nature's Kid Golden and he wanted to be first in line for his return to the Promised Land.

Virginia's cabin was tucked away in a stand of quaking aspen and surrounded by lodgepole pines. Sagebrush, whortleberry, and willow covered the ground between the cabin and the lake. The moon was just soft-shouldering over the mountains as Ranger walked up the steps and knocked on the door. Virginia opened the entrance and it was the opening to the Taj Mahal, revealing all of the secrets and mysteries within Virginia's temple. It was a movement that holds millions of years of evolution. She was wearing a blue negligee folded long and simple around her body. Ranger's eyes entered, but his body dissolved at the doorway. She had filled the cabin with flowers, candles, and music. Ranger stood at the door while his mind and tongue eloped on a highball to Winnemucca. Virginia took one step, grabbed his arm in a secret hold called the Sacred Deliverance, and threw him into the room. And then she knelt down on one knee, raised her arms, and started a cheer:

> Boomachoppa, boomachoppa, hey, hey, hey!
> Tonight we're going to be laid in the hay!

She jumped into the air and threw her arms around Ranger's neck and shoulders. "Let's have some wine."

"Virginia . . ."

"Come on scaredy cat, you'll need this . . . so will I.

You're the best thing to Jesus I'll ever find. I've been a professional virgin long enough. Besides, you dumbshit cowpoke . . . I love you. I always have. After you disappeared I didn't go out with anyone for six months. Six whole months just for you. And now here you are . . . Ranger Slim, as handsome as ever." She shoved a large glass of wine to his lips and tilted the glass. They stood facing each other, drinking the wine without talking. Their eyes were moving, speaking their own feasting language, preparing for the next move.

Virginia finished two glasses of wine. "I've practiced this scene so many times I know exactly how much hooch I need to take me where I want to go. I've had enough." She sat down on the couch and tugged on Ranger to follow.

Ranger wanted more time, but he knew he couldn't wait. He could feel his heart chugging away like an old Monterey fishing boat breaking the silence within his own private ocean.

In the long, slow-motion slide down into her arms he felt himself in shutter frames, and then, as their lips and seven years of waiting met there was only the deliverance. He didn't need his spurs to move out of the chute. As always, when the chemistry is perfect, and the smells are beautiful, and the mouth and skin taste like the flowered earth inside the flowing river, there is only the perfection. He suddenly didn't care if she thought of him as a second-stringer for Jesus . . . he was finally almost home. He wanted everything to be a double-encore experience for her so she would go to her bishop and tell him, ". . . it was wonderful, and I'm never going to stop."

Ranger had his pants down around his ankles, but he couldn't kick them off because of his boots. Virginia had already taken off his shirt. He was wondering how he was going to get his boots and pants off gracefully and still keep everything working. Riding herd and twelve steers break away in twelve directions at once. . . . Oh boy!

Virginia made a slight move and said something about the bed. He nodded yes, and somehow they stopped, and she got up and blew out all of the candles except one. Ranger finally got his pants and boots off without breaking any of the furniture, and they dived into bed.

The sanctuary inside. Under the covers there is the privacy of the oceans. The secrecy of the ritual to be performed within the boundaries of the universe. It was the beginning of life all over again.

Ranger moved slowly with his body, and she moved slowly with hers as they searched for the goals of their own passions. Within to within to within they began their circling into the high summer night. Ranger moved his hips into the air so they would merge as lovers . . . slowly into each other. As his body was on the edge of his virginity to leave behind and begin again a new virginity; as she opened as the morning flower to the new light; as they were both poised on the balance of their bodies, infinitely and delicately waiting for the smallest of a thrust that would guide them forever into a communion of flesh and spirit, the bed began to shake, and then the cabin was jumping, and the forest began to roar, and the mountains and the moon were rocking, and then the world crashed and Ranger was thrown downward—bursting into Virginia's body as they were locked into a Brahma-embrace—being whipped by a greater power than their own lives. He felt his cock being thrust deeper and deeper into Virginia's body—farther than he had ever imagined the greatest of animals could penetrate.

"Oh . . . my god! An earthquake!" he heard his voice

begin to shout, and then Virginia slapped a hand over his mouth and stopped him.

"No . . . oh no . . . it's God. Don't stop . . . oh, don't stop."

And then Ranger heard the mountain slide down the canyon as his body was being bucked, sunfished, and crow-hopped all over the bed. Virginia's eyes became moons of illumination as she opened up more and held onto this great powerful beast who was taking her beyond anything that she had ever imagined. They rode on through the quake—horse and rider through the great world championship virgins' rodeo—bareback—higher and higher into the air and crashing onto the bed, back up until they exploded into thunderbolts of orgasms. They began to shout and scream as their bodies demanded more, and Ranger fell deeper, and Virginia pushed higher, until they could no longer maintain the balances of this wild, rocking earth animal that had become their guide. And with the last huge bucking and sliding of the earth they were forced apart and Ranger was thrown across the room knocking him half-unconscious.

Virginia was still on the bed with her arms raised to the box seats of the holy arena of heaven. The cabin was slowly being launched down the hill into the lake. Virginia began to moan, chant, and cheer into the night—an expression of ecstasy and complete acceptance to the great powers of the first-string stud in the sky. Shaking her fists she began her affirmation. . . .

Hallelujah hallelujah, divine intervention!
Great merciful fucking god, divine intervention!
Holy holy grandslam holy, divine intervention!
Holy holy grandslam holy, divine intervention!

The cabin was shot into the lake and Ranger was thrown out the back door. He grabbed onto a small tree and just before he passed out he looked up to see the cabin floating in the middle of the lake. Virginia had climbed onto the roof and she was riding the ridge like a pornographic beatitude on the back of a giant, steaming water bible.

Ranger was flown to Bozeman to be treated for a brain concussion, neck bites, and multiple lacerations on his back and arms (a first-class cataclysm can hide many secrets). The next day he was given a ride in a Cessna back to West Yellowstone by two national TV reporters and their crews. They kept asking Ranger questions about the quake—what was it really like? What was he doing when it happened? Ranger couldn't talk. Numbed flat to the bone. He kept shaking his head and laughing silently in his gut, pulling himself down into the seat until his newly shoplifted, mirrored sunglasses were the only messages they could receive.

Ranger searched everywhere for Virginia, but he couldn't find her. She had completely disappeared, perhaps transcended . . . hot body and all. He began to wonder whether that night with her had really happened. He kept going into the restrooms to check out his cock to see if there were any signs left from his rites of passage. Still the same. No secret marks or mysterious tattoos had appeared, but there was beginning to be a very strange look on Ranger's face. A new inner smile jumping around inside his body. A strange trickster-boarder . . . paying room and board . . . top dollar, and Ranger was beginning to laugh again.

Ranger was told at the airport that Virginia and her father had flown out the day after the quake. He was given a letter: a blue envelope with blue paper, and Virginia had drawn on the paper a winged Arabian stallion flying through a triple rainbow'd body of God (who was looking very virile, sexy, and well satisfied with himself). Ranger walked out into a meadow and sat down on the grass.

Dear Ranger Rose or whoever you are,

Two nights ago I was made love to by a great being. I remember you were there at the beginning, but then something very strange happened, and I was being taken by somebody more powerful and beautiful than you. All I could feel were beasts and wings and great thunderbolts of flesh consuming me until I had lost touch with any sense of reality. I had hoped that we could be together, be friends and make love, but I realize now that I have been chosen to be the mother of a new God-Child. No mortal could have done what I experienced two nights ago. I'm leaving for Hawaii where I will have this child. I know that I conceived that night, and I must prepare for this sacred event. I hope to see you someday, perhaps later on in heaven. God bless you, Ranger.

Come come Ye Buckarina Saints,
Virginia Spring

Ranger rolled back into the grass, kicked his legs into the air, and threw himself over onto his stomach. With his face into the earth, his complete life up to that moment came spinning through him like a migrating galaxy. The highs and the lows, and beyond that, just being. And the long shot . . . supreme ecstasy. Ranger began to laugh. A few chuckles and giggles, and then he started to hoot and shout and beat his head against the grass. Fortunately for Ranger no one saw him go through this Houdini double-dribble as he exorcised all of the lazy second-stringers who had been living with him for so long. He laughed, rocked, and cried for a long time, and then he broke out with a strange, haunting cowbuddhian maniacal Tibetan roundup scream. A sound that could challenge the highest of authority. A cry that could turn robins into six-legg'd, monkey-faced lizards; a moan that could flip all of the Vatican's gold into popcorn farts and belly button fluff. A wailing that could change cesspool graffiti into the Ten Commandments. Ranger was up on one knee, shaking his fists at the invisible and illusive Almighty Deceivers of the Damned. He stood up and poked his head through all of the many layers of human bullshit and self-minded thinking until he discovered the inevitable of all inevitables. Daylight! Sunshine and clean air. He didn't stop but kept on reaching for the sun until he had broken his six foot three inches into the clearing. There they all were: mountains, trees, flowers, clouds, sky, birds . . . his closest friends for the past seven years, and he was finally seeing them for what they really were: mountains, trees, flowers, clouds, sky, and birds. Everything and Nothing and Everything . . . again.

Ranger pulled a ball out of the sky and started to dribble. Easy at first, but as soon as he rediscovered his touch he went through all of his old moves: behind the back and the floater; between his legs and chasing the caboose; half-moon spins and the high-pocket drift; and a double-cross lay-over with a reverse spin called the dancing arrow polka. With the exercise over, Ranger settled down and broke into the game with jump shots, set shots, fakes, steals, picks, fadeaways, layaways, pumps and double pumps, reverse spins, floating lay-ups, stuffs, dunks, and then the Grand Dunk: leaving the ground from fifteen feet out, going into a full twist as he moved the ball behind his back the opposite direction and then slamming it into the hoop. POW! By the time Ranger stopped, the game was over because the bad guys had thrown in the towel when the score became triple-infinity to ZeeRow-zip. Ranger walked out into the middle of the meadow and bowed to all of his fans as he accepted the trophy which was the Granddaddy of all trophies: the Cowboy Buddha dribbling twelve planets while tap dancing and tai-chiing at the same time. He lifted it in the air for everyone to see as he turned in a circle. He held up one finger to show everyone how he felt about his earthquake renaissance. The middle finger, presented to all of his demons, dragons, and wart-nosed, back-shootin' gargoyles, who had been riding inside his body, rent-free, for so long. To them . . . and all of their kids and children's kids . . . Old Numero Fucko!

"Fuckum all!" he shouted to all of the invisible dwellers of the sky, plus one eagle who was trying to decide whether to have rainbow trout at Jenny Lake, or just hang around and see if any ham sandwiches were left in the picnic grounds. "Fuckum all! Especially the ugly ones. They thought they had won, but I fooled them. Bastards! I fooled them. I was only red-shirting. Now, I'm back. And they'd better have their moves a lot smoother and quicker because I'm rollin' and I've got all of mine back plus a few more. So watch out! My pickup has been smashed flatter than an English saddle. My clothes, wallet, and my all-time favorite . . . old Numero Five-X rat-infested Beaver Stetson are all floating in the middle of the lake and I ain't down. Virginia is gone and I ain't down. She thinks she's gonna have my kid and I ain't down. My kid. Ha! She thinks it's God's. Damn! Do you hear that, God? I've fooled you this time. I beat you. You know? Beat you at your own game. I didn't have to pull off a plus-eight on the Richter Scale quake to get laid. That was a mean trick, God. Real bad! Look at all the people you killed just so you could sneak into Virginia's pants. Was it worth it? Huh? Was it? Well . . . I'll tell you something and I want you to listen. I'm cutting out of here. Understand? Leaving. Going home, and you ain't gonna stop me. Not this time. I've finally got you figured out. Yeh . . . figured out. And you're nothing but a con, a dirty old man, a fly-by-nighter, and a flimflam man. I can't believe it. You! Well . . . I'm finished. Through. So leave me alone. Just back off and let me be. Fuck off! Get lost . . . adios and sooooo long." Ranger started walking through the meadow. Ten steps beyond his farewell he spun around to check his tracks. Nothing. He raised one fist and shook it out into space. "*Adios,* motherfuckers . . . Aaaa-deee-ooossss!"

With his trophy in one hand and the magic ball in the other he walked through the town, spinning with this newly discovered feeling of ecstasy and tranquility. His walk was about ten feet tall and just about that much off the ground. "It's all perfect," he kept on chanting to himself. "It's all perfect. I can feel it now. Everything. And it's all perfect." On the beginning side of town he slipped into the corral where he had delivered the four horses. He picked out a strong-looking mare with soft, dark eyes, and a long, flowing mane and tail. In the barn he found a bridle, blankets, saddle, saddlebags, and an old plaid coat that had been used for a dog's bed. He filled the bags with grain and took an old sleeping cowboy hat that was hanging on the barn's center support post. He walked the horse through the trees until they were a mile from the barn, and then he mounted the Appaloosa. He was going back home. He was going to find his mother, the moon woman of the alfalfa fields, and he was going to find his older brother . . . Jus' One More Cowboy, Jonquil Rose. He was going back to that great long valley that touches the White Clouds and reaches out into the Sawtooth Mountains. Home. A little west and to the south. All downhill. Before the sun could pull down its shades and declare itself a magnificent sunset, Ranger Rose was long gone.

*The First Light
of Sunday*

She is called Syringa Rose, and she has lived in the mountains all of her life. Within her mind, within the deep-pooled lakes of her imagination she has lived in many of the magical places of the world. But she has never wanted to leave the land that was for her, her own boundaries of physical migration. She is possessed with the need to be one with the earth—living the sacred geometry that has created everything, being inside the spiral that moves beyond the senses. Living without praise or blame. Being her own ceremony—folding her life into the plants and animals who become her own breath as she gathers and moves through the land of all of her ancestors: deer, hawks, fish, planets, trees, dreams, buffalo, stars, and the old migration trails of the natives. She became the dreamer for all of those lives who are still flying around within her liquid footsteps.

Affirmation. Living her own passions and releasing them again without possession. Owning nothing but her own life. She learned about time from the voices of birds and the flooding of stars.

Horse miles, and the pace of the growing corn.

It was the first of September and fall was strong in her arrival. Mountain fall, and dangerously arrogant. Syringa had been canning all week, and this night, Saturday, she was almost finished with the peaches. It was just past midnight and she was feeling tired—a long way from first light. She needed to be outside to feel the air that was so fragrant with the new smells of the changing season. She made a pot of spearmint tea, cooled it with brandy, and added a spoonful of Camas prairie honey. She released the knot that tied her hair and it fell into a reddish-brown cascade with streaks of silver running like an infinite river through dark, vermilion clay.

She stood outside the door, drinking the tea, slowly allowing the night to move through her senses. The moon was full, high and ghost-owl white, illuminating the valley like a moving ship reflecting ice. Syringa felt herself move from the moon's intensity. Stage fright. Butterflies flying within her body as she gave herself to the vastness of the sky. Crickets were singing, and she could hear the river moving over the rocks, polishing the stones as a laughter of granite. The horses in the corral were silent, but she could see their shapes as they leaned against the fence.

When she finished the tea she walked into the garden. She touched the corn, full and ready to be picked. Small ears because of the mountain sun and the short growing

season. She walked through the late squashes and pump-
kins with their great round bellies hanging onto the
earth's cord. Umbilical and Buddha.

She moved through the garden as silent mother. Their
lives beyond language.

She walked into the alfalfa fields. The plants were to
her waist, and it was time for the second cutting. She
knelt down and touched the plants—running her hands
over the tops, letting them stroke her palms—caressing
them like tiny breasts against the flesh of her aroused
mind. The finest of the fodder the Arabs called it. Alfac-
facah. The food that created the dynasty of horses. The
horse mother pushing into Europe. A centaur's dream. Alfalfa. Allah. Food of the gods. A moving wind of migrating muscle.

She changed her balance and fell back into the field,
lying down among the plants as she entwined her legs
around the long stems of the alfalfa—bringing them between her legs and holding them like a lover's long hair.
A woven tongue nibbling the plants. Her body began to
evaporate into the earth—down into a spiraling web of
ancient prayers, old costumes, and timeless inhabitants.
Down into underground lakes and chambers of gold
where the roots of the alfalfa dive to find the sacred
water.

The releasing of skin—the container. Her body fell into
flight.

Evaporating, the migration outside the vessel. Moving
as vapor in a long, slow glide into the mouth of her own
body—transcended from the rainbow's Kaballah.

She began to move through the layers of her lives—
through the great powers of her own continent into an
inner cellular river of light. Vast assimilations of yellows
and white with green pulsating edges. A mandala life in-

side the centering of her own powers. The light flooded her body—orgasmic and spiritual in its elevations of electricity.

God
Flight
Lover

A love affair with the two worlds of the one body. Male and female. The powers of the evolutionary cell moving as one. A dynasty of oneness.

Air
Fire
The phoenix

Suddenly she jumped up and looked up at the ridge. A deep feeling of birth was riding through her body—a sensation of being conceived by a long invasion of male. A mother's consciousness riding out through her own hips. Glacial and astrological—time being held in a constant by the parallel curve of space and her own body—a total melting of forces. He was arriving. She knew. A delivery of life through the hips of the mountains.

She walked back to the house holding the new fire, allowing it to be nourished like the beginning of a new season. She washed the dishes and put them away in the cupboard. She arranged a bouquet of flowers on the kitchen table. As she was leaving she looked back into the kitchen. It felt good—the center fire. The pine floors were clean and her hand-woven rugs were vibrating gentle stories of dreams and songs.

Syringa walked to the tack shed, picked out a bridle, blanket, and saddle, and put them on a bench by the hitching rack. She led a mare out into the clearing. Two Rivers, a leopard Appaloosa. After she had Two Rivers ready to ride she talked with her for a long time—telling

her what they were going to be doing. The mare knew.
The music of voices told her. Each tone was a translation
into her own comprehension of language. The perfection
of music. When Syringa had finished she mounted the
mare and they headed into the mountains.

She held Two Rivers to an easy trot until they cleared
the trees that led into a long valley, and then she released
the tension on the reins and they moved out into a long
sliding canter. A night drumming of hoofs, owls, and the
drone of the trees. An early morning raga.

Two hours later they were on the ridge—open at the
top with two small lakes fed by melting snow fields.
Below her was the valley—a resting place of gravity—
reclining to accept the thrusting of avalanches and the
consumation of rainbows. A lap of flowers, tall grasses,
and small pools of water gathered between streams.

Syringa dismounted and removed the bridle from Two
Rivers. She sat down on the ground, moving her body
into the earth until she felt satisfied with the pocket of
softness below her. She breathed in—all of the night
smells—opening her body to the sounds—awakening into
the sensations of being alone inside the rolling of darkness and the circling of earth.

> The infinite patience
> To live without waiting
> Keeping the jars full of water
> Wind chimes
> A perennial rocking of earth.

Hours later. The moon was on the far side of the valley, closing itself off from the fading darkness. First light
—a shower of rain—the breaking of the dark side and the
balancing of hands.

He came. Riding down through the cut leading into

the valley. The opening. The phasing of two planets until
eclipsed into the deliverance of the circle. Her son.
Ranger, who had disappeared seven years ago, was now
returning from the center of his shadow—being released
by the contraction of his own destiny. Syringa watched
him riding an opalescent sun-rose Appaloosa from out of
the darkness. He was tall, long-legged, and moved easy
with the horse—a single-footer that was as smooth as
coasting hills. Two Rivers picked up her ears. Syringa put
her hand over the horse's nose. "Shhhh . . . quiet," she
said, as she slipped on the bridle.

Ranger broke into a fast trot as he cleared an outcropping of rocks. Syringa couldn't find his face, which was
still hidden by the long shadows of the trees and mountains. She waited . . . until he had ridden one hundred
yards past her lookout, and then she jumped on Two
Rivers, tongue-clicked a command, and they moved into
a slow pace centering their bodies into the valley.

She held the horse back until the sun had broken out
from behind the mountain. The clouds—flat-bottomed
and long-legged—were capturing great colors of apricot
and rose inside their bodies, and the sky was expanding
with its variations of morning blue. Syringa kept her eyes
on him as she rode closer—watching him—his life, and the
way his body expanded the air around him. She heeled
Two Rivers into an open run, closing in as the Appaloosa
lifted them over the earth.

Syringa began to whoop in a high bird cry. A calling
that she had used when she was a young mother for her
two sons playing by the river, or working out in the
fields. The calling to the fire. And then she slapped the
morning silence with a long, high scream. A shrill, vibrating sound indigenous to the voices of eagles and desert
dwellers in flights of victory. A screaming of birth and ec-

stasy. The voice shot through Ranger's body and he immediately spun around—a quick pivot of his Appaloosa to face the instrument of the noise—the mysterious rider who had come up behind him. He saw her as she was pulling hard on the reins to check Two Rivers from over-riding them. There was an instant when they were suspended in the air, checking their horses as their eyes locked into each other's faces. Finding the memory. A mysterious face from years ago. Syringa didn't need to understand the closing distance between them as she nudged Two Rivers through the last barrier. There were tears on her face, and her hair had blown loose from the tie—flying behind her—lifting into long wings.

Finally he saw her. This moon woman of the alfalfa fields, having aged seven years for him in the last three seconds. His mother. A sound in his mind that made him realize that he was no longer the stranger as the years of being away—being lost in his own body—fell into their own death. He was finally home.

Ranger flexed his body to jump from his Appaloosa when he saw that Syringa had leaped from her mare and was flying toward him. He had only enough time to open his arms before she landed into his laughter, calluses, and dreams. And then they were falling, through their bodies, back through the cells of each other—into the very essence of their journeys to find the source of the music. Home. Where the roots of the alfalfa descend for fifty feet to drink from the flowing river; where the alfalfa woman drinks her tea and brandy, and listens to the songs from the old migration trails. Ranger heard his name being called over and over again . . . "Ranger . . . oh, Ranger, my son, my son, Ranger." The tears were running down his cheeks into her face and hair as they continued to fall through the first light of Sunday.

Save the Last Dance for Me

"It's Cowboy but it ain't
cowboy"

Cowboy Proverb

Buddy Sunday stood on the edge of the road with his thumb locked into the Wyoming wind. Flat-out open at ninety the cars and trucks ran down on him like falcons diving on fat rubber ducks in a child's dream of the real world. He had used all of the tricks in the cowboy's bible for hitching between rodeos: nude when patrol cars pass; lying across the blacktop waving a "Free Pussy" sign; climbing up in a tree and trying to drop into the backs of pickups and hay trucks; giving everyone the finger, hoping some God-fearing rancher would become incensed or outraged, stop on a buffalo nickel, and try to punch Buddy's neon and chestnut lights out; a phony detour sign; looking tall, lean, sexy, and 69 per cent indifferent to the hottest of honky-mamas flashing by in their strawberry roan XKE Jags on their way to the Row-day-ooh.

Nothing worked. Indians, cowboys, bishops, heathens, grave robbers, franchised meditators, dirty old ladies, and collectors of antique Porsche pickups all passed him by as if he were a permanent fixture of the road put there by the Wild West Security Bureau. "Buckaroos and buckarinas. Here is a perfect example of the down 'n' out twenty-year-old bull rider who has not placed in one rodeo. He spends his nights in bars playing his old pawn-shop trombone for any old tin-eared dipsomaniac he can bushwack. His hair is too long, his mustache too droopy, his satin shirts with pearl buttons much too flashy for cowboy, and his boot leather is made from soybeans. In fact, the only thing cowboy about him, according to the Buck Higher Manual of Rodeo Dress, is his silver buckle, which has the Cowboy Buddha riding a Brahma bull out through the third eye of God engraved in the center, and even that leaves us with a Dubious Eye. So, why would anyone who has visited every rodeo between the Garden and San Berdeaux be even the slightest bit interested in picking up this lowlife, riffraff, star-grazing cowboy?"

Buddy sat down on his rigging bag and rolled a cigarette. He looked at his body, thinking perhaps, by some strange act of God, he had been doomed invisible. No! He was there! He could feel all of the bruises on his body from the last rodeo. He pounded on his legs with his fists; stomped on his toes with the heels of his boots; he took off his sunglasses and looked at himself in the mirrored lenses. Yup . . . he was there all right. Polarized, but not in the least bit Pulitzerized.

This wasn't the loneliest road in Wyoming, but after five hours of standing in the hot sun it was closing in fast for the Lonely-old-road of the West Award. This road had been built by the Mormons as a polygamist's underground highway to smuggle their surplus of ugly daughters to the cowboys in Idaho and Wyoming. And even now, no one wanted to stop, fearing they would be bull-dogged and piggin'-tied into a shotgun marriage by the ghost of Brigham Young.

Buddy had nine hours left until the first event, and he knew, deep down inside his rodeo heart, that this time he was going to draw the meanest, rankest bull in the parade, and this bull was going to be one big, bad, maahtha-fukkkaaahhh! He was going to ride him right down into the ground and come up with an eighty-five in the golden trophy. He was going to push, grit, bear down, stomp, sweat, and eat that bull until ol' One Ton was jumping higher than the clown's smile; spinning faster than props out of water; hooking so bad he was giving himself twelve new assholes. That bull would be backfiring so hot a new canal would be dug between the Salmon and the Sweetwater. It was that simple. Buddy Sunday was going to win . . . if he could only get his cowboy ass down the road.

Buddy leaned out from under the shadow of his hunner-duller five-X beaver with eaves so big if they could flap he would be flying to the stampede. Nothing. Not even a mirage.

"When the goin' gits tough, the tough git goin'," the old cowboy tune sings, but when there's no place to go but down the road, walking in soybean boots, gettin' tough ain't the answer. Buddy opened up the case of his old pawnshop trombone and took out the three pieces of his personal magic show and put them together. He took off his silk bandana and polished up the silver—giving the bell a couple of B-flat shots of mescalito snoose. He got back down into the case and found his bottle of Elixir of Trickster. He held the bottle up to the sun sizing up the contents. "Well . . . Cowboy H. Boooodhaaa! I fergot that I gave this bottle to the waitress so she could wash her hair." He opened up his rigging bag and scooted around inside and came up with a half-full bottle of champagne and a bar of oatmeal soap. "If this ain't gunna be one of the best cowboy 'ngenuities, I don't know what could be!" He sliced off small pieces of soap with his knife and stuck them into the bottle. He swirled and twirled the bottle around until there was a Wyoming Laundromat going crazy inside the magnum of super-market champagne. He put the bottle on the ground so the mixture would calm down. "Ain't much . . . jus' enough fer three good bubbles an' a turkey fart." Buddy did a few deep-knee bends, push-ups, and side-straddle hops to loosen up for the performance, and then he poured his new batch of Elixir of Trickster into the bell of his old trombone.

Buddy raised his trombone to the sky and aimed it with his newly installed Dead-eye Scope one century past Centaurus—a dusty hole where all old rocking-chair cow-boys are suppose to be bunked. He closed his eyes until all he could see was the Cowboy Hall of Fame riding high on Persimmon Hill, and he blew out a bubble that was long, low, and incredibly slow. The bubble floated down the road fifty feet in front of him and when he opened his eyes there was an old school bus painted Oklahoma Mud and filled with every old derelict cowboy who ever rode the Good-night-loving Trail to Pumpkin Creek. The bus came within ten feet of Buddy's invisible stage and then it started coughing, hacking, bucking, and humping, and finally collapsed. A ball of snoose the size of a basketball came rolling out the door before the bus disappeared into a black cloud of Cowboy Lung.

"Sheeeeet," Buddy mumbled through his mustache to a coyote who was sitting by the side of the road trying to read a road map to find out where a rancher had stuck a fresh band of sheep. The next bubble was lean and clean and sparkled in the sun like rainbows flying through multifaceted Tibetan crystals. The wind picked up the bubble and blew it over the road. When this iridescent planet had grown to the exact size of Buddy's mind it exploded into a million Buddhist raindrops, which fell through the sky in number-five drops, landing in the juniper trees and sagebrush. "Damn! All I want is a ride and what do I get? Perfection." Buddy stuck his head into the bell. "Hey . . . down there! I can't stay here all day. Get it together . . . yahear! I've got to git down the road to win this rodeo. Wait until I'm dead to pull off this kind of bullshit." Buddy swirled the remaining mixture around in the trombone. "Come on, baby. Let's git it right this time. Anything will do 'cept a UFO . . . jus' gimme a ride. A George Dickel salesman; an old farmer with thirteen beautiful long-legg'd daughters; a tuna boat . . . anything headin' west." Buddy rubbed his belt buckle, polished his boots on the backs of his Levi's, said a tenderloin prayer to the Cowboy Buddha, made the sign of the Tibetan knot, and then let it fly. Woooosh! Out it came. A perfectly shaped hourglass just about 36-22-36. It flew into the air and hovered over his head. "Come on . . . where are you?" A picture began to form inside the bubble and when it came into focus there was an old 1939 Chevy panel truck and on the side in faded letters . . . *Miss Rodeo, USA, 1939, Cody St. Kid.* The truck settled on the ground and the door was kicked open.

"Hey, cowboy! . . . jump on in. Woooweeee . . . do I like your style."

Buddy threw his rigging bag into the back of the truck and climbed into the cab. Behind the wheel was a perfectly shaped fifty-six-year-old woman (add three inches all around for spiritual ballast). Her eyes were steel gray with a few rust spots on the edges; her hair was blond and beehived to the top of the cab. Turquoise rode her skin like Navajo traffic lights on suntanned dirt roads; her boots were years ago custom-made with silver toe and heel caps. And her pants fit like she had jumped into a hot spring with them on forty years ago and she was still trying to dry them out. To a drunk she would look twenty-seven and beautiful, but to Buddy she just looked like his grandma trying to get laid at the Winnemucca Fellini Party.

"You're a bull rider . . . I can tell by your face. You got a handle to go along with that handsome body of yers?"

"Ah . . . Buddy . . . Buddy Sunday," he said, hanging onto his trombone as he let fly with an avalanche of silent curses to the Cowboy Buddha, who was at this moment sneaking around with the coyote sizing up a band of sheep on Bear River.

"Ahhhh . . . Buddy Sunday. Good name. It's got a nice cowboy sound to it. Mine's Cody. Cody St. Kid. Miss Rodeo Nineteen Hunderd and Thirteee-nine . . . Oh boy! A good year for cowboys." Cody put the truck into first and laid a patch of Michelins right across the state line. "Where ya headin' . . . Buddy?"

"I'm trying to git to the Stanley Basin Rodeo. I'm s'pose to be ridin' the bulls . . . if I ever git there."

"Well, kid, we might make it and then we might not. The White Buffalo, that's my truck, runs like she's hooked into a stampede and then sometimes she just likes to bunch up and graze on the grass. Never can tell what kind of a performance she'll put out. But what the hell, there's always another rodeo. They jus' keep comin' at you like rapid-fire dreams of lost lovers . . . if ya know what I mean, cowboy?"

"Yup . . . sure do. Well, sort of anyway." Buddy tipped his hat onto the same angle as his nose, leaving enough eyeball coverage for one finger of horizon. Cody reached over the dashboard and cranked open the windshield. "Ahhh . . . that's better. If you're hongry I've got some grub in the back. Hep yerself. All good for you. None of this between-rodeos cowboy shit. It's all natural as my naked body . . . if you know what I mean. And there's a bottle of tequila. That's hunner per cent natural too. Made from cactus." She looked over at Buddy. He was wrapped right down into a deep sleep. "Well I'll be a fifty-pound Idaho potato in heat. He didn't even bother to say his prayers."

When Buddy finally woke up, Cody was parked underneath a long row of poplars by the Big Lost River in the middle of the Arco desert. He lifted his hat and periscoped out. "This don't look like Stanley Basin to me, the mountains are too flabby. What's goin' on?"

"Well darn," Cody said as she opened her door. "Looks like the Buffler has decided to bed down for the night. Nice place don't you think? A little shade, and not a rodeo in sight until tomorrow."

Buddy jumped out of the truck and opened the side wing of the hood. "What the hell is wrong with this thing? Can't it go?"

"Hey, Cowboy Sunday, get the ginger out of yer ass. There's nothin' we can do unless you're some kind of bedazzled wizard. Here . . . help me throw out this gear. No sense gettin' all busted out. She'll be fine in the morning. We'll roll into Stanley and catch the last two days."

"Sheeeeet," Buddy sidewinded out of his mouth as he started throwing their gear out of the truck. "Ya jus' cain't waltz into a rodeo one day late and 'spect to ride. This ain't the olden days any more . . . lady. They run these Row-dee-oohhhhs like Swiss cat houses. Even the goddam riding stock all piss-'n'-shit on time. Damn! Every cowboy who can jack himself up to a bull or a harse is gunnin' fer the big silver buckle in the sky. Sheeeet!" He grabbed his rigging bag, threw it down next to a tree, and sat down.

Cody came over to him and sat down. She'd seen it all so many times before and it never got easier. "Well, Buddy ol' Kid . . . I know I ain't the sweetest thing in the West, but I've still got a few dances left in me and we can have some fun. That's what rodayowens all about. Beats workin' and there's always another rodeo. Say . . . does that thing work you got there 'tween yer legs?"

Buddy looked down at his Bermuda triangle, studied it for a few seconds, and then rolled back up to Cody. "What do you mean . . . does it work? Hell and goddam! I'm a man, ain't I?"

Cody started laughing, her mascara chipping around the edges of the arroyos. "Hey . . . kid. I didn't mean that . . . yer whooper. I can tell already that works. I was talkin' 'bout yer trombone."

A faint smile cracked across Buddy's lips. Embarrassed and caught dead to rights, but coming out clean. "Well . . . sure it does . . . it's a beaut!"

"Why don't you play us a tune . . . something sweet and romantic." Cody was just about ready to purr . . . her body curling.

Buddy picked up the trombone and started playing with the slide . . . running out from first to seventh position and back . . . and then trilling around third and fourth. "It doesn't work that way. It's tempermental . . . real sensitive . . . jus' like a whoaman."

Cody swallowed that one . . . giving in. "I can see by the way yer carryin' it aroun' that it's special . . . cowboy. Oh yeh . . . I wish somebody would rub me like that."

Buddy was rubbing the bell with his scarf, thinking to himself. He closed his eyes to catch the movie on the front of his eyelids, trying to figure out what was going on inside his head. A few shakes of the head . . . chuckles . . . the laughter saying . . . Yeh . . . oh yeh. When Buddy opened his eyes he looked out into the vast desert . . . smiling. "Cody." He slapped her knee . . . finding a ballast for his tongue . . . his imagination. The knee felt so good his hand began to melt into her thigh. "Cody . . . I'll tell ya what. This trombone is strange . . . real strange. Kinda like yer truck. It only works when it wants to an' it needs a special formula . . . plus . . . ya gotta have a lot of belief and try. Now, if we could scrounge up the right concoctions I cud whup us up a rodeo that would make the Pendleton, Calgary, and Cheyenne Rowdaze-oohs look like a box of Cheerios. It would be the all-around gran' champyun piss-cutter . . . it would be better than the Second Comin' . . . cuz I'm gonna git my old friend and secret hero, the Cowboy Buddha, as the Peerade Chairman . . . and then you'd better step back and watch out cuz you ain't seen nuthin' compared to a Cowboy Buddha Super-deelux Rompin 'n' Stompin' Stammmpede! We'll have a grand parade, trick riders, chuck wagon races, fireworks, the meanest bulls north of the Rio Grande, and the finest cowboys in the circuit! Think ya could handle that?"

Cody coiled back, eyes as big as Sunday morning prayers. "Cowboy . . . I'm game for anything that rides, flies, or spins. Let's git going. Whatcha need?"

Buddy was rubbing his hands together . . . thinking in up-time. "I need everything ya got that makes bubbles. Where's yer medicine bag?"

Buddy helped Cody to her feet . . . almost elegant. Cody walked over to her truck and stuck her head into the back. "In here, but you'd better help me. It's heavier than the Lord's Ass on Monday morning."

Buddy ran over to the truck and opened her bag. "Well, I'll be a bull-nosed, flat-ass'd chicken smuggler. I think we've got everything we need . . . we're cowboys and we don't look down. First, I want a bucket of water. Better yet . . . some champagne. Got any?"

"French or domestic?"

"Hell . . . let's have both . . . I ain't prejudice."

Cody reached into her rough-'n'-ready ice chest and pulled out two bottles. Mumm's and Schramsberg. "How's this?"

"Great . . . jus' great!" Buddy opened the bottles, shooting the corks at two crows that were hanging around trying to look mystical. "Goddam bugger eaters . . . git out of here! You know what those birds like to eat? Assholes! Ya see 'em on the highways jumping on the road kills . . . 'n' all they eat are the assholes . . . leave the rest for the backpackers. That's what those health food factories make their pemmican out of . . . diesel-flattened rabbits and kangaroo mice. Didja know that? Oh . . . where was I? Now, what I need is something to make bubbles. Bubble bath . . . soap . . . anything."

Cody started rummaging through her bag. "I always wanted to be an alchemist. Swooosh . . . goose turds into silver dollars."

"Once ya see what Ole' Trom d' Bone can do you'll think we're the greatest all-round owlchemists in the West. That bottle of Alka-Seltzer . . . drop it in." Cody emptied the bottle into the bucket. "What else you got? What's in that bottle?"

"Hummers."

"Great! We'll git this show rollin' right off its tracks. Hummers, jumpers, beans . . . anything that sings . . . fast 'n' mean."

The speed went into the bucket. "Douche powder?"

"Be my guest," Buddy said as he gave Cody a one-quarter bow to her blind side.

"How 'bout some of this good tequila . . . can't hurt ya. Like I said . . . it's organic and Pancho Villa didn't win the war on tacos and beans alone."

"Dump it in."

"Vitamins?"

"Yeh . . . good fer the bulls. Good fer the cowboy . . . 'specially me. Help me git over these bruises from the last ride." Buddy started mixing up the goop with the trombone slide. "Ohhhh . . . it's lookin' gooooood. We need some more bubbles . . . any shampoo?"

"Yucca."

"Well, shit, ma'am . . . we ain't gonna drink it!"

Cody hit Buddy over the head with her douche bag. "Yucca is a shampoo, dummy . . . made from yucca plants."

"Oh . . . well sheeeet, Yuccarina . . . dump her in."

Cody poured in the shampoo. "Want some perfume?"

Buddy took the bottle, uncorked the lid, and stuck it up to his nose. "Yum yum . . . French underwear."

"Hey you! Don't snort the stuff. It's twenty beans a bottle."

Buddy shook the perfume into the bucket. "Cody . . . ya'll been to a lot of rodeos . . . right? So why don't ya take this foldin' chair an' sit down under that tree. Yer the hotshot director, an' I'm the visitin' magician. Ya jus' tell me how ya want this golden rodeo to be. Anything ya want . . . ya got it!"

Cody took the chair, a bottle of champagne, a crystal

glass, and a footstool and sat down under the tree. "Anything?"

"Yup. It's yers." Buddy finished stirring the brew and poured it into the trombone. He walked over to Cody. "All right, Cody St. Fancy Pants . . . we're ready to begin. What would you like?"

Cody took an inspection sip of champagne, looked through the glass, and stuck her boots up on the stool. She closed her eyes and when she opened them a twirling dervish was riding her grin. "All right, Dr. Sunday?" A nod. "I would like an old-fashioned three-story wooden hotel right over there by the river. There is a first-class restaurant and bar downstairs with lots of mirrors, crystal, brocaded drapery, and an excellent French cook. The rooms have brass beds, French antique wallpaper, marble counters, bathrooms and sunken tubs, Belgian lace curtains, Persian rugs, maple floors, walnut banisters, and a parquet dance floor that will hold one hundred cowboys. I'm a silent partner in the hotel. I own . . . say 99 per cent. Next door I want a high-class dress shop, and across the street I want a beauty parlor. On the corner is a bank that has just received a shipment of gold. Tonight, the Messiah Brothers are going to ride in and blow the safe and escape with all the money. Oh . . . while we're at the bank, stick in one hundred and ninety thousand dollars for me in a savings account. Now, five miles north of town there is a big spread that is owned by the banker. He has a Victorian house, barns, stables, and about five thousand head of Mexcun stock and a remuda of about fifty head. Mix them up. A-rabs, Appys, Morgans, pintos, quarters for the boys, and in a special stable there are three thoroughbreds that we'll start racing next year. There is a bunkhouse full of good-lookin' cowboys. Now, I want the town to be peopled by about five hundred

. . . give or take a few. A church is tucked in a stand of quaking aspen and pines. Any kind . . . it don't matter. I'll never go but it's good to look at . . . like the bank. Got all of that? Over there is the rodeo grounds. Not too big 'n' not too small. Jus' big enough so everybody in the town can be seated. The pens are full of calves, steers, bulls, saddle 'n' bareback broncs, and the cowboys are behind the chutes gettin' ready for the first event. The parade has already begun and the clowns are making everybody laugh. Now . . . have I left anything out?"

"Indians?" Buddy answered, looking a tad frazzled by the size of the order.

"Oh yes . . . we must have the Indians. We are surrounded by friendly Indians. They have some of the most beautiful land in the West. Lots of it and they could care less what we are doing because we haven't messed 'em over. They just think we're nuts and we think they're weird . . . everybody is happy. Throw in 'bout five million bufflers, a million deer and elk, antelope, eagles, hawks, owls flying over us like robins in summer, egrets, blue herons, whooping cranes, pelicans, snow parrots, and a whole pack of timber wolves that are out in the mountains trying to sneak into town to carry away the minister's delicious young daughters. Now, the rodeo is 'bout to begin an' you've entered three events. It ain't been rigged, so you'll have to ride your ass off in order to win. I'm the rodeo queen and soon the parade will come by and pick me up. Right now, I'm just going to sit here and watch it all be created . . . like a slow-motion implosion. Think you can handle all of this . . . cowboy?"

Buddy was shaking his head and laughing into the face of his trombone. "Cody . . . sounds like yer asking a short-order cook for a seven-course meal with a different wine 'tween each swallow. It's gonna be rough, lemme tell ya. I should be usin' a tuba. But hell an' goddam! I signed on fer tough, didn't I? You bet I did."

Buddy swung his trombone into a little dance, pumped the slide a few times and brought it in a double-helix to his lips. He gave his knees a mountain river bend just before the rapids and when he hit the straightaway he shot out a bubble that was as big as twenty-five thousand buffalo scrotums all sewn together with invisible gold thread. The bubble arrived like it had been living inside the trombone as the last great Western Trombonanza of Hysterical Truth. Inside the bubble was the town, the ranch, cowboys, buffalo, bankers, sheriff and deputy, strangers skulking around the general store, the rodeo grounds, stock for the rodeo, and the Indians were out in the boonies doing whatever Indians always do. The bank was full of money, and the Messiah Brothers were camped down by the river waiting until midnight to blow the safe.

"Hey, Jesus," Adolf Messiah said to his kid brother, "you got everything ready? We don't want no more fuckups . . . *Ja!*"

Jesus Messiah turned around and looked at his kid brother. "Adolf, how many times have I told you I know exactly what to do . . . so take it easy and pass me that bottle of schnapps . . . señor."

Adolf walked over to his brother and kicked the dynamite box out from under Jesus' ass. "No boozing before a job. That's an order! Here . . . eat some prunes!"

Jesus slowly got to his feet and eased out two .410 pistols. "Pass me the bottle, señor, or I'll blow your fucking head away from your anal retentive mustache . . . Mein Herr."

Buddy looked down at his masterpiece . . . scratching his head and feeling almost eight on a Ten Scale of

Godlike. "Could be better but what the fuck . . . this is
the West, ain't it?" He could hear the parade brass-plop-
ping its road-apple way to the Mustang Rodeo Grounds.
"Hey, Cody . . . look at it! It's jus' 'bout what you ordered." Buddy didn't hear a peep. No hummmmms, lip
smacks, hurrahs, or six-guns exploding at the southern
borders of heaven. He looked over at Cody. She was
rolled up in sleep. He walked over to her and peeked in.
"Hey," he said softly, "you 'sleep?" Nothing. Not even the
whisky eye. Her mouth was open and a small dribble of
saliva was spelunking down her chin. "Mmmmm . . . so
this is where the headwaters of the Big Lost start." A
small snoring purr was resonating from her throat. He
took the glass from her hand and touched her face. He
looked at her, studying her face, body, and up-against-
the-wall aura. The false eyelashes, which drooped instead
of swooped; her pants, which were faded and symbiotic
to her attractive ass; her boots, which needed a fifty-
dollar overhaul; her wrinkles, which were the curtains for
the stories of her turquoise. Buddy stepped back and
picked up the trombone. He closed his eyes and found
the perfect photo in his mind . . . a rejuvenation of the
painting of Cody on the door of her truck. He dropped to
his knees and with the image riding a prayer through his
wild white-water fantasies he began to speak to his trombone. He asked for compassion, understanding, and con-
sideration. He asked for a miracle, and he asked for a
no-trick clause, and no hidden shenanigans between the
iridescences. "I don't 'spect you to walk on water or talk
turkey with the whales. I don't 'spect you to exhaust yer
resources and I don't need one-hunner-pur-cent purfec-
tion. Jus' 'bout niny-nine would be hunky-dory. A deal
. . . partner? Do this fer me and I promise you the finest
of silver polish and champagne. I'll git you the lushest

deep-piled blue velvet case money can buy. It'll be covered with tooled leather with a handle made from buffler horn. Engraved Coeur d'Alêne silver will hug the corners and I'll never leave you laying around in the harse shit . . . no more! Three fingers, no . . . five fingers to the Cowboy Buddha . . . I promise."

He gave a gentle blow like kids blowing dandelion seeds, and a bubble flew out of the bell that had a feeling of the Madonna running inside the breath of a White Cloud's meadow; it had the sound of Chopin on a pedal steel; the smell of alfalfa and wild roses. It floated over to Cody and eclipsed her body . . . tucking in all the loose and scraggly edges. When she awoke she was seventeen and the most beautiful rodeo queen ever to ride the golden palomino through the echoed streets of rodeo tunes.

When Cody came around she jumped up and looked at her new riding clothes. "Buddy . . . what have you done?"

Buddy was putting the trombone back into the case. "I thought you'd like to be seventeen and West of the Rockies deelicious . . . again. Like before in the olden days."

Cody skipped over to the truck and looked in the side mirror. "Oh, my oh my . . . I can just verily remember how it was. And now . . . Oh . . . yes . . . I was . . . am . . . yes, am so beautiful." She spun around and faced Buddy. "How do I look . . . cowboy?"

Buddy was leaning against the tree, thumbs hitched down into his Levi's, sucking on a grass stem . . . rolling a cigarette with his imagination. "Cody . . . yer the most beautiful whoaman I've ever seen. Jus' remember . . . save the last dance fer me. Go on now . . . they're waitin' for ya."

Cody ran over to Buddy and kissed him on the cheek. "Thanks . . . everything is just like I imagined it to be. The town, hotel, the rodeo grounds. I think we should call the town St. Kid, Idaho . . . whatcha think? See you after the rodeo . . . Kid Cowbone." Cody mounted the palomino that was waiting for her and they rode off to join the parade . . . her gumdrop butt waving good-by.

Buddy watched her until she had disappeared, and then he put on his chaps, grabbed his rigging bag, and walked down behind the chutes. There they were . . . the Greats! Buddy looked around and counted fourteen All-around Cowboy title holders getting ready for their events. They were sitting in their saddles, taping their hands, legs, feet, and arms, working over their riggings, stretching their bull ropes, and rubbing them down with rosin.

"Hey . . . who's the kid?" he heard someone say.

"Ah . . . that's Sunday."

"Oh yeh . . . ain't seen him around before."

"You will . . . that kid has a lot of try."

"I saw where he'd draw'd some rank stock. He'd better have a lot of try . . . heart too."

Buddy had drawn Mortar and Pistol for his bareback horse; Jalepiños for the saddle bronc; for his bull he had Old FED (Find, Engage, Destroy). The parade was just leaving the rodeo grounds and the clowns were starting to kick around inside the arena . . . warming up the audience. Buddy wasn't listening to what the announcer was saying as he walked back and forth getting himself all psyched up for his first ride. He was thinking how he was going to ride, putting it all through his mind exactly the way Mortar and Pistol was going to react when he broke out of the chute . . . trying to think through the horse so their minds would be, hopefully, in sync . . . only with the opposite desires. He saw himself raking his spurs over the shoulders, pumping hard like a runaway locomotive, and he was going to marry his hand to the saddle handle like they were inseparable Siamese twins. Nothing was going to break him loose. Buddy was three turns up so he walked over to the chute with his rig and climbed the wood. Mortar and Pistol was an Indian Red, not too big, but he had heart and was known to be top rank. He would never run but just buck, spin, sunfish, contort until the rider felt like he was a jellied doughnut inside a paint-mixing machine. "Good . . . tha's good," Buddy chatted to himself as he eased down on the horse. "Now . . . you ain't no chute fighter are ya?" Mortar and Pistol took him without kicking up any trouble as another cowboy helped him cinch up his rig and set the flank strap. He tied on his glove and slid his hand into the han- dle—fishing and pumping his fingers until he felt he had the grip that could never be broken. Buddy got his legs up, toes out, and ankles locked as the announcer was calling his name. The chute cowboy got ready to pull in the flank strap as Buddy gave the nod and the gate was flung open to the moon. Mortar and Pistol exploded out into the arena with Buddy pumping his spurs, knifing him out, as the Red struck to the left, whipped up and back, shot to the right, and then bucked three times straight up into the air. Buddy never stopped whipping out the licks with his spurs as he was thrown back onto the rump and then lashed frontward as the horse went into a perpetual three-sixty centrifuge. Buddy was look- ing really tough, giving his ride lots of action and class, letting them know that Sunday had signed on for tough. He held on, bearing right down into the rigging, moving with M&P and showing the judges that he was out there to ride and not have a dirt supper. The whistle sounded just as Buddy was being spun right into a double-helix.

"Eighty-one," the announcer shouted. "Top score so fer. Let's give a big hand to Buddy Sunday. It's been rumored around that he is called the Trombone Kid. So let him know what a good rodeo fan is all about. Sunday . . . the Trombone Kid!"

"Long live the queen," Buddy shouted as he went behind the chutes to get his saddle ready for the bronc ride.

When it was time for the bulls Buddy was even with Jesse T. Rivers for top money. All he had to do was stay on Old FED for the count and he would be riding the big money and come out with the silver buckle the size of his grandmother's heart. Buddy took his rope off the post and went over to the chute. He had changed spurs so the rowels were locked and his boots were tied on. He looked down on Old FED, the Brahma Houdini who had only been ridden twice to the count in the last three years. Buddy and the chute cowboy put the bull rope around the bull's torso with the two bells hanging down below the brisket. Buddy had worked his glove over with rosin until it was as sticky as a back-seat screw in a midget. He took up the rope slack, wrapped the thongs around his glove, tying it off with fingers and teeth. He pulled the rope again until it was tight, wrapped the flat rope around his hand, and closed his fingers . . . letting the tail stay in front of his hand. He gyro'd his hips, hunched down, stuck his free arm out as a sky hook. He set his legs for the licks and closed his eyes for a second run-through of the next eight. It was all there before him. Ride for glory.

The Nod. Explosions like dynamite thrown into a full silo the bull blew out of the chute, whompkicking his hind legs and slapping Buddy onto his head. Perched like a judge over the mad bomber, Buddy was counting hairs until he was shot straight up, cracked onto his back, and then whipped downward as the bull tried to pull Buddy onto his horns. Buddy was flying rag-dolled all over the bull's back but he kept his spurs raking as FED snapped into a triple spin hoping to drop Buddy into the well. Buddy froze his hand into the rope until he had no feeling left in his fingers as he felt all of his organs begin to twist up into his throat. He was riding through the spin, trying not to be sucked down under the bull, and then came another blast as the bull shot up into the air gyrating south as Buddy was still spinning north. When the whistle was blown the bull lunged into a clown, lifting him into the air, as Buddy was thrown backward into the dirt. When Buddy hit the ground the bull was down on him working him over, trying to get his horns into protein and fur. Buddy rolled away from FED as the clowns tried to divert him by jumping over his back and pulling on his tail. Again, the bull came down on Buddy, almost knifing his head with his hind feet. All Buddy could see were a giant sack of dangling cojones and a whang the size of a Louisville slugger. There was only one thing to do or Buddy would be eatin' his shorts. Bite, or bite the dust. Buddy sprung up onto the bull belly, wrapping his arms and legs around the bull. He closed his eyes and chomped down as hard as he could on Old FED's swinging sack of delicatessen progeny. Old FED shot straight up into the air, bellowed, snorted, and farted tracers at the box seats. When he landed he took off after a clown who was running across the arena, jumping up into the air like he was being shot, as the trap door of his long johns fell open and a red goose dressed as a matador jumped out. The goose opened her cape and began to call the bull into her stage. "Hey . . . Toro," she quacked. "Toro . . . hey!" The bull looked back at Buddy, mean as sour owl shit, and then charged the red goose. *"Olé,"* the crowd roared as Cody St. Kid held up Un Numero Uno for Buddy to see he had won all of the prizes . . . plus the queen.

BAAAAAA - WHOOOOOOOOOOOOOOOOOOOOOOO-OOMMMMMMMMMMMMMMMMMM!!!

"What was that?" Buddy said to Cody as he dumpflipped a glass of champagne into his mouth.

"The bank. The Messiah Brothers have just blown the safe," Cody answered as she wrapped a Chinese silk robe around her body and looked out the window. "I never did like bankers." She danced back to the bed and poured two glasses, giving one to the Top Money Winner of the St. Kid, Idaho, Stampede. Buddy was laying on the bed, naked, except for a huge silver belt buckle hooked to a hand-tooled, virgin'd leather belt, and his Stetson. No boots or hard-on. "Hey . . . cowboy! You were great! I'd never seen anyone in all my years of rodayowe'n ride like you did tonight. Oh . . . we should try it again, just as soon as you finish your champagne."

"How does it feel to be seventeen again?" Buddy asked Cody as he balanced the glass on his forehead.

"Ah . . . Buddy, may it never stop. Look at this hotel. It's beautiful! And look at all of these fine clothes. It's a dream come true. I could go on like this forever . . . easily fore-ever, Buddy. But . . . how do you feel?" Cody pivoted on the bed, cocked her head into Buddy's eyes, as her hand was running downriver nearing the rapids.

"Sore . . . damn sore from that last dump. I chipped a tooth when I was chompin' away on Ole FED. I'll live . . . but I don't know if I'm gonna survive you. Hongry-er than a stoved-up grizzly . . . ohhhhweeeee! Whoa . . . oh . . . heh . . . wow . . . this ole hotel is really rockin' 'round. Maybe we shud go down and join 'em?"

"Ho . . . you jus' want to go down there and show off. Let's wait. Later we'll go down and dance and see that everybody gets fed breakfast. I jus' want to be right here with you. Breathe it all in, make love with you some more, and drink the rest of the champagne. You know, cowboy . . . it's not everyday a young rodeo virgin queen gets to have such an elaborate comin' out party. Look at me. I've got the prize cowboy, the best room in the hotel, money in the bank . . . oh my, this sure beats workin' for a livin' . . . hey, cowboy?"

Buddy removed the glass from his forehead and gave Cody his best I-Don't-Believe-It-or-Not stare. "Seventeen, my hard cowboy ass! Don't you remember? Ah . . . what the hell. You're the sexiest sweetheart of the West, fifty-six or seventeen. Ya sure do look good right now." Buddy poured the champagne over Cody's breasts and started licking them. "Oh . . . oh . . . I always wanted to do this . . . oh . . . hmmmmm . . . yummmmnnn . . . oh . . . it's so gooooood."

Cody grabbed Buddy and started kissing him as she pulled him on top of her. "Let's see how you rode that bull one more time . . . cowboy?"

The top floor began to keep time with the bottom, bucking and stomping on its granite foundation. There was so much noise running through the floor boards that Cody and Buddy didn't hear the sheriff, Jesse T. Rivers, come up the stairs. When no one answered the door Jesse very politely stepped back two boot lengths and kicked it open. Buddy was inside a triple spin, riding right off the crystal chandeliers and going down on Cody for the last great stampeding finale. Buddy turned in mid-air, looked at Jesse T., and fell onto the bed missing Cody by five feet. "Damn! We didn't ring for the sheriff."

"Hold it right there, Sunday . . . yer unner arrest!"

Cody pulled the covers around her body, tucking herself into safety. Buddy was looking for his Levi's. "Unner arrest . . . what fer?"

Jesse T. walked over to the table and picked up the trombone. "Fer settin' up that bank robbery, holdin' a roa-dee-oh and peerade without a purmit, and seducing this lovely-young-thing."

"Bank robbery, my sore, busted ass!" Buddy shouted as he was stumbling around with his jeans, cross-stepping, and cuff-stomping. "I didn't have anything to do with smokin' that bank. Ah sheeeeeet!" Buddy threw his Levi's on the floor. "Goddam . . . these Levi's are jus' like a cheap hotel . . . no ballroom." He turned around and faced the sheriff . . . hands on hips.

"Hell you say," Jesse T. fired back. "We caught the Messiah Brothers before they could git out of town. They confessed everything."

Buddy jumped at Jesse, hoping to snag the trombone. Jesse T. side-stepped Buddy, whipped out his six-gun, and aimed it one-round-high above the buckle. "Stay right there, Sunday . . . settle down."

Buddy eased off . . . trying to remember the beginning. "What in the hell do you mean . . . settle down? I created all of this. Everything! This is my fantasy an' yer trying to drag me off to the hoosegow. Gimme back my trombone an' I'll show you . . . I'll erase all of you. Send ya back into a dime-store novel . . . back into sagebrush an' Alka-Seltzer."

Jesse T. spun the revolver six times, bringing it right back to Buddy's centerfold. "No way . . . Sunday. We like it here. You might of created all of this, but we've got laws now. We've got a good little town here and we plan to keep it this way. This is the West. We don't like anyone comin' in here an' gettin' fancy with us. Git yer clothes on."

Cody wasn't saying a word. She just pulled up more covers and settled in for the night.

"How old are you, Miss St. Kid?" Jesse T. asked Cody.

"Seventeen," Cody answered, dropping her eyelashes onto her peaches and cream complexion.

"Seventeen! Seventeen! Jesus! Sheriff . . . this whoaman is fifty-six years old. She's old and damn near worn out from too much rodeoing. I'm the one who made her into seventeen so she could be the queen."

"Yeh . . . yeh, so you cud git into her seventeen-year-old pants. Sounds to me like you've been thinkin' with the wrong head . . . Sunday." Jesse T. cocked the hammer on his pistol. "Seventeen will git ya twenty . . . any day."

Buddy sat down on the bed, his head resting in the cradle of his callused hands. "Let's all calm down. I can explain all of this if you'll jus' give me back my trombone."

"Give it back to you? Why, I'd jus' as soon turn over my six-gun. I'm told you could do some real damage to our town with this trombone. I'm holding this as state's evidence."

Buddy grabbed Cody's arm. "Tell 'im, Cody. Tell 'im how'd you blew out of my trombone on the Wyoming border. How we made this whole thing up cuz yer truck, ol' buffler, couldn't make it to Stanley. This town, rodeo, the Messiah Brothers . . . everything. Tell 'im!"

Cody poured out a glass of champagne, took a sip, and set the glass on the rosewood night table. "Ahhhh . . . this is excellent champagne. Jesse T., would you mind ringing for room service?" Cody looked up at Buddy. A look that has kept the whole world in perpetual motion. Survival. "Now, Buddy, just relax. I'll find you a good lawyer. I have no bad feelings about what happened so I want to help. I won't press charges so it will just be the bank roast and the permits. I like it here . . . even though I am the banker's daughter. But then, what can a beautiful seventeen-year-old banker's daughter do but be the queen?"

"Oh, sheeeeeet!" Buddy said as he fell back onto the bed.

"You toss a good story, cowboy," Jesse T. said to Buddy, "but you'd better save it fer the judge. Get yer clothes on. We don't want the likes of you comin' in here and messin' with our wimmen." Jesse T. was checking the cleavage. Perky. Cody caught the long shot.

"Why don't you let the wimmen decide that? Hey . . . what's all that noise?" Buddy jumped up and ran over to the window. "What's those people doin' down there?"

"That's an angry mob, Sunday. They want to string you up for instigatin' the robbery. They don't know that I found you in bed with the banker's daughter. We'd better sneak out the back way." Jesse T. walked over to Buddy and gave him a poke with the barrel of his shooter. "Move . . . cowboy!"

Buddy looked down at the crowd. They were angry, walking back and forth, shouting to Jesse T. to bring out the bull rider so they could string him up. Over by the general store a group of buffalo hunters and skinners were fixing their gear to leave early in the morning to hunt the buffalo. "My god . . . what's goin' on? Hasn't anyone learned anything? Are you still locked into the same stories? Does everyone keep makin' the same mistakes?"

"Looks like to me, Trombone Kid, yer the one who's

made the mistake. We like it this way an' that's the way we plan to keep it. Come on . . . get a move on!"

Buddy turned around and looked at the sheriff. "Damn . . . all I wanted was a ride . . . an easy ride to the rodeo. Jus' one good ride." He walked back to the bed and put on his clothes. "Well, Cody . . . looks like you've got yerself a home. Guess that's what ya always wanted."

"That's right, cowboy. It's a good town with honest folks. A place where I can raise a family. I've seen it all and this is where I want to be. So long. I'll be seeing you around . . . cowboy."

"Move it, Sunday. Let's mix ourselves a walk. They'll be breakin' down the doors if we don't git goin'."

Jesse T. motioned to Buddy to get moving through the door. A narrow-hipped, six-gun nod. A gesture that has been practiced behind the barn by every kid who has been through all of the reruns from Dodge to Silver City. The West hangs on like a fused vertebrae within the liquid spine of the earth . . . reliving its life over and over, using the same characters from matinee billboards to musicians on the wooden stage. It's a good story . . . even when it's written in longhair. The West. Full of unwritten laws and wild dreams; mountains so high they bring visions rolling down with their rivers; meadows so full of wild flowers, streams, and tall wild grasses, translations are needed by everyone who attempts to understand their bodies. A strange reality where truth rides hard and beauty ain't no camouflage. The West, where Buddy signed on for tough . . . and, as they say behind the chutes . . . "that's what cowboyin's all about."

A Weaver of Light

Golden St. Augustine was sitting in the back of his old pickup rolling a cigarette. The sun had just cleared a strange-looking beer-bellied cloud and the early evening air was beginning to cool. He leaned back against his gear, opened his shirt, and pushed his hat back on his head.

Golden reached into his chuck box, pulled out a bottle of brandy, and took a long drink. A small liquid fire rolled through his body, penetrating the loneliest of corners. "Amazin' stuff," Golden said to the label on the bottle; "a few more dances with yer sweetness and truth and those mountains over yonder will be in perpetual sunset." Golden didn't need much, but he needed it. He was becoming lonely in the mountains, especially during the long winters where he was stoved-in like a hoot owl up a grizzly's asshole.

A few trucks humped by with kayaks poised like insignia of hierarchies on their way to the Middle Fork. Patriots of the white water, captured into the rivers and mountains with different ideas about how to live with the earth. "After you" has been rotated by a decree of mysticism and whiskers to mean through the astrology of language . . . First Me! One young man in a twelve-G, four-wheel, winched and double roll-barred cinched pickup looked over at Golden and shot him the clenched fist. The signal? The sacred sign? Golden pointed an index finger at the pantheistic vampire and shot him right through his ecology sticker. No peace or victory signs, no homecomings or deals made with bear hugs . . . jus' a straight, forty-four mountain magnum shot from brandied-brown eyes. "Keep movin' on . . . Don Juan."

The difference, Golden wanted to say as he had them strapped to trees, shooting flies and hornets off their danglies with his hunting bow, is being able to live on the earth and leave no tracks. Learn how to disappear into your own silence and give up what is not important. A wilderness ain't a wilderness with ten thousand backpackers, river runners, mountain climbers, water ouzel lovers, deep-knee benders, and golden eagle fuckers. Not one of you could last a week by yourself. If you could, you wouldn't need all that hardware. Three years junkied to your Master, charge on! . . . to hang your ass over a fallen dream and crap out your vision on a wild onion. "Ah . . . fuckum all, especially the liberated ones," Golden mumbled down the throat of the bottle. He rolled his shoulders up two notches and slapped his stomach. It was hard and flat from thirty years of chopping wood and running all over the Selway, Bitterroots, and Beaver heads. He pulled out a piece of lint from his belly button and stuck it into a small tobacco sack. Someday soon, he felt, his cabin would disappear into some organized government yodeling program as the wind tasted more and more like aluminum.

Golden finished the cigarette and snubbed it out on the bed of the pickup. He jumped out of the truck and walked around to the cab. His name was on the door—faded letters along with his profession. Hunter and Guide. Perhaps he thought he should change it to Dreamer and Drifter . . . riding out the legend into unsocial insecurity.

Golden pushed through the batwing doors of the Cowboy Hotel and walked in. The last time he had been in the Cowboy Hotel the walls were covered with hunting trophies, old rifles, traps, skins, and pistols. They had been replaced by rugs and blankets from Nepal, Tibet, Morocco, Mexico, and Arizonan and New Mexican Navajo. He walked around the room looking at each weaving. "Good," he thought, "no more ghosts." He had always disliked trophy hunting. The head becoming more important than the life of the animal. His customers would fly in for the hunt, bag the animal or have Golden shoot it, and then fly off with the head on ice. Their money, and his winter's food. An easy arrangement. As far as he was concerned they took the asshole and he got the spirit.

He sat down at the end of the bar next to a large window that looked out onto the mountains. Old peaks, snaggled and rugged, cutting into the sky like ancient battles. The sun was just beginning to drop behind the mountains and the clouds were picking up the light as it bent its way through the rainbow—long shafts of rays

were slicing across the sky flooding the testimonies of
Buddhists, Cowboys, and Heathens.

Syringa Rose stood in the hotel's kitchen looking at
Golden. Seven years ago she had lived with him in the
Bitterroots. She left him just before hunting season because she couldn't watch the killing. It was not her nature. He couldn't leave, and she didn't want to stay. Their
planets were still sifting different stories.

She took off her apron and smoothed out her hair. She
was excited and not afraid to see him. She knew that
someday they would be together, perhaps not as lovers,
but as teachers and friends to each other. She pushed
open the doors and walked over to him. Golden was still
locked-through the window at the mountains, but when
Syringa was close he began to pick up her presence and
turned around.

"Well I'll be . . ." he began, "look at this will you . . .
Syringa! Where did you come from? Damn!" He leaned
backward to check out what he was seeing. "Well, I was
just thinking about you, how I was going to ride down to
your little spread and pay you a visit. Holy Moly. And
here you are. Damn!" Before she could speak he picked
her up and gave her one of his finest and least civilized
hugs. "Syringa . . . it's good to see you."

Syringa sputtered but her words became lost in his territory of six feet six with arms and shoulders like avalanches. Her body, more spirit than meat, melted. There
was nothing she could do but be absorbed. She would be
found sometime during the first thaw. Golden finally put
her down on the barstool and stepped back to look at her
again.

"My . . . Golden, you're as big and handsome as ever
. . . the years just make you bigger and stronger," she
said, trying to recover from the rondayvoo-crunch Golden

had given her. "Well . . . it's been a long time. I've been thinking a lot about you, too . . . wondering how you're doing. What brings you down so far?"

"Well, Syringa, wow . . . it's so good to see you. I've been feeling just like an old hermit with only his false teeth to talk to at night. Hell, I was just lonely. Today's my birthday. I wanted to celebrate with something alive besides the standard Garden of Eden crew. I've given up the hunting business . . . ain't taken anyone out in over a year. That should make you happy, I'm sure. I've changed. It's changed. Now, I look at these mountains and all I see are mountains. Ain't that something? Well . . . let's have a drink."

Syringa felt a smile the size of a whooping crane's history sweep through her body—wings floating with laughter. "This is going to be on the house, Golden, as long as you want. Dickel . . . is that what you still dream about?"

"Yeh, that's right, when I'm not dreaming about you."

"Oh yeh . . . ?" Syringa went behind the bar and poured out two shots of whisky. "To you and fifty-six. Happy birthday."

"Numbers, what do they mean?"

Syringa touched their glasses. "Synchronicity, let's say."

"Well, here's to synchronicity and you," Golden toasted as he shot the whisky into his mouth. "Ahhhhh . . . that's good for one year of my life . . . only fifty-five to go. Say . . . who owns this place now . . . you?"

"Well, sort of. Infinity owns most of it. Remember her . . . Jonquil's wife. She's in Nepal right now . . . doing just great."

Golden studied the hotel. "Well, this place really feels good. It's soft . . . warm. Damn! Some of the West is changin' for the best despite all of us old farts who are still hangin' on to our grandfather's bedtime bullshit . . . still thinkin' it's eighteen-eighty 'n' all the redskins have been pacified. Ha!" Two men and two women came into the bar and sat down at the end of the counter. Syringa put the bottle of Dickel in front of Golden and went over to help the two couples.

The jukebox was punched into action. One hundred and twenty tunes waiting to be spun out into everyone's cowboy heart with runaway boots and stampeding lovers. Sideswiped, sidetracked, but not dee-railed. Broke, broken up, broke down, but not broken. Cowboys dancing with their asses stuck out in the wind like hitchhiking thumbs. Country and Western haiku . . . once again. . . .

> Cowboys dance with their
> asses stuck out in the wind
> like hitchhiking thumbs.

Another well-wisher slid a drink down the bar. "Happy birthday. May the sun never set on the rowels of yer spurs."

"Bowels?"

"Rowels!"

"Oh. You-too-buddy."

Golden heard his own music. All he had ever wanted. The waterfalls booming down through the canyons; the wind sweeping over the frozen lakes, and the vast great silence of winter. Hawks, herons, the staccato of aspen leaves, the sound of one earth breathing. This was the music he danced to every morning when he would jump out of bed and run to the lake for a sunrise eye-waker.

"It's 'the scrotum tightening sea . . .'"

"Who said that?"

"Some writer," old Sammy Jump said. "I'm reading yer mind and I think yer far too serious."

Golden looked around the room. It was all becoming close to squirrelly. He was feeling ancient. Not tired, old, but geological. Deep, scarred, and somewhat shitfaced. Shitfaced but not shitheaded. One more round and one more ceremony. The marriage into old. Into wise. Into mellow and old. The Mellow Old Fart Company. That's what he wanted painted on his truck, and then he'd have a grand ceremony marking his movement into old age as a graceful fart-face. A peaceful and most humble fart-face. Best yet.

"I'm going to marry myself to the Dreamer," Syringa said seven years ago when they were smoking fish by the lake. "Marry myself into my own dreams and to all of the dreamers who have lived before."

"You drunk? I hope they're a good lay. Sounds illegal to me."

"Golden. Why don't you go fart up a rope?"

"Huh?"

Golden had thought a lot about marriage although he had never found anyone who would share the life he needed to have. Consequently, he became more involved with his own life as a marriage into himself, his body, into his own woman. She. He-she, she-he. Living inside his own marriage. Growning into his own male and female and having the responsibility of being both.

Weaving through his own genitals and ultimately into his own light.

"Would you make me a loom?" Syringa asked Golden that one summer.

"For you?"

"No . . . for you. You could weave your own clothes, and weave your own coverings. Beautiful woolen blankets and coats instead of hanging your body with skins. Dead animals . . . blah!"

"I think you're trying to weave me around your feminine finger . . . Syringa Rosebud."

"You have sheep in the valley and there is a spinner in Salmon."

Shedding old skin.

Weaving from caves, caravans, and temples.

Wood for the loom. Wool for the body. Dyes from the earth. And from the sun you take the colors and from your dreams you weave your stories and mythology. It is your journey.

The bar was filling up with people hungry for the evening's massage. Golden had built a fire in the fireplace and the light was playing on the walls illuminating the rugs and blankets. Their colors were alive with their own histories, telling stories as they lived on the walls. Stories of people, hands, earth, rain, fire, and the continual migration of life. The power of the rainbow and the growing of food. It was a long way from stuffed animals with glass eyes.

Syringa came over to where Golden was sitting and sat down next to him. She was drinking tea and brandy. She studied his face, trying to look deeper than the grand view of mountains and wild alpine lakes, farther than the clouds running in thunderheads over the ridges. She was searching for that strong, earth-vertebrae that rode through his body like herds of wild horses. A man who had created his own life, beyond stories, where great blue herons, eagles, and buffalo herds ran and flew through his body as cells in his blood. A man who believed that it was impossible to own any part of the earth.

"Do you still have horses?"

"Only two. I had to get rid of them when I stopped

hunting. I couldn't keep them in feed during the winter. I took them into a low, beautiful valley to become legends and mysterious ghosts raiding on the minds of back-packers and river runners."

Syringa put a spoon of honey into her tea, stirring the drink slowly with the bar spoon. "I'm going riding tomorrow. Why don't you come out to my place and stay awhile?"

Golden licked his lower chakras and stuck them into the wind to test Syringa's direction. He grinned, trying not to look horny.

Syringa continued. "How about a wonderful hot springs that spills into a stream where a deep pool of water has mixed itself to just about one hundred and five degrees. Give or take . . . depends on the weather. I bet you could use a hot bath and a good massage." Syringa watched Golden's face. She knew and called out her reserves. "How about homemade breads, jellies, soups, and I'll even find some venison just so you can keep your teeth polished. And . . . when was the last time you got . . ."

"Stop . . . stop right there. Enough's enough. You want me to start dancing on the bar doing some crazy, perverted borealis mating dance?"

"I'd love it. Naked?"

"An erection as big as a whale's."

"Humping the Cowboy Buddha's mother."

"Sheeeet! Humping the Cowboy Buddha!"

Syringa held out three fingers. "Give me three . . . I lost two in the thrasher."

"All right. . . ." Golden fumbled around trying to snag his pinky with his thumb but he had never been very good at sports.

"Party's over . . ." Syringa said as she slid off the stool.

"Mountain men have big thirsts." Syringa left to wait on two new customers. Cowboys crossed with a hip version of a rock star slightly used. Last year's model with low mileage. Another creation on the stagecoach translation. Pointed boots and turquoise smiles crossed with styled hair and dreams of faded denim. Strangers riding shotgun inside the incognito of themselves. They could be anyone: lawyers, doctors, ancient Sanskrit detectives, or airbrushed dildos.

Syringa had said, "Treat everyone as your teacher no matter whether it be a redneck, six-gun owl, or the Buddha hawk." Golden looked at the fancy cowboys, trying to see beyond their license plates. Twins or maybe pseudoalleles. He lowered his eyebrows down across the horizon onto their sunsets; he squinted his eyes and wrinkled his nose, trying to locate their auras, halos, white light, or just a good, old-fashioned, touchdown feeling. Nothing. He opened his eyes and looked at them head on. They still looked like Philadelphia necrophiliacs to him. "Ahhh fuck 'em! I'm too old, drunk, and stubborn."

An Indian woman came in and sat down at the bar. She was in her late twenties sliding into thirty-five. She was attractive in a way that made you think of Appaloosa horses and temples in Tibet. She had a few scars around her cheeks, and she wore half Levi's and half velvet somehow sewn together so that you couldn't tell which side she was fighting for. Turquoise rode her arms like invading blue-faced mongols. Cowboy boots walked her feet. She looked somewhat drunk, but acted sober; and she ordered straight whisky without checking her bank shots. She never bothered to look around, check out the hotel and bar, or size up the customers. It could have been any bar in town. All she wanted to do was drink without reruns or commercials.

Unfortunately, the commercials began. The two four-barrel cowboys sucked in on her—drafting on her ass—with strange eye winks between them. Their secret code. The asshole brothers with their superstudded, dildo minds purchased from the savings of five hundred wrappers from organic hot dogs (soybeans and pig fat).

"Get lost!" the woman graveled out of her oystered voice chamber. It didn't take. Their cocks were bigger than their brains, riding the express between their mouths and their scanty underwear.

"Where you from?" the twin called Billy Scripture said to her, putting his drink next to her shot glass of whisky.

She looked up and studied her diminishing reflection in the etched mirror. "From? What does that mean? You wouldn't believe where I'm from. Would be like asking a glass of water where she's from."

"Oh, Jesus," the other brother, whose name was Billy Verse, said. "I think we got a heavy on our hands." Before they could make their next move she turned to both of them—giving them a face from both sides of her head—comedy and tragedy coming out of the middle chute.

"Listen, goddammit! I came in here to get drunk and listen to the music. The music ain't too bad, and the whisky is good. So why don't you fuck off! Go outside and hump your pickups. Blow up an outhouse, or take your grandmother to a porno flick. Jus' leave me alone."

The twins were impenetrable. Hardheaded to the absolute cowpie of themselves—a geometric advancement of dumb. They blasted down two more drinks and continued. "I've seen you before. Yeh . . . really. Perhaps in Sante Fe, Flagstaff . . . maybe Spokane."

She floated her mind down into her drink. "We all look alike . . . shithead."

"How much?"

"What the fuck you talkin' about?"

"Easy. How much you sellin' your ass for . . . these days."

Billy Scripture ordered three more drinks. He paid for them with a fifty, leaving the change on the counter.

"Listen," she said, "I'll give you this town if you'll leave me alone."

They had all the time in the world. The hustle was on and the meaning always changes depending on the prize. A "no" was "yes" in their male world. To them, They all wanted It. You just had to break them down. Like horses, if you couldn't ride them you turned them into bucking stock.

Golden finished another drink. Sammy Jump was down on his knees trying to eat-out a woman who had on the only skirt in town. She lifted up her dress and continued talking to her date about log house condos. Two couples were dancing to a Texas song—the words whiplashed in sadness, brutality, and penitence. Confessions in blood. Ah . . . makes the sinnin' so much better next time 'round.

Golden walked outside to take a leak. The Buckaroo Room was filled up to capacity with a nose orgy. Scripture and Verse watched him leave—checking out the competition.

No moon but a million stars.

Golden watched the sky as he relieved himself. He turned around in a circle as he looked at all of the stars and constellations. He knew them and he didn't know them. He knew their names and sometimes he felt he could understand their meaning through refracted silence as the opening to the question. How to take a whiz and watch Aquila the Eagle, Delphinus, and Boötes—like all of the old astronomers when they first raised their heads while taking a leak. The beginning of flight into the tensions of the universe. Discovering the abstractions like the acupuncture points of the body. Bringing it all inside.

"Jesus, am I shitfaced." Golden gave his whang a double-polka to shake off the fat ones, and then two-stepped it back into his jeans. "Shit! I can't even remember the questions I was gonna ask. Something about what I'm s'pose to be doing . . . hunting my own food. Killing animals. Hiring out as the bwana of the Bitterroots. Fat-ass'd hunters who couldn't kill a hot dog by themselves. Perhaps the answer is not to believe in the original question. Is there a God? Ah, fuckit!" He walked over to an old pickup that had broken down twenty years ago and had never been moved. Everything was still intact except that the motor had frozen up like a constipated ice jam. Twenty winters of fifty below.

Golden smoothed his butt over the front fender and leaned his back against the hood. "With whisky, old-timer, the answers are only laughable. Without it, the whole sourdough of existence should have stayed in the grub box." Golden rolled a cigarette, thinking through his feelings and laughing at his cross-eyed calculations. He hung the cigarette on the edge of his mouth and struck a match with his thumbnail. "Well, old-timer, what you have given us is the fascism of biology. Ain't nothing more. Perhaps it would be okay if I was being hunted down for food. At least that's a balance . . . keeping the human nervous and honest. The only thing we do now is hunt down ourselves with our minds and that's only geological. It ain't even a victory. Like the squeeze of technology in an eternity of soybeans. Ah, shit! Goddammit! The human condition, old-timer, has absolutely swallowed us up. Perhaps, if we could all realize that there ain't nothing more, it would be different. No rewards, heavens, retirement condos next to your bungalow, no spaceships to ziparoo us away to some advanced honky-tonk, no guaranteed reincarnation or juju—once a shit-beetle always a shit-beetle. Sorry, folks, what you got is what you got . . . too bad! Maybe we'd all get down and make it work, try and make this place last for a while." Golden slapped the fender of the truck. "Jus' like you . . . heh? Trucks never wear out, only parts. But since we can always buy a new one, no one gives a shit. The only thing you got to look forward to is a steady diet of rust and raggedy-ass snow storms. Too bad, earth. Smoothed flat and sucked dry. So what is it old-timer? Sorrow? Pain? A big joke? All three mixed together as a steady diet of humanity. Sheeeeet! I don't believe a word of it." Golden slid down from the fender. "But even then, god-dammit! It's amazingly beautiful once you get the hang of it. Past the bullshit, the mumbo-jumbo, and you're home free. And then, at its best, it's a damn good magic show."

Scripture and Verse came shouting out the door with the Indian woman. She was staggering but the two brothers were holding her arms as they guided her to their van. They didn't see Golden tucked away in his own midnight crossfire. At first he thought he should find out what they had in mind with the woman, but he didn't want to butt in. She didn't look like she was being forced. Perhaps, he thought, they were what she was looking for in the first place. Hard to believe, but like the spoon as the male and female, flipped over the receptive becomes the mountain. Maybe they just wanted to play Cowboys and Indians. There was a bumper sticker that read, When This Camper Is Rockin' Don't Bother Knockin'.

Golden went back into the bar. He was glad to see the Flying-A-Brothers gone. Syringa was behind the bar,

cleaning up, putting away the glasses. All of the customers had left except for Sammy, who was sleeping
under the mother-of-pearl inlay rosewood pool table.
Golden watched Syringa for a long time, studying her
presence. The illumination that radiated through her face
was like the sun filtered through aspen leaves. Everything
that came through her was returned as a refinement—
from her breathing to her swearing. When they had spent
the summer together she had taught him what it was like
to see through the eyes and body of another human—
another mind and sex. She had been the first woman he
had ever allowed to penetrate beyond the first cavalry of
his maleness. "Don't be trapped inside your own body.
Let it change, and think about evolution. Use your body
as a healing instrument, a filter, and not as a weapon.
Learn how to talk with yourself, with me, and with everything that is alive . . . as a friend and not as a conquest. Take the time. All language is only vibration. Send
it out and it will return." She was soft and gentle and
never did she let herself poach upon his own secret for-
ests. When she talked with him it was like she was speaking with herself, or to the sky. She would put out her
ideas. They were never meant to be obeyed . . . only
heard as healing sounds in the mountains.

After Syringa left his mountain hideout, Golden spent
all of his free time learning how to hunt with his mind.
Using the bow and calling the animal to him. The body-
hunter, the bow and the arrow, the deer, were all vibrating on the same wavelength and they became all of the
same being. He fasted and learned how to wait. Sitting
for hours, all day, waiting with the one image in mind.
Calling . . . until the deer appeared, giving that life to
him. He was hungry and there was no food in the cache

box. He learned how to listen to the voices of the wind. He learned how to dream.

As he watched Syringa, something even stronger than love was flooding his body. He was finally beginning to realize how much they were the same male and female going back for centuries like amber separated from the mother tree, washed down through the great rivers of Europe until they apeared in Egypt on the same piece of jewelry worn by the same mother queen.

Golden went back outside. On the porch he heard noises coming from the area where Scripture and Verse had their rig parked. He started walking toward the van to find out what was going on. The Indian woman was shouting and yelling inside the truck. Golden started running toward the noise when the back door was kicked open and the woman was thrown out into the dirt street. The twins jumped into the front, started the motor, and took off, spinning and kicking dirt and gravel all over the woman. In five long strokes Golden was over to her. When he bent down to see if she was hurt she jumped up and ran for her car. She fell across the front seat, hit the jockey box, and pulled out a pistol. She scooted back out and threw one arm across the top of the car and leveled the pistol at the van, which was already turning the corner. Golden slowly started walking toward her. She relaxed her arm and put her head on top of the car. She started mumbling something to herself but Golden couldn't hear what she was saying. Then, she slowly turned around, raised the pistol bracing her wrist with her left hand.

"I'm going to blow your fucking head off!"

Silence.

"Those two motherfucking white-eyed bastards took all of my money and my jewelry. All of it! I was going home to be with my kids. I was finally going home. Goddammit! You could have stopped them. I saw you lurking over there by the old pickup. Asshole! You could have stopped them."

He looked up at the stars. His friends and guides. What did they say? He didn't feel frightened. To be hunted you have to run. He looked back to her, trying to absorb her face. All of it. The tears and the sorrow. Hundreds of years of being on the run, chased, duped, raped, imprisoned, severed from her religion. How easy it would be for her to pull the trigger. He believed in her more than he believed in anything else. No matter who she was, or what she had been, she held a power within her that arrested all of his fears. He finally knew who she was. "What are you supposed to be in my life?" He spoke to her silently. "Have you called me to you? Did you call me from my cabin this morning? Must I accept? Have you called down the mountain? Are we finally the same? Have I finally become what I have always lived?" Golden heard another voice coming to him. The voice of Syringa from another conversation or perhaps another lifetime. He knew. She was right and he finally understood.

"Are you my teacher?"

"What? What the fuck are you talking about? I'm going to be your motherfucking end. That's what I'm going to be. I've had it with all of you white fuckers. All of you!"

Golden tried to slow down his heart. Just a slow drumbeat into one invisible life. To bring her to him—learning how to hunt. He breathed . . . slowly. He had time. "Are you going to teach me how to die? Is this what you're here for?"

"I'm going to blow a hole through you the size of a pickup truck."

Golden started moving toward her. His head was clear as he breathed in the mountain air. Inhaling, that great breath. Exhaling, his being. He was going to walk right through her. He could feel it.

"Jesus . . ." she yelled at him, "you've seen too many movies. It's not going to work. I've shot someone before. I can do it."

Golden continued to walk. She thumbed back the hammer. He heard the clicks. "I think you are my teacher," he heard his voice say over and over again. His palms were open. He was close to her now. Neither one of them could miss.

"Don't come any closer."

Syringa was standing ten feet away silently talking to the woman. Voiceless. Speaking to her through her mind . . . trying to make her see and feel through Golden's body, to find his spirit that is her own and of her people. A beautiful life that needs to be free from ownership and the demanding migration of greed. "See through him . . . his spirit is yours. His past lives are from your people. He is the buffalo, the fire from the sun, the eagle and the hunter. He is the life that has carried the dream, the vision of perfection within our own calluses and tears. He has lived alone in the mountains so he could live without owning anything but his own body. It is your gift he has been given."

Golden sat down on the ground. He closed his eyes. His body became very calm like a high mountain lake, smooth and silent when the sun is rising over the peaks. He didn't have to say anything more. Silence was his celebration. He finally knew he didn't have to understand his life any more. He had arrived.

"Stand up!"

Syringa was slowly walking up to Golden. She was

moving inside the circle, into the woman's life of earth and sky—stepping into the fire as she translated the differences of their lives into one mind—into a ceremony of their spirits. A healing of the great river that is flowing through all life, invisible within the mountains. Syringa sat down and entered the ceremony. She touched Golden's arm telling him she was there. They were together.

The Indian woman looked at them, at something she had always wanted to destroy and be rid of . . . forever. To be given her life again as it once was with her own people without cities, white people, and reservations. She wanted her life to be honest with the earth like it had been before without the tragedy of conquest by deception, without the suffering, and without the endless desert of ignominity. She looked up into the mountains where her people had gone to hunt and fish, trade with the other Indians, and bathe in the hot springs. They were all there. Her ancestors. And soon she would join them . . . soon.

She put her mind into the hand that held the pistol to give her courage, to steady the flight. Her hand felt strong, her fingers were like talons swooping in on a rabbit. The running was finally going to be over.

She lowered the pistol and looked down to feel her target. She only needed to see them once. She adjusted her mind into the final contraction, but the pistol could not find them. It closed empty with air. They were gone. She shook her head, blinked, and looked again. Nothing. It had only been a second as she watched the mountains but now they had vanished. She looked all around her but she couldn't see any sign of them. Even the emotions of anger and hatred that had captured her were gone.

The night was dark and silent, the wind softly sweeping her face . . . there was nothing to destroy.

She dropped the pistol onto the ground and looked up into the sky. To the stars who rode through the night in her own body as storytellers and messengers. She looked up and felt the singing, the chanting, and the prayers. The songs to the earth and to the life of her people. She felt the anger that had been with her through her whole life leave and disappear into the sky. She was alone. She was alone with the night and with herself and with the stars that will always be there for her—for her children and her grandchildren—moving through the darkness as weavers of light.

The Floating Rose

Jonquil Rose . . . Jus' One More Cowboy, had decided it was time that he went off to seek his vision. It had been too long since his one-quarter Apache wife, Infinity Cactus, had run off to Nepal with a Baby-Blue-Eyed-Hippy-Mountain-Climber-from-Los Angeles, and he still hadn't been able to get his life back into all-around Cowboy Fightin' Shape. He kept thinking about what his mother had told him many times as he was growing up: "Your ass might fit the saddle, son, but does the saddle fit the horse?" He knew what she meant, kind of, but then he didn't know at all. Horses he could understand . . . yes. Humans . . . maybe one in ten . . . as long as they were male. "Damn!" he said to the moon that was pole-vaulting over the White Clouds, "maybe that's why Infinity ran off to Knee-pole." He picked up Mariposa

Lily's reins and chugged himself into the saddle. "I can't even voodoo myself into gettin' a new motor fer my pickup. I'm buried up to my axles and spinnin' fast . . . right down to solid quicksand. I need some help, Mariposa Lil', I need a vision."

Jonquil sent out the word to all of his old sidekicks that he was going off to discover his vision and within a week there was a Three Hunnerd 'n' Sixtee degree hump-and-jump fandango going on at the Quick Draw Saloon. Millions Wordsworth, photographer, Zen speed explorer, and juggler of mountain ranges, flew in from Better Deal with enough liquid and solid fuel to keep the party aloft for months. Joaquin Latigo, famous Mexican vaquero and dead-eye whipsnapper, arrived in translation with hand-tooled boots full of freshly erupted volcanic peppers and tequila, and a brand new Cowboy Buddha Dictionary of Smoke Signals and Rope Tricks. Roland Riggs, Honcho-of-the-Highway, rolled up in a Won-Hunner-Thou Road-runner Peterbilt that could sleep an orgy and haul half of the Mexican marijuana crop across invisible borders in one smooth cross-topped ride. Studley Wonder . . . Gin-Singed-in with six man-eatin' ravenous mountain beauties that he whored, boarded, and hoarded all by himself. "Sheeeeeeeeeeeeeeeet . . . there's never enough to go all the way 'round 'less I haul 'n' ball 'em in m'self. Whars the bedroom an' the deadly drugs?" Bobby Wire, a pianissimo on the ground, but a Grand Finale on the back of a cross-bred Brahma, in between rodeos, jumped out the fire escape of 747 with three cases of Schramsberg's Blanc de Noirs and landed in the middle of the first go-around . . . right on time. And, the famous metaphysical outlaw, sundancer, raincharmer, and Cowboy Buddhist Chanter, Dr. Copernicus Flood, Trader-at-Large, arrived in a rainbowed Bugatti and immediately had all of the six-guns checked at the bar. He tacked up a large sign over the century-old rosewood backbar: "God Loves a Good Rodeo."

It was obvious to everyone who stuck around, beginning with the first fight, that it was a man's party. A Macho Machissmo Machine . . . a celebration of the yang, bang, and the whang. The strangest collection of Grindstone Cowboys ever to rondayvoo since the first rodeo on the Pecos River in 1883.

"Till the fences are buried!" Studley Wonder proposed by jumping up on a table, snapping off the Desperado Bullet Quickstep, and whipping out two bottles of champagne from his empty holsters. "BAM BAM . . . yer dead, Roland Riggs . . . gotcha right through yer pacemaker." The corks went caroming off Roland's head, spinning his hat, and ended up in Dr. Flood's first baseman's mitt. "Till your ass is inundated in alfalfa and pussy . . . that's what you really are trying to say . . . heh, Mr. Wonder?" Flood dropped the corks into the drink he was blending for Millions Wordsworth.

"Ya betchur sweet ass . . . McFlood."

"When's the ro-day-oo comin' t' town?"

"This is it . . . cowboy."

"Well . . . git down on yer knees and let 'er buck."

"Yeh . . . let us fuck."

"Hey, Flood . . . ya ol' wizard. Let's have 'nother round."

"Yeh . . . an' some mountain oysters . . . put the sting back into my ass."

"Let's drink to Jonquil . . . and visions."

"Sheeeeeet . . . only redskins and women have visions. The rest of us poor bastards got t' work."

"When's the last time you ever worked?"

"Ever' time I look into yer ugly face. I've got to work

my steel-polished ass off tryin' not to laugh or jus' git downright sick."

"If you weren't one foot taller than the meanest Brahma north of Mek-see-co I'd kick the b'Jesus right out of ya . . . and that's the unvarnished truth."

"Go git 'em, Bobby Wire . . . kick ass!"

"Yeh . . . don't let his size scare ya. It ain't how big they is, but how fuckin' mean and tough ya're."

"Quick too . . ."

"Nuts, guts, and speed. That's what counts . . . huh, Jonquil?"

"Fuckin' A . . . cowboy."

"Hey, Jonquil . . . how'd ya do at the Floatin' Feather Stampede?"

"Floated right out on my ass all night long."

"Hurd ya went home with the queen . . . though."

"Naw . . . that was ten years ago."

"Her mama?"

"That was five years ago."

"Well sheeeeeet . . . the grandma?"

"Now ya got it. We played strip poker till three an' then I trimmed her bunions with my huntin' spurs."

"Atta boy. . . ."

Dr. Flood picked up his guitar, leaned back on a bar stool, and began to sing his songs of the Cowboy Buddha.

> The Buddha man with a butterfly soul,
> a spirit that sliced the night.
> The first time in my star-gazed life,
> anything seemed flat out right.

"Hey Joaquin . . . ya ol' meskin. There's a fly on Studley's ass . . . see if ya can snake it off."

Joaquin picked up his sixteen-foot Diamondback bull-

whip and frenched it out into the dance floor, picking off
the fly that had decided to ride out a dance on one of
Studley's copper rivets.

"Did ya kill him?"

"Oh no . . . señor. I theeeeeenk I just sprained his
ankle."

"Good . . . we don't want no violence 'round here."

"Go on, Dr. Flood, sing some more."

"Hey . . . any of you old farts ever seen the Cowboy
Buddha?"

Millions was sneaking around in the exposed beams
trying to get a good snap shot of Roland and one of his
girl friends, Betsy Spoke, as they danced nude, cowboy
style (naked except for boots and hats . . . Code of the
West). "Hey . . . I'm a Cowboy Buddhist," Millions said
as he swung over to another beam.

"Fuckin' sheep don't make ya a Cowboy Buddhist . . .
cowboy."

Millions swung down from the rafters and shoved a
pair of three-hundred-dollar handmade goatskin boots
with mule-ear pulls into Studley's face. "See there, redhot
. . . I'm a Cowboy Bootist."

"Sheeeeeeeeeeeeiiiiiiiiitl!"

"Hey, Flood, make us some George Dickel milkshakes
. . . I'm hoongry."

> Now his grandfather was a slinger,
> and a tough man to hit.
> Who became the cowboy legend,
> riding an epileptic fit.

"Hey, Flood . . . whatcha do with the money?"

Flood stopped singing and looked over at Roland. A

lopsided grin peeked out from under his eight-inch mustache. "What money . . . diesel ass?"

"The money yer parents gave ya fer singin' lessons."

"Go get him, Joaquin, snap off his peckeroo, if you can locate it, and I'll ree-ward you with one of my finest, most intoxicatin', deadliest, elixorated melanges known in these most picturesque Rockies. Not only will it take the hump off your back but it will put it right where it beelongs. And that, my sad-eyed friend, is a Copernicus Promise."

"Sheeeeeeeet . . . he ain't got a pecker. He gave it to the gypsies last month to have it made into a wallet. . . ."

"Yeh, yeh . . . and when he plays with it it turns into a suitcase . . . we know."

"Ah . . . throw 'em out . . . throw 'em out."

> His mother was called Tao-la-la,
> a vision from the East.
> Who died when she was earthly young,
> taming that angry beast.

"Hey . . . I'm seein' triple. What's it mean?"

"Look't here, Jonquil . . . Shammy's havin' a vision, and she ain't even left town."

"Sheeeeeeet . . . maybe the mountain came to us."

"Hell yes . . . why not. We know all 'bout this vision bizznuss . . . hey Flood?"

The party continued through the night like a cockfight lost at sea. Jonquil kept talking about leaving at first light but he could never sober up enough to figure out which way it was to the mountain. The second day of the blowout became Real Loose, somewhat ornery, and all of the women made a fortress out of the tables, benches, speakers, and chairs and went on strike until the men quit acting like the worst male chauvinist assholes in the West. The barricade lasted for over an hour, and then Millions brought out a cowgirl's boot (size 9½ . . . big mama) full of 100 proof, 88 per cent Interpol Coke. Led them right out of their blockade by their noses. "Realities of life," Millions said to Dr. Flood, "a boot full of snow is the best shock wave to start a sudden avalanche."

"Ayemen."

The third day of the farewell fell right flat on its face. "Mus' of been the punch ol' Flood made out of his exotic potions of ol' remedies, paradies, and melodies," Millions said to a breast, thigh, and a hip . . . all from different bodies.

"Don't quite know what went wrong," Flood said to Jonquil. "I followed the recipe right down the dusty trail . . . except for the opium liqueur."

"Sure ya did . . . seein' triple."

"Oh . . . I thought it was amazingly potent. Well, my dear old friend, let this be a good lesson to all of us," Flood said, as he eased down into an old, five-woods, rocking chair. "You can't cut hot apple pie with a chain saw."

"We sure tried. . . ."

> He sang and danced and tossed his stars,
> and gazed at the changing moon.
> He lived with thirteen turquoise birds,
> and sang the buffalo tune.

Jonquil eased his body out of the saddle stool. "Damn . . . looks like the boys are slowin' down, Flood. Ass-HOLES . . . all of 'em. Can't drink, fuck, or fight worth shit anymore. I think I'm jus' gunna sneak right out the

back door while the gettin's good. I'll jus' git my ass up
on the mountain, strap myself to a wildcat, and wait until
I git my vision. But first"—Jonquil winked at Flood and
held up one finger—"my good doctor, I've got to take a
whiz." Jonquil whipped out a cowboy flamenco, toes
flashing and elbows flying, before he made a beeline for
the can. He pushed the door to the Buckaroo Station but
it wouldn't budge. "Damn . . . some ol' preacher's son
has passed out in there." He sideslapped on down the hall
to the door that read "Buckarinas and Rodeo Queens
Only," pushed it open, and waited for any signs of feminine activity. "Nope . . . beavers mus' be gnawin' or
sawin'." He looked down the hall, cocked his hat to incognito, and slipped in, locking the door as it closed.

"Ahhhhhhh sheeeeeeeeet," he said as he flipped on the
thirty-watt bulb. "I'm sorry, ma'am . . . I thought it was
empty." Jonquil spun around to make tracks for the old
outhouse.

"That's all right, Jonquil, I came here to find you."

The words hit Jonquil right in the middle of his kundalini and they began to vibrate, rocking back and forth
until they finally ignited inside his head (whisky being a
slow conductor of electricity). He turned on the heels of
his boots, slowly . . . but, by the time Jonquil had completed the pivot, the bell on the Buckarina Meter was
banging out a whole symphony of hosannas, a glocken-
spiel of Sunday morning praise for a first class with a
deadly ass supreme dee-lux buckarina beauty rodeo
queen sweetheart . . . hallelujah and High-Men! Jonquil
removed his hat and held it just below his belt buckle.
He rubbed his face hoping that he just might be able to
excavate some of the three days of destruction. He sent
his belt buckle on parade so this incredibly beautiful
woman would notice the "Champion . . . All Around

Cowboy" engraved around the flowered edges of the silver and gold miniature arena. "Well, ma'am . . . you . . .
you . . . are a beauty to behold . . . I mus' say. But . . .
I'm wonderin' . . . if this ain't some kin' of a joke my ol'
sidekicks might be playin' on me?"

This woman of the Buckarina John was staring right
into Jonquil's eyes . . . even Steven. Which put her exactly at six feet, discounting the leather stack on the heels
of her low-vamped blue python cowgirl boots. Her dark
red hair billowed and smoked around her head like an
eternal flame escaped from a sundance; two thin, tightly
woven braids hung down the edges of her face tied off
with swan and owl feathers. Her skin was ivory-rose, and
her eyes, set deep within the chambers of her face, were
jade within opals; her eyebrows were hedges of sorrel riding on the ridges; and her mouth was full, smiling, and
unpainted wild cherry. She was covered with maroon
silks, cottons, leathers, and silver. She looked as if she
were defying gravity ready for flight. She was the El
Dorado of womanhood, the Yosemite of natural beauty,
and a seraphic Sequoia of dignity. She was a million
moons of Yin surrounded by thunderheads and blue
herons flying through a sky of rainbows and lotus pools.
"No, Jonquil," she said very softly, "this isn't a joke. I
came here to find you."

Jonquil thumbed a ride his way.

The woman twisted her finger into Jonquil's chest.
"Yeh . . . little old cowboy you . . . Jonquil Rose."

Jonquil shook his head hoping the whiplash would
scare off the raggedy old crows that seemed to be nesting
inside his brain. He sat down on the toilet, jumping back
up when he realized that he hadn't offered the lady first
chance. ". . . 'Cuse me, ma'am . . . it's the best in the
house."

She sat down, and Jonquil turned the fifty-five-gallon barrel that was used as a wastepaper basket over and rode on top. "Ya comfortable . . . ma'am?"

"Yes . . . are you?"

"Sure . . . I'm always comfortable when I'm hoverin' an' perchin'. Mus' be the eagle in me." Jonquil fiddled with his shirt snaps, tried a bank shot into the mirror hoping not to see how bad he thought he looked, stuck one boot up on the sink. His eyes returned to the woman. "Ya got me all spooked . . . sort of. I'm wonderin' if y'all mind explainin' a few things to me. Y'know . . . I've never been much of a conversensationalist in the whimmen's can. Know what I mean . . . ma'am?"

The woman smiled at Jonquil, an easy smile, as if they'd been friends for years. "There's really not much to explain, Jonquil. We've been waiting three days for you to show up on the mountain. Finally, we realized that you were never going to be sober enough to make it there, and so I came here to find you. And Ta Dum, here you are . . . looking a lot better than we expected."

Jonquil buried his head in his hands and peeked out through his fingerprints. "Damn! I didn't know anyone would be waitin' fer me. Have I blown it?"

"Oh . . . I don't think so," the woman said, laughing at Jonquil. "We're a lot more tolerant than most visionary guides."

"Oh wow . . . that's good." Jonquil began to feel a little better. He pulled his hands away and looked sideways at the woman. "We? Ya keep sayin' we. . . ."

"The Cowboy Buddha . . . who else?"

"Hua . . . the Cowboy Buddha?"

"That's right, Jonquil. We had an idea that we were going to have some trouble. The report on you is that you're jus' about as stubborn as an old army mule, and—

sometimes—as wild as a Nevada mustang with ginger up his ass. The Cowboy Buddha said that . . . not me."

"Well I'll be a bee-wildered duck flying North in the winter. I had no idea it worked this way. I figured ya had to hobble yerself right down to the ground, naycud, with nuthin' more than a few rattlers fer shade, an' then tape yer eyelids open and put fishhooks in yer scrotum. Rain, snow, or hunner deegrees . . . waitin' fer the Word. Hmmmmmmmm . . . it ain't that way no more?"

The woman was giggling at Jonquil and her eyes were moist from her laughter. "It could be that way for some humans, Jonquil, but why suffer? Look at you and these incredible mountains. This is Stanley Basin, Idaho, one of the most beautiful valleys in the world. You're a cowboy and a rodeo star, somewhat jaded I must admit, but still a hero to lots of people. You have chosen all of this for yourself. Enjoy your decisions, Jonquil . . . enjoy the go-around. Put the whips away and stop trying to feel guilty about something you had no control over. You haven't done anything wrong as far as we're concerned, except being a little macho."

Jonquil put his boot back up on the sink and studied the toe as if it were a reversed crystal ball . . . looking for the right question. "I never thought 'bout it like that. I figured ya was 'spose to make it tougher . . . git right down an' bleed an' pay fer all the good times you've ever had . . . an' pay fer the fuckups too. No?" He looked at her as she was shaking her head. "But still . . . my 'Pache whoaman ran off with that asshole baby-blue-eyed dippy-hippy mountain climber from Los Angeles, an' I blew up my good ol' pickup in my anger an' frustration and it seems like it's been on the downhill slide since my last good laugh."

"Jonquil . . . oh Jonquil, everything is all right, believe

me. Infinity is doing some work for us right now in Tibet. It's been very exciting for her . . . something she really needed."

"And the assHOLE?"

"The ass . . . oh . . . yes. The B.B.E.H.M.C.F.L.A. Oh . . . Infinity dumped him right after she arrived in Nepal. He was somewhat of a dud . . . anyway." She reached over and took Jonquil's hand. "Look at it this way, Jonquil. If Infinity hadn't taken off I wouldn't be here. And I'm sure that you've never seen anything as lovely as me in your whole life . . . right?"

Jonquil looked at the woman and fell off the barrel, madly in love. "Yes, ma'am . . . yer absolutely right. But . . . even that's damn scary."

She gave him a floodlight smile, and the old thirty-watt ladies' john began to feel more like a Kama Sutra fantasy chamber. "You could stop calling me ma'am. My name is Jimmi Maroon. Jimmi with an i . . . cowboy."

Jonquil ran his hand out on his arm. "Well, I'm pleased to make yer acquaintance, ma' . . . what? Jimmy Maroon . . . Jimmy Maroon? Why, that's the name of my ol' fifty-five stovebolt. How'd ya pick up that name?" Suspicion lurking in the squints of Jonquil's eyes.

"Well, Jonquil Rose, that's what we were picking up from you. You would have gone to the mountain looking for your vision when all you really wanted was to have your old pickup back with a few extras . . . like me. So . . . Ta Dum . . . here I am!"

"What? Ya knew that?"

". . . 'Fraid so, cowboy."

"And . . . and . . . well sheeeeet, ma'am. If that doesn't make me the last great drop kick in history . . . right into my own recyclable ass. And you . . . yer . . . ?"

"Just like you've always dreamed about. All those times

you've spent under the hood, or lurking under the frame
. . . cooing and ohhhhhing, rubbing and snorting." Jimmi
stood up and turned slowly around in front of Jonquil.
"Well . . . do you like?"

"Ah sheeeeet, Jimmy . . . do I like? You're a real vision
jus' by yerself. I can't believe it. I jus' can't beelieve this
is happenin'."

"I can see you've got excellent taste, Jonquil. Why
don't we hightail it out of this joint?" Jimmi pressed her
thirty-six magnums against Jonquil's body, cocked and
ready to fire. "Don't forgit, with an i . . . not a y."

"I got ya." Jonquil grabbed Jimmi's hand and flung
open the door. "Come on . . . let's git outta here." He cut
down the hall and out the back door. On the porch he
stopped to look around, sneak around the corner and
take his whiz, open his body to the night air, and check
to see if he wasn't hallucinating from some of Dr. Flood's
triple elixirated Rocky Mountain Juju. He leaned against
the building and watered the sagebrush. "Ahhhhh . . .
that's much better. Hey, Jimmi . . . are ya sure I ain't
dreamin' all of this?"

Jimmi walked around the corner and put Jonquil's hat
on his head. "This is your dream, cowboy, but you ain't
dreaming." She punched him on the shoulder. "Come on,
I've got something to show you." She took his hand and
guided him to the front of the saloon. "See, cowboy . . .
I've got everything ready to ride."

Jonquil dug in his heels. "Whoa . . . whoa there.
How'd ya git Mariposa Lily and ol' Hipshooter?"

Jimmi shook her hand loose, took Hipshooter's stirrup
and reins, and swung into the saddle. "Come on, Roses,
you're lookin' a little knocked-kneed."

"Yeow . . . not only are ya knockin' my knees but yer
humpin' my mind." Jonquil took Mariposa's reins and

creaked up into the saddle. "Oh . . . easy sweet Lil' . . . easy. Yer old man's silver pin ain't slippin' so easy." When he was ready he looked over at Jimmi. "Where ya takin' us . . . ma'am?"

"For a long slow waltz, Jonquil . . . a long slow waltz."

Two

At first light Jimmi and Jonquil arrived at the mountain hideout that she had prepared for his vision. Jonquil had rode himself sober, but the three days of debauchery was beginning to wear through the leather. The one-hunner'd-'n'-sixtee-five pounds of nuts, guts, and speed was beginning to look more like a hunner'd-pound sack of number-two spuds. Jimmi, looking as if there was no end to her Three-Dee-Pizzazz, floated off Hipshooter and fanned the campsite. "It's the best I could do on such short notice, Jonquil . . . my favorite camps had already been scheduled. But this isn't too bad . . . heh?" Jonquil grouched off Mariposa, shaking off the bumps 'n' grinds, before he looked around.

"Oh wow . . ." he said as he rocked back on his boots, "this is neater-than-heck lookin'!" What Jonquil was looking at was a minor paradise: five waterfalls cascading into one deep pool that was filled with yellow water lilies that looked like small spaceships sliding through a dark purple sky. Behind the waterfalls was a hot springs with a natural platform hanging over the pool. There was enough grass to keep the horses (who were already stripped down and belly deep in the long green) satisfied for weeks. Just cockeyed to the pool was a small clearing where Jimmi had erected a tepee. "I had this made especially for you, Jonquil Rose."

"Hey . . . look at this wannigan, a thirty-six poler. I'd bet there's enough room in there to have a pool table."

"Come on inside and see the bed."

"The bed?" Jonquil said, giving Jimmi his notorious three-weeks-on-the-trail lusteye.

"Yeh . . . the bed. I had it made out of barbed wire . . . jus' for you . . . cowboy." Jimmi opened the entrance flap and followed Jonquil through the opening.

"Hey . . . look at this would ya . . . buffalo robes with an eagle-down-filled mattress. Virgin eagle, I hope?"

"Today, Jonquil . . . everything is virgin, even you, which is going to take some left-handed jiu-jitsu on my part."

"Ah, come on . . . ?" Jonquil picked up a rabbit skin. "And . . . what are these for, m'lady . . . coverlets for the mice?"

"You'll see . . . cowboy."

"Nothin' nasty, I hope."

Jimmi took the rabbit skin from Jonquil. "Jonquil," she said, holding him in place with her eyes, "to quote from one of my teachers . . . 'I'm always a lady, Jonquil . . . always a lady.'"

Jonquil, held in a stall for a moment by Jimmi, broke loose and banked around the tepee. "Hey, wish my old sidekick, Don Coyote, could see me now . . . would he . . . hey!" He looked over at Jimmi with a thirsty purpose. "Ya didn't by any chance . . . ah . . . order some beer?"

Jimmi folded her arms, cocked her head, and wagged out an amazing disbelief. "Jonquil . . . you're suppose to be searching for your vision."

"Yeh . . . I know, I know . . . but I jus' thought that . . . well sheeeeeet, ma'am . . . fergit it."

"Well . . . jus' in case, Jonquil, I put a few cans in one of the streams."

"Really?"

"Yeh . . . really. Why make it difficult for you?"

"Well I'll be a . . . sheeeeeet . . . really?"

"Check it out. I wouldn't be putting you on about something as important to you as your beer."

Jonquil sprinted through the entrance and ran around the camp until he found the beer, returning with two cans. "Jimmi . . . this is incredible. Two cases. I mean . . . well, I can't believe it." Jonquil popped one and emptied it in a three-second ride. "Ah . . . that's much better. Oh . . . I'm sorry, I brought this for you."

Jimmi shook her head, laughing under her smile. "Thanks . . . I never thought you'd ask."

Jonquil started dancing inside the tepee. "Hi ei ei yi yi ei ei yi yi ei ei yi yo yo yo yo . . ." He grabbed one of his boots, pulled it off, and threw it out the entrance. He stopped in front of Jimmi and started unbuttoning her blouse.

"Jonquil . . . slow down!"

"I know, I know . . . but I jus' can't wait to see ya naycud. Ah jus' can't wait."

Jimmi reached through Jonquil's arms and started unsnapping his shirt. "Just remember, cowboy . . . this ain't no grab-ass contest."

Jonquil was about to throw Jimmi's blouse into the air. "Well sheeeeet, ma'am . . . I mean . . . I didn't. . . ."

"That's okay, Roses, I don't want to dampen your spiritual activity, but I'd like to have equal time with the beer."

"Okay, okay . . . I'm slowin' down. I'm shiftin' on down to grandma . . . right down into low . . . you'll see," he said to Jimmi as he grabbed his other boot and threw it out the smoke hole. "Oh . . . look at ya, jus' look at ya. I can't look, yer jus' too beautiful. I jus' know it

. . . I can tell already." Jonquil slapped a hand over his eyes and continued to undress Jimmi with one hand. "Lookit! I'm am-BYE-dextruss, Jimmi . . . no . . . no . . . you're makin' me am-BYE-hiss-stare-ee-cul. I don't want to look until the wrappin's gone. Oh . . . this is worser than Christmas."

Jimmi slipped out of her panties. "All right, cowboy . . . it's time to prop open your eyelids."

"Jus' a minute . . . jus' a minute right there. Oh . . . yes, I can feel ya naycud. It's comin' right through me. I can feel yer breasts right now and yer clear 'cross the tepee. An' . . . what I'm feelin' is jus' goin' t'be so much better when my eyesight ree-turns. Cuz seein' is bee-lievin' 'n' bee-lievin' IS the fanDANGgo of truth . . . amen. OH . . . here I go. I'm gunna do it . . . NOW!" Jonquil took his hand away from his eyes and looked at Jimmi Maroon. "Ohhhhhh . . . ahhhhh . . . wow . . . ahhhhh . . . yes . . . yesireeee! Ohhhhh . . . I can't look no more, yer jus' too beautiful." He grabbed his bikini underwear and pulled it over his head so that his eyes were covered. "Oh . . . that's much better. I've got to give myself time . . . it's been soooo long. Jus' let me sneak up an' smell and taste ya fer a minute or two."

"Come on, cowboy . . . be a man. You can take it . . . heh?" Jimmi walked behind Jonquil, put her body against his back, and started guiding and pushing him toward the bed. "I'll give you a nice, soothing massage . . . would that help?"

"Help? I don't think so, ma'am. Maybe if I chopped off my toe I would calm down." Jimmi pushed Jonquil onto the bed.

"Lie still and try not to poke a hole in the buffalo robe."

"Damn! Ya sure are strong. I think I've found my

match. Ohhhhhhhhh . . . ahhhhhhhhh . . . that feels so good." He patted the robe. "Hey . . . ol' buffler! How's it goin'?" Jonquil put his ear onto the robe. "Yeh . . . okay . . . I gotcha. All right . . . all right." He turned his head, removed the underwear, and tried to look over his shoulder at Jimmi. "Hey . . . ol' buffler says it's all right to make love on him . . . as soon as yer ready."

Jimmi leaned down so that her breasts touched Jonquil's back, rubbing them gently back and forth. "Jonquil . . . we are making love. If you need to stick your whang into something right now perhaps the skinner left the asshole behind the tail."

"Ah sheeeeeeeeeeeet."

Jimmi worked on Jonquil's neck, head, and shoulders, staying away from below-the-belt until he had given in to her hands. Jonquil couldn't fight any longer, she was much too powerful for him, and he finally slipped down into a smooth, soft, arena of sleep. The three days of carousing had finally ended. Jimmi rolled Jonquil over and worked on the front of his body, moving uphill. She put his head into her lap and massaged his eyes, cheeks, temples, and forehead. When she was finished she snuggled down beside him and looked into his face. "Hey, sidekick, how's it goin'?" Jonquil was layered so far down into his dreams he only heard the purring of her body. Jimmi kissed him on the face, wound her body through and around his body, and curved into his breath of sleep.

When Jonquil awoke it was only with one eye. He stared at Jimmi, trying to remember how this beautiful woman had entered his life. He slipped his hands under the robe and felt her body. He closed his eyes, shook his head, and looked at Jimmi again. He couldn't believe what his hands were telling him. He zigzagged his eye around the tepee, trying to retrace his ride . . . somewhere back to three days of Pillage and Plunder at the Quick Draw Saloon. There it was . . . the thirty-watt bulb. The timid eye felt safe to come out and shied open. "Jimmi Maroon, Jimmi Maroon," he whispered. "Yer sure a heck of a lot finer lookin' than my ol' pickup . . . any day. Is this still part of my vision? Hey . . . now I remember, we never made love." Jonquil's cock began to rise . . . periscope up and torpedoes ready for action.

Jimmi woke up when she realized that Jonquil had shifted from no-man's-land into combat. "Hey . . . know where you are, cowboy?"

"I'm not sure, but I ain't complainin' . . . ma'am."

Jimmi eased over on top of Jonquil. "Bet you don't remember what shit and two are?"

"Thirty-six, twenty-two, thirty-six."

"You cheated." Jimmi kissed him on the mouth. "You have soft lips . . . real soft. And you taste like sagebrush and soft spring rain . . . kinda ancient." She kissed him on the eyes, running her tongue over his eyelids. "Mountain musk, aspens, granite, with a faint flavoring of horse shit. Nice . . . real nice."

"Wanna trade places?" Jonquil said, trying to keep the lid on the geyser.

"Naw . . . I like it up here."

"Like to be the boss . . . heh?"

"Roses, if this was a circle you'd never notice."

"Huh . . . ?"

"Relax, Jonquil, I don't want you to explode in three minutes. It's early, and we have until we're finished. This ain't gunna be some eight-second ride . . . cowboy."

"What? You mean you ain't offerin' belt buckles?"

"Stick with me, kid, and you'll get something a lot better than a standing ovation, and the rodeo queen. Easy

. . . easy, Jonquil, ride easy." Jimmi arched her back and took Jonquil's cock and put it inside her body. She slid down on him, tightened her muscles, and then relaxed. "I don't want you to come, Jonquil."

"What . . . ?"

"Think you can do it?"

"What the fuck fer . . . ?"

"What do you need to come for . . . we ain't having a kid?"

"But . . . but . . . damn, Jimmi Maroon . . . I like to come."

"Yeh . . . me too. Listen, I'm trying to teach you something . . . remember? Build it up and then let it go. Keep it all within you, and don't lose it . . . and forget about tryin' to impress me with your action. We can make love until the Cowboy Buddha's birthday. Ya scared?"

Jonquil scrunched up his face to show Jimmi that he was thinking. Question marks for ears. He fluttered his hands. "Can I use these . . . m'lady?"

"You betcha, cowboy . . . as long as you can float."

Jonquil tapped his forehead. "Ah ha . . . I think I'm beginnin' to understand. . . . My ass might fit the saddle. . . ."

Jimmi finished the saying . . . "Does the saddle fit the horse?"

"Hey . . . how'd you know that?"

"Every woman knows that one . . . Jonquil."

"Yeh . . . ? Well, coach . . . what would ya like me to do now? Go out fer a pass, yodel, or do some fancy rope tricks with my tallywhacker?"

"Rosehips . . . shut up and screw."

With the darkness Jonquil got up and built a fire inside the tepee. He went outside, gathered some more wood, and put the sticks by the bed. "Hey . . . it's gettin' cold," he said to Jimmi, as he jumped back under the buffalo robes. "Might snow on the higher peaks."

"How do you feel?" Jimmi asked Jonquil as she rubbed his legs with the inside of her thigh.

"I feel . . . I feel strange. Strange, weird, challenged. I didn't know it was possible to stay inside a woman fer so long. It feels good . . . like I stuck 'round fer the whole game."

"No competition . . . heh?"

"Ya . . . something like that, sweet Maroon."

"Equal time . . . Roses."

"Yeh . . . like sixty-nine?"

"How 'bout one hundred and sixty-nine?"

"How's that go?"

"Go around one more time until you can't tell whether you're male or female."

"Damn . . . what if I git lost in the dark and my cock ends up in your ear, or maybe . . . wah . . . in mine?"

"Who cares."

"Ya don't?"

"Jonquil . . . ol' kid, your mouth can do as much damage as your talking totem pole."

"That's cuz I'm a Gemini . . . m'sweet."

Jimmi curled her body and slid under the covers to the camp of the talking totem pole. "Me too, Kid Roses . . . me too."

In the middle of the night they got up to take a hot bath and watch the moon.

"The moon mus' be in . . . what's that word, pedigree?" Jonquil said as he hummed his body down into the water.

"Perigee. . . ."

"Yeh . . . that's the word. Mus' be why yer lookin' so good . . . heh?"

"Yeh . . . and you're looking sooooo big," Jimmi said as she dropped under the water.

"Yeh . . . yeh," Jonquil said to himself, looking down. "Not too bad. Mus' be all the protein I ate at Cafe Sixty-nine."

"Hey, Roses," Jimmi called out, "want to ride into town and shoot some pool?"

"Handicaps?"

"Sure . . . why not. I'll spot you five balls."

"I'm doin' better in the robes. What else ya got in mind . . . captain?"

"How about the Japanese Basket Fuck?"

"The Japanese Basket Fuck? Oh yeh . . . I saw that one time in a puppet show in Hong Kong. Yer in the basket an' I'm on the ground waitin' fer ya to spin on down and twist my dick up into a passionate swirl. Sounds great . . . but whose gunna pull the rope?"

"No one . . . we use hydraulic lifters. It's called low riding."

"Oh . . . I git it. They run off the steam that I'm gunna be generatin' from watchin' you strafe me with yer pussy."

"Naw . . . a currant bush, dummy."

Just before dawn, Jonquil was sitting by the fire, roasting a piece of buffalo meat. "I never thought it was possible . . . not to come. I feel like I've been tranquilized with dynamite. How would ya like yer meat, m'lady . . . burnt, burnt-burnt, or burnt-burnt-burnt?"

"I like it just like you . . . triple burnt. This is the West . . . ain't it?"

"Last time I looked out the smoke hole it was. But . . .

y'know . . . I'm beginnin' to feel invisible. Like . . . when we're makin' love I've completely forgotten 'bout myself. That ain't never happened b'fore. Know what I mean?"

"Yeh, sure do. I really do. Your heart is becoming really sweet right now, very soft and gentle."

Jonquil put a few small pieces of wood on the fire. "Jus' b'fore I went into the Buckarina John and found ya, my ol'-time sidekick, Dr. Copernicus Flood, was singin' his song 'bout the Cowboy Buddha. One part went like:

> That Western man who rode the land,
> but never went inside.
> To float within the mystic's dream,
> wearing the buffalo hide.

Is this what yer tryin' to do with me, Jimmi?"

Jimmi looked up at Jonquil and smiled. "Yeh, sure is, cowboy. Low ridin' in the fifth dimension."

"Damn! All this time I never knew I'd come equipped with overdrive."

"Ta Dum . . . the Floating Rose," Jimmi said as she slid underneath Jonquil. "Ya know, you've been incredible. You gave in and let me become your guide. You're a good act, Roses, y'know. We make a good team." Jimmi put her arms around Jonquil's neck and shoulders and kissed him on the mouth. "Now, I'd like for you to come inside me."

Jonquil was just beginning to purr in three/four time when he heard Jimmi's request. "What?" He raised his body up to clear a path for her request. "Damn . . . are ya puttin' me on, Lady Maroon?"

"No, Jonquil, you'll understand. Come on, it's okay."

"Well, ma'am . . ." Jonquil said as he tried to look

through Jimmi's face for any new metaphysical hocus-
pocus. "Ya sure ya ain't got the bridge mined?"

"Hunner purrcent . . . cowboy."

"Yeh . . . ?"

"Yeh . . . come on."

Jonquil put his arms around Jimmi and kissed her on the
lips. "Well, mama . . . open up yer fur coat . . . I'm
comin' home."

"Come on home, cowboy."

He smiled into her life, caught her breath, and kissed
her all over her body with his lips and eyes. Time disappeared from his maleness as he released himself into the
body of their lives making love. He had finally surren-
dered. From somewhere he heard music. A smooth, joy-
ous tune that reminded Jonquil of something Jimmi had
said earlier. He spun into her arms as they began to
dance a long slow waltz on the mountain. A dance of
grace and dignity, as they touched each other so gently,
breathing through their love so quietly. When they
reached the top they swirled through the dawn until they
floated out of their bodies, becoming a chromium of sky
within the sun . . . dancing the edge along the curve of
the morning light.

Three

They broke camp quietly with smiles. Jonquil made a
travois from two fallen lodgepole pines and struck down
the tepee. When they were ready to leave, Jimmi walked
through their camp touching the trees, plants, and drank
some water from the stream. "She's been a good teacher,
Jonquil," she said. Her face said everything as if this
piece of earth had been telling Jimmi what to do. Jimmi

picked a small bunch of sego lilies and put them in Mariposa's and Hipshooter's headstalls. "You too, old ancient earth spirits . . . thanks for waiting so patiently."

Jonquil had attached the travois to his saddle, and he and Mariposa followed Jimmi and Hipshooter down the trail. They kept their pace at a slow walk, which seemed much too fast for Jonquil. He felt the ending was coming much too soon, and he didn't know what to expect. She hadn't told him her plans. She kept on moving down the trail. A mile or so from their camp she turned around and laughed. "Hey cowboy . . . ya forgot your beer."

"Well I'll be a reconditioned virgin . . . so I did." Jonquil kept on riding. "Let's see. One beer in over . . . over . . . well ain't that something . . . I can't remember how long we've been on the mountain. Seems like weeks."

A mile further down the trail Jimmi began to expand in the saddle. She knew what was happening to her as she rubbed her belly, smiling down the trail. By the time they had reached Feather Creek she looked seven months pregnant, and when they came to the old fire road she was ready for the delivery. She stopped Hipshooter and waited for Jonquil to catch up.

"Hey Jimmi . . . I think ol' Hipshooter might have a rock caught in his foot. Maybe I ought to take a look," Jonquil said as he rode up alongside Jimmi. "Whoa . . . I'll jus' . . . Yeow!" Jonquil pulled back in his saddle so that his eyes could tell him something different than what he was seeing. "Oh boy, Jimmi, ya sure fooled me with that stuffin'. Ya really looked knocked up."

Jimmi sidestepped Hipshooter over to Jonquil, took his hand and put it on her belly. "This ain't no paddin', cowboy . . . it's your kid."

Jonquil whipped off his hat and stood up in his stirrups. "Damn ya, whoaman! How come ya keep doin' this to me. Get me all set up and then . . . BLAM, ya thump me right on my cowboy ass." He reached over and felt her surprise package once again. "Sheeeeeeet, I jus' came in YOU this mornin'. Ya don't git poked out like that in a four-hour ride down the mountain. It might work that way fer water ouzels, but not fer humans."

Jimmi took Jonquil's hand. "It's all right, Roses, I can have the kid right here in the woods. You'll understand soon . . . I promise." She kicked one leg over the saddle and slid off Hipshooter onto a large granite boulder. "Stay here, I won't be long, and don't worry. This is what you wanted to keep you flying . . . Kid Rose. I'll try not to scuff up the paint." She took a small bag from Hipshooter's saddle and walked over to where Jonquil was standing. "Hey," she said to him as she punched him on the arm, "you were great, Jonquil . . . just great. You'll be all right now, I know it. In a few days you'll be jus' like you were a year or so ago. Floatin' Rose . . . jus' one great cowboy. You'll see." She kissed him on the mouth and put her head on his shoulder. Jonquil put his arms around her, tucked his head into her hair, and closed his eyes.

"Hey . . . Jimmi . . . Jimmi Maroon, ya ain't leavin', are ya?"

"Wah cowboy . . . of course not." She broke from Jonquil's arms. "See ya at the waltzin' dance . . . fancy pants."

When Jimmi was out of sight he ripped his hat from his head and threw it on the ground. "Goddam whimmen . . . ya jus' start figurin' 'em out an' 'fore ya can git a good night's sleep they buck ya right out of the saddle. Oh . . . shit an' good goddam!" And he jumped on his hat and flattened it right down into the middle of a three-day-old meadow wafer.

Several times Jonquil took off through the trees, but he stopped and returned to the horses . . . shaking his head. He finally settled down on a log, determined that he would hold fast until she returned. That vow only lasted a few minutes until Jonquil was up checking Hipshooter's foot. "Ah . . . I think ya were jus' fakin' me out, ol' boy. Probably in cahoots with Jimmi. Everybody else is 'round these parts." He sat back down on the log, but before he could stick a blade of grass into his mouth, he was off running through the trees again trying to pick up Jimmi's tracks. Hat in hand and boots sniffing, he cut through the trees looking for signs, hoping that she hadn't doubled back on him and was already sitting down by the horses laughing up a storm. He finally broke out of the trees and came to a small clearing that led into a large meadow. Jimmi was at the far end, squatting, and holding onto a small pine. She had a blanket wrapped around her hips, and sweat was running down her forehead and he could see the veins and muscles in her arms, neck, and face. Jimmi was biting her lower lip, rocking on her feet, and pulling the tree with both hands. She was going through a contraction as the force of the life that was inside her was making its last great efforts for birth. Jonquil almost broke, but then he saw her relax as she dropped her head down onto her chest. She took a towel and put it between her legs and then she looked up at Jonquil. "It's beautiful, Roses . . . looks jus' like you. Take care of it . . . cowboy. You've found your vision. So long Jonquil . . . we had a great waltz together."

"What . . . ?" Jonquil took off running. ". . . What are ya talkin' 'bout, Jimmi?" She stood up just as the life she had given birth to began to grow up around her, pulling her inside its shape. "Hey, Jimmi . . . what's happenin' to ya. Where'd ya go?" Jonquil was so busy running, cussing, dodging brush, and jumping streams that he didn't notice that what Jimmi had given birth to was a 1955 Jimmy Maroon pickup with four on the floor and compound low, nubile, la cherried-deeluxe. And, by the time Jonquil made it to the pine tree that Jimmi had used for her midwife, the pickup was full grown and ready to ride. "Hey . . . whoa . . . I mean hold it right there, Roses . . . slow down. Are ya seein' what I'm seein' . . . ol' cowboy?" Jonquil jumped back in his boots and then faded right down to his knees. "Jimmi . . . hey, Jimmi . . . what have ya done? I didn't want ya to leave. I was feelin' real close with ya . . . real close. Sheeeeet . . . it ain't fair, Jimmi . . . it ain't fair." His head was hanging low, but slowly he began to peek out from under his confusion to focus his mind onto what Jimmi had given to him. Jonquil stared for a long time, studying the 1955 Jimmy Maroon, wondering if it would disappear as soon as he made a pass. He tried to put Jimmi's puzzle together, but it wouldn't work. There was still something missing. Jonquil eased up on the pickup, slowly, just to make sure it wasn't alive and would try and run him down. He touched the door and felt the paint. "Oh . . . hand-rubbed lacquer, look at it shine!" He walked around the pickup, shaking his head and biting his hand to check out the reality of his vision. "I never figured it would be anything like this, not even from the Cowboy Buddha." He leaned over the front fender and put his head on the hood. "Oh Jimmi, sweet Jimmi Maroooooon . . . we're really back together again. It's been a long time on dandelion wine, but yer back. My old, but REE-juvinated, VIRginized, ree-LIABLE, high-flyin' Jimmi Maroon." Jonquil looked up at the mountain. "Hey . . . thanks, partner. Ya did good. I'm sorry I gave ya so much trouble, but so did YOU. I don't quite understand it all, but someday I'll git it all figured out. Maybe the answer's in the box ya left in the back of the pickup. Tell Jimmi hello fer me. She was more beautiful than a thousand rodeo queens . . . a real vision jus' by herself. Yesirrrreeeee . . . an adios . . . Cowboy B . . . adios." Jonquil kissed the hood and jumped up. "Hey . . . I'm ready to ride." He whipped open the door, slid in like a rosewood pool cue through loving fingers, and started the motor. "Ta Dummmn! Ohhhhhhh . . . listen to her sing such a beautiful waltz . . . a real sweet waltz yer playin' fer me. Jimmi or Jimmy Maroon . . . yer jus' so fine my nineTEEN fifty-FIVE . . . cherried ROSE WINE."

Four

The boys, hung over and hanging down low, were gathered on the front porch of the Quick Draw Saloon looking like old varnished replicas of the West. It took a good slow-motioned eye to even notice that there was life after hangovers in those statues. Millions Wordsworth was posed-in-sepia next to his tripoded Leica waiting for Jonquil to return so that he could record for many-good-laughs-later the Wildcat Look of three days on the Mountain. Dr. Copernicus Flood had just fired up the coffee with good measures of peppers, tequila, Brahma sweat, and eagle farts (an old shaman's recipe for eternal recovery).

"Well sheeeeeeet, I wonder what ol' Jonquil is up to today?"

"I'll bet he's got one rumblin' tummy that's dancin' a mean polka on the back of his ribs."

"Let alone a frozen ass. Ya'll know how cold it got last night? Damn! It's the middle of summer and look at the new snow on the peaks."

"I'll bet he's wonderin' jus' how fur a man's got to go to find the truth. I mean . . . sheeeeeeet, all this ol' redskin mojo. I know where my zipper, mouth, and wallet is . . . and that's all a good man needs to know."

"Hey, señors . . . I theeeeeeeeenk you are all full of sheeeeeet. That Jonquil is one tough hombre and he will return with his vision. I know he will," Joaquin said as he two-stepped his whip.

"Ya cud be right, Ol' Mex."

Joaquin cracked his whip. "You only theeeeeenk I'm right, Studleeee Wonder?"

"Yup . . . ol' Joaquin Latigo's right once again . . . dead right."

Bobby Wire and Roland Riggs were in a poker game. Silver dollars stacked a foot off the table with beer cans rattling on the floor. "Well, I hope the fuck he gits back soon," Riggs was saying as he dealt out the cards. "I got to git that load of soybean boot leather down to Texas. It's the hottest item since jalapeños underwear."

"Hey . . . look at that rig. Wooooooooooweeeeeeeeeee . . . is that cherried or is that cherried?"

"Looks like an old professional virgin to me."

"She looks like Jonquil's old stovebolt gussied up."

"Throw a road apple at it, Bobby Wire . . . see if ya still got yer arm."

"Sheeeeeeet, Rosehips' ol' truck never looked that good."

"Gentlemen," Flood said, "if you would ree-move your booze-and-drug-ruined heads from the asshole of the last five-day storm that has just passed through us you would be able to see clearly that the driver of that rig is the one and only . . . our good friend, Jonquil Rose . . . Jus' One More Cowboy."

"Are you shittin' us, Flood?" Studley asked as he stood up and dropped one of his sweethearts, Molly Taps, onto the floor.

"Mr. Studley Wonder," Flood said, as he leaned against a post and looked up at the sky, "I have an incredible imagination, but I'm not a delusionist of the obvious." He stepped off the porch to greet Jonquil Rose.

"Yeh . . . look fer yerself, assHOLE!"

"Well, I'll be a double clutchin' ass bandit. That's him all right comin' in slow 'n' easy. He never got that outfit sittin' on some mountain."

"Heyzeus Booodeeeeest, I theeeeenk we've all beeeeen baaaamboooooozled."

Dr. Flood picked up a broken pool cue. "If I hear one more deracination upon Rose's character I will be forced to reduce my behavior to your level . . . which I have noticed in the last five days ain't been no spiritual gold mine of oriflammeous morality."

Jonquil pulled up to the Quick Draw Saloon as smooth as silk panties wrapped around honeydews. He stuck his elbow out the window, pulled down his sunglasses, stared at his old sidekicks, and shook his head in disgust. All they heard was a sigh and a groan from Jonquil. They looked at each other, shrugged their hangovers, sneered, and turned their attention back to the main attraction.

"Hey, Jon . . . !"

"Cool it, Bobby Wire," Dr. Flood shouted under his breath, "he's been to the Mountain."

Jonquil stepped out of the truck and hung one arm over the door, still sizing up his friends and letting them have a good, long, uninterrupted testimony of his ree-juvenated presence.

Studley broke up, doubled over, and started laughing into May Liberty's beehive-do. Flood removed his multi-plumed hat and began to beat him over the head. "I said keep yer magpie mouth shut, Wonder. We're waitin' for the Word."

Jonquil was dressed in a powder-river-blue suede coat with a western yoke, arrowhead pockets, and leather horsehead buttons. His silk lace shirt was open at the collar, and he had a maroon silk bandana around his neck; his pants were kid maroon leather jeans and as smooth as the ride he rode in on. His boots were full-quill ostrich leather with inlayed roses, and whisper vamped tops; his beaver and mink Western opera hat was lily white. He was looking Cowboy to the square roots of his vision, and once again . . . he was the best show in town.

Jonquil left his pose alongside Jimmi Maroon and walked up on the porch. "Gennelmen . . . I mus' admit that all of ya look like an alcoholic tornado had jus' blown through town. Yer a damn eyesore to this beautiful valley. A scenic disaster area. Ya'll should sign up fer the gov'ment bew-tee-fa-KAY-shun project, but there ain't enough money in the federal REEserve to do any good. But then . . . I can unnerstand how it is when yer left alone without any strong right arm fer Dr. Flood's leadership. I do unnerstand." Jonquil opened up a small leather bag and handed out sunglasses to all of his friends. He walked to the end of the porch and pointed to the Mountain. "I've been up there . . . on the Mountain. And I mus' tell ya that it's been rough. Damn rough! But I survived . . . yessirrreee . . . I did, as ya'll can see. The Cowboy Buddha paid me his ree-spects and I've come back with the Word."

"What's the word, Jonquil?"

"Where'd the pickup come from?"

Jonquil held up his hand. "First, I would like to introduce ya'll to the new Jimmi Maroon . . . with an i." Jonquil stepped down off the porch. "This pickup was my ree-ward fer hangin' tough on the Mountain. I was hoongry and I was cold but I rode it out."

"All right. . . ."

"Go git 'em, cowboy!"

"I stayed right there with my convictions. I gritted my teeth, bared my chest, and looked the Cowboy Buddha right square in his third eye and told him . . . I need my truck."

"Hymen . . . Hymen!"

"The Cowboy Buddha told me that I was one of his fav-O-rites, and if I wanted my truck back . . . it was MINE! He told me that anyone who would climb the mountain, fast, suffer, tie himself to a tree that had been struck by lightnin' five hunnerd and thirty-two times, go without beer, poontang, and fasten his eyes open with bobwire dee-SERVES to have his ol' Jimmi Maroon back once again."

"Right on, cowboy, right on!"

". . . an' my pickup was ree-TURNED! It was res-rrr-RECTED . . . right back to life. The Cowboy Buddha blew the spirit right back into my ol' pickup and now she lives once again. Hallelujah buckaroos and buckarinas!"

"HALLELUJAH!"

"Jus' look at the paint! Look at it! Seven coats of Jimmi Maroon lacquer, hand-rubbed bee-tween each coat. An' crank yer necks down under and ob-serve the underside of this amazin' carriage. Git right down on yer knees, my good friends, jus' like you'd be prayin', and check out the chromed drive line, the chromed shocks, and the chromed rear end."

"Look at her! It's a miracle . . . a fuckin' miracle."

"And while yer down on yer knees jus' look at those tires. Are ya not seein' the apex, the peak, the pyramid of the rubber tree? My dear ol' sidekicks . . . those tires have gone through the transsubplantation of life. They have gone through the transistorization, an' they have gone through the transcontinentalization of life. Yeh . . . they have been reborn an' they have been ree-IN-car-NATED into the treads fer the most famous an' bee-U-ti-FUL pickup in the Western West . . . Jimmi Maroon!" Jonquil walked around to the front of the truck. "Side-kicks 'n' sidekickerinas . . . beefore I pop this hood I would like fer ya'll to make sure you've got yer sunglasses in place. Bee-cuz . . . I'm not insured and I can't be re-sponsible fer eye fractures an' dislocations."

"We've got 'em on, Jonquil . . . we're ready."

"Sheeeeeeet, I thought the E-clips happened last year."

Dr. Flood looked down the line and raised his pool cue . . . glowering at the interruption.

"What ya are goin' to see, my dear 'roos 'n' 'rinas, is one of the greatest miracles of this century. It is more amazin' than the pedal steel, the pickup truck, an' the double clutch. It IS even more miraculous than the Cowboy Buddha jugglin' nine planets at the same time."

"Glory, glory, Cowboy Buddha. . . ."

"Glory, glory, Cowboy Buddha."

"Are ya ready?"

"We ARE ready, Rose Garden."

"Are yer glasses in place?"

"Right ON . . . cowboy."

"All right." Jonquil reached under the hood, released the lever, and stepped back.

"Ohhhhh . . . look at the LIGHT!"

"Hua, hua . . . turn it off, Rosehips . . . I'm blinded."

"My eyes, my eyes! It's more powerful than the sun on a sunny day."

Jonquil stood by his truck and stared directly into the motor. "Look into this rollin' machine an' ya'll see the Truth, an' the Truth will easy erase yer wicked souls; the Truth will eradicate yer sins; an' the truth will eroticize yer lustful eroticism; an' the Truth, my good ol' friends, will eradicate yer down 'n' out whisky ways into trail drivin' dusty days. NOW . . . tell me what ya see under the bonnet of my Jimmi Maroon."

"Chrome . . . that's what we see Jonquil, we see CHROME!"

"What else?"

"Chrome and more chrome."

"Give me some real answers. Yer lookin' at the surface, my friends, only the soupperFISHull. Millions, my ol' snappin' drifter 'n' dreamer, ree-lease yer lust to capture our souls in yer X-RATED box, an' give us some of yer Dee-troit X-PURR-Tease."

Millions adjusted his own mother-of-pearl polarized shades and swooned his eyes under the hood in search of the Sacred T. "Ah yes . . . I see . . . a taaaaaseTEE but WICcud vet checked 'VETTE . . . three-twenty-seven SEVENTH HEAVEN."

"An' . . . come on, Millions, I'm countin' on ya . . . cowboy."

"Oh . . . flyin' A supercharged day! It's a front line, negative whine, multiple spin supercharged grin!"

"Come on . . . come on."

"Ya found a smidgin' of the Truth, Millions, but there's more."

"Oh . . . I can't bee-lieve what's under the eaves. . . ."

"Yeh . . . ?"

"A nitrous oxide injector system. ONE for the carbs and one for the cab to aid the driver in peddlin' his gas."

"Yuv got a taste, Snapperoo . . . jus' a taste. NOW . . . let's have some more cuz I wanna know what's on the floor."

Millions fell into the hood and came back up; he looked under the frame and returned again to let Jonquil know he knew what was hidden in the gears. "Jonquil . . . you've got a Sri-light, Brahma-flite tranny-granny with four on the floor . . . AND a little float on the boat that is sometimes called an Five-Dee Overcoat."

"Yeh . . . but there's more . . . what else, ol' Words?"

"Power, Jonquil . . . I see POWER!"

"Come ON. Ya haven't found it yet . . . there's more!"

Millions shook his head. "I give up, Jonquil . . . I haven't been to the Mountain."

Jonquil backed off and slipped up on the fender. "Right, ya haven't, and I know ya can't see what I'm talkin' 'bout bee-cuz it's hidden. AND . . . like most truth . . . it's bee-yond our senses of recognition. YOU were blinded by the glitter an' the gold, the size an' the speed, the paint . . . ain't ol' friends where it's AT! Now . . . hidden inside that three-twenty-seven is . . . is . . . the music fer the WORD."

"Well sheeeeeet, Jonquil, don't keep us waitin' no more. Let's hear it."

"It's comin' . . . . it's comin'." Jonquil slid off the fender and jumped on the porch. "I've been to the mountain an' I've come back with the WORD. And . . . let me inform y'all that the WORD is fer all of us. We can all benefit by the WORD."

"Jonquil! We can't stand it NO MORE!"

"Give us a break, alfalfa flake."

Jonquil held up his hands. "In time, my friends, in

time." Jonquil stepped over to Molly Taps. "Ma'am . . . would ya mind steppin' down to the street with me?"

Molly stood up, curtsied, and took Jonquil's hand. "My . . . Jonquil, you do look handsome. It would be a great honor for me to accompany you down those stairs, Jonquil Rose . . . my pleasure."

"Thank you, ma'am." Jonquil guided Molly down the stairs and showed her a small toggle switch on the pickup's dash. He asked her a question and handed her a comb. "An' now my ol' West of the Dee-vide friends, while Molly is smoothin' off the edges of yer five-day endurance ride I would like to thank all of ya fer comin' here to be with me while I rode out my vision. Anytime . . . one of ya ever dee-cides to go on his or her vision I'll be there. You betcha! Helpin' ya ride it through like y'all have helped me. Now . . . y'all's probably wonderin' why I'm duded up like this. Yup . . . I knew you'd be curious. Well . . . it's bee-cuz I've found the Word. An', yer probably all dee-railed tryin' to understand what's comin' down the road. Well, it's the Word. And . . . yer probably a-wonderin' what will happen to me now that I've got the Word. Well . . . I'm a changed man, a conVERT, a REE-juv-I-Nated Cowboy Boodist. But . . . don't y'all fergit that the ol' Jonquil is now a NEW Jonquil . . . Jus' One Great Cowboy . . . but still that ol' Jonquil Rose . . . Jus' One More Cowboy." Jonquil looked over at Molly and winked. "And now . . ."

"Yes . . . Jonquil?"

"The word is . . ."

"The word . . . cowboy?"

Jonquil held out his hands, palms up.

". . . an'?"

"TAAAAAA DUMMMMMMNNNNnnnnnnnn!"

"Ta Dum . . . ?" A chorus reverberated from the porch.

"Yup . . . Ta Dum." Jonquil smiled at Molly and she flipped the toggle switch. The chrome air filter that covered the carburetor began to turn as it played an old Viennese waltz, "The Floating Rose." Jonquil bowed to Molly, took her hand, put his arm around her waist, and began to dance in front of the Quick Draw Saloon. "Ta Dum, Ta Dum, Ta Dum, Dum Dum . . . ," Jonquil sang, as he looked at Molly and she gazed at him, a tear in her eye. "Ta Dum, Ta Dum, Ta Dum, Dum Dum. . . ." Dr. Copernicus Flood grabbed the broken pool cue, jumped in front of his amazed and bedazzled sidekicks, and began to wave the cue. "Come on, ya ol' heathens . . . let's sing with Jonquil . . . let's sing the WORD. 'Ta Dum, Ta Dum, Ta Dum, Dum Dum. . . .'" He hit Studley over the head with the cue. "Come on . . . Studley Wonder . . . sing! Put your arms around all of your sweethearts and sing, cantus firmus. It's the WORD! Ta Dum, Ta Dum, Ta Dum, Dum Dum . . . that's it . . . but stay on key. Ta Dum, Ta Dum, Ta Dum, Dum Dum . . . all right, my whisky-soaked angels . . . you're beginning to sound like canaries. Now, all together . . . Ta Dum, Ta Dum, Ta Dum. . . ." The Boys continued singing the Word as Jimmi Maroon played the melody and Jonquil Rose and Molly Taps twirled and swirled a long slow waltz down the old dirt streets of his hometown in floating rose, three/four, jus' one more cowboy time.

Black Rose of the Yin

Nomad Spring was sitting in the middle of his cabin floor facing Mount Tamalpais. He finished his meditation just as the sun came out from behind the mountain. The light entered the room, flooding the last remaining particles of darkness. He watched the redwood walls begin to glow in the new light. The room was a miniature canyon filled with waterfalls, plants, and dark red vermilion walls. Natural dyed rugs and hangings told the stories of Nomad's last seven years—silent, visual historians. A journey through India, Nepal, Kashmir, Pakistan, and Afghanistan, and then of his return to this mountain that lived over the Pacific Ocean.

Nomad walked out onto the deck. His body moved gracefully over the floor. This had once been a studied lesson, but now he moved as easily as water running through a timeless stream bed. He was beautiful to watch. His eyes were like two dark moons inside a smoked ivory skin. His shiny black hair hung down to the small of his back. Each day he gave his body a ceremony —a gift for the ancient human structure that carried his life. A form that will, with dedication, move so easily, creating the most amazing geometry of dreams, fantasies, and creativity. A haiku of an earth vessel. He was a temple without mirrors.

Nomad had been living alone for the last three years since his return from Asia. Now the sacred mountain, Tamalpais, and the morning sun were his East; and the Pacific Ocean and the setting sun were his West. The rest was centered within his cabin, his body, as he went through his rituals of living within his discipline of yoga, meditation, running, reading, tai-chi, growing and preparing his own food, and planting redwood and pine trees on the slopes of the mountain. He had planted ten trees for every one that he had used in building his cabin. His food was from the earth, and the water from the mountain. He was searching for a way of living, a truth, that somewhere, or sometime, had been offered to him—perhaps as he was flying through his mother's womb. It was not his concern that his body live forever, but what he searched for was to have his incarnation as beautiful and simple as possible. Each day was a celebration to the earth. It had given life, multidimensional art forms of creatures who were all living within the balances of the planet. To spin within this invisible fulcrum was his sense of religion.

Nomad went out into the vegetable garden. He walked through the many different plants that would someday be taken into his body as food. He spoke to them, telling them how beautiful they all were, and how their lives would never end. They would pass through his body, giving him strength and pleasure, and then, they would again be giving life to a multitude of inhabitants living within the soil. An infinite cycle of earth-business. "We, my friends, must take care of this earth. The sun, air, soil, and water give you life, and I, by our own decisions, have been chosen to be your gardener. You give me life and I must return that promise by working to transcend my body into a caretaker for this planet. Someday I hope to be as clear in my life as you are right now. I'm learning, and you are my teachers."

Nomad felt the soil, rubbing it between his fingers, checking for the amount of moisture within the dirt. "Tonight we will water. I will come out here, turn the water loose from the stream, and sit with you as you drink. Perhaps you have some new stories to tell me, maybe I'll have one for you."

He walked over to a small orchard of fruit trees: apples, plums, lemons, avocados, and pears. He checked their leaves for aphids. His long fingers caressed them as lovers and friends. They knew him. This human who walked through them as gardener and singer. He went over to the blackberry bushes and looked at the fruit. In another month they would be ripe. He smiled, thinking about the pleasure he would have in eating their bodies. He looked up in the sky to watch a hawk suspended in flight, held motionless by the wind moving off the ocean. A deer was standing twenty feet away from him, poised, ready for any movement that would signal a retreat from her grazing. He watched her for a few seconds and then turned around and walked back into the vegetables. "Someday, I'll plant a garden just for the deer so they can have all of their favorite snacks. I'm sorry I had to build a fence around you, but if I didn't the deer would sneak in here and run away with you. For now, I must keep you here. The deer can go over to the rich people's gardens. They can afford it."

Nomad went back into his cabin and put on a pair of cutoffs. He hung his mattress over the railing of the deck, bowed to his house, and started down a trail through the eucalyptus and Monterey pines. Monarch butterflies were all over the summer blossoms, taking in their nectar; a mockingbird was sitting on a line pole going through a montage of birdcalls. And within her voice was a red-crowned sparrow saying over and over again, "Oh, sweet life . . . oh, sweet life."

At the bottom of the hill he crossed the highway and tucked himself into one of the side roads that led to the beach. The ocean was at low tide and the beach was a fine, hard track curving into the water. Nomad ran through the soft sand until he reached the ocean. He looked up and down the beach. It was empty, except for a gathering of gulls that were standing in a triangular formation held in a deep trance by the solitude of the morning. The beach was three miles long and Nomad was one half of a mile from the southern end. He started running slowly toward that end so when he turned he would have the three miles for his run. After fifty yards he kicked into a moderate pace, shaking his arms and rotating his shoulders to loosen his neck and back. He started playing with the waves, moving in and out with them as they ascended and descended onto the sand. He came upon a flock of Lesser Pipers running like mechanical toys, eating the food that was uncovered by the waves. One hundred yards from the end of the beach Nomad saw something move near a large rock. A horse was standing at the edge of the water watching him run. He slowed down as he searched the rocks for a rider. He couldn't see a saddle or bridle, or anyone else on the beach, only horse and tracks. The horse was searching for smells, splaying her nostrils with her ears stiff and pointed. She was the finest horse Nomad had ever seen in his life. She looked like a black royal Arabian taken from a painting done by the king's artist. Nomad stopped running and walked toward her. She threw her head and danced a quick backstep.

"Lady . . . it's all right," he said very softly. "I would just like to know who you are." She didn't move. He watched her eyes for some information that would help him understand what was happening between them. He had the strange feeling that she knew who he was. It was in her eyes—something he had seen before. Suddenly, his conscience was pulling at him, to return to his running, but he refused to listen. He didn't want to stop. He had to know. He had been alone for so long and now he had encountered someone who was more attractive to him than his daily ceremony of living within the mountain. Or, perhaps, it was exactly the same. He had perfected his life to a place where he was ready to meet such a being. He looked at her, and he could see her in a thousand paintings from China, India, Persia, and Europe. He moved in closer, and she turned and walked away. He felt his heart begin to pound and he knew that he had to be with her.

He turned around and walked to the water. He could see the Farallon Islands flying like white whales on the horizon as they moved north one inch a year. He planted himself into the sand and closed his eyes so that he could feel everything around him. A long mountain valley came into his inner focus, and he saw her running through an open meadow leading a herd of wild horses. There were no houses or buildings, but he could see a river and some people were camped on the bank. The horses moved down through the valley and then they disappeared. Nomad opened his eyes, but he didn't turn around. He knew that she was watching him. He could feel her eyes, and he could feel how she was standing with her thick mane and tail blowing over her body. She was so mythical in her presence. Perhaps she was a great queen from the wild Tibetan herds, or a great Indian buffalo runner. Was that it? He felt that he had discovered something. A feeling that captured an intuitive answer. Indian. But that was as much as he could understand through his feelings. The buffalo? Was she one of the great Indian buffalo horses who had been treated as well as any great chief? But why was she on the beach? Nomad looked at the sand and the ocean. He wondered if he were still living inside his own lifetime. Everything looked the same but something was different. The beach seemed cleaner, the air a different quality. He looked at his body, his skin, and it was darker, like the colors of the walls in his cabin. Again, he closed his eyes hoping to recapture the image he had seen of the valley. Suddenly, he felt her breath on his neck, a soft nose on his shoulder. He stepped forward and waited. The breath was gone and then it returned. It had the smell of wild grasses and mountain streams. He moved sideways and as before she followed. He walked ten feet away and stopped. She came up behind him and put her nose behind his ear . . . breathing, slowly breathing. He reached up and placed his hand on her nose. Warm flesh and hot air covered his palm and neck. They entered his being, flooding down into his body. He slowly turned, an open pivot, and looked into her face. Her eyes. They were Indian into black fired pottery with a rose in the center where he could see histories of horses and dynasties of wild herds flying over the hills, cutting through the wheat, bluestem, and buffalo grasses. He saw

them in the canyons, along the rivers, and in the high alpine meadows running with their great freedom of un-
fenced earth. He could see, and she knew that he could
see her in so many lifetimes of her spirit.

"Why are you here?" he asked softly. He slowly
reached out and touched her neck. She shied, and then
returned her head to his hand. He began to rub her back,
sinking his fingers into her coat, which was so elegant
with its colors of blues and blacks. He walked around her
body, touching her sides, flanks, and rump—his hands
moving as if they wanted to be lost forever in her life. He
looked for marks that could identify her as being kept.
He looked at her feet to see if she had been shod. "Did
you fly here?"

She began to walk, and Nomad followed. She moved as
if the whole beach was her land. He wouldn't have been
surprised if she had walked onto the water and started
running toward some mystical island that only great
beings know about. He began to run and she ran with
him. He jumped into the air and let out a whoop and she
snorted, rumbled, and gave him a laughing whinny.
Nomad started walking on his hands, and she came up to
him and knocked him over with her head. He jumped up,
did a front flip, and finished off his acrobatics with two
cartwheels and the splits. "Hey . . . what do you think of
this? I haven't done anything like this in a long time. Too
much discipline. I have forgotten how to play." Nomad
ran through the water, splashing, kicking, and stomping
in the surf. And then, he ran up to her, took hold of her
mane, and vaulted onto her back. She back-stepped, and
then settled down. "Now . . . don't buck me off." He
shifted his body until he felt that he was centered on the
right vertebrae of her back. He pressed his knees into her
sides and leaned forward. She picked up his movement

and began to walk. "I've never ridden a horse without reins." He looked on the beach hoping to find a piece of rope or seaweed that he could braid for an Indian bridle. The beach was clean. "Well, I guess you've got the lead, but no headstands or reverse spins . . . hey?"

She began to walk down the beach. Nomad moved in closer, pulling up his legs, and she changed into a trot. Easy, as if she wanted to find out how well he could ride. She stayed in a trot for about one hundred yards and then she picked up into a canter. Nomad moved up closer to her neck, folding his body into hers as she opened into a gallop.

"Woooooeeeee," he shouted into the wind, and then he cut loose with a series of short, chopping whoops, trilling the last sounds as they came from his mouth. She responded by reaching out for more of the hard sand, cutting just on the edge of the surf. He didn't have any trouble staying with her. His body was so flexible and strong and her gait was as smooth as the touching of their two bodies. Nomad looked up into the sky as it pulled them into it. Somewhere running through the clouds he could see a picture of an Indian warrior riding through a vast space of earth covered with grass and buffalo. He saw him riding hard down through a canyon toward a river—riding for the joy of being alive. He felt his body slide into the clouds, chasing the horse and rider.

The morning sun was on their backs and Nomad looked behind him to see the light bouncing from her body. Her muscles were flowing in long, graceful runs being released into the sand. He leaned forward, curving his head closer to her neck, touching and caressing her, pulling closer into her life. He began to feel that at any moment they would clear the beach and move through all of the myths and stories as the winged horseman. She reached into another pace, another distance within her body, and Nomad felt as if he were riding through her. They were being born into another being—horse-human, female-male, myth into myth, dreams into dreams.

The wind stopped. The sound of her hoofs striking the sand disappeared. Everything was silent. Nomad could not feel his own body and he had lost her as horse. They were air-borne and beyond their lives as skin coverings. They sailed. Their bodies were flying through a channel that was a vast ribbon of migration—the wind and ocean currents—a sweeping of migration. Flight—transcending the mind's gravity, the quintessence of dreams. The mind of a feather. And then they returned. Nomad could hear her hoofs once again pounding on the sand, and the wind blowing past their bodies. She began to slow down as they reached the end of the beach. She returned to a trot as easily as she began. Nomad was riding flat on her back with his legs hanging down along her sides. He felt empty, without the person he was before. She walked to land's end—the ocean was rushing through the bar into the lagoon. He slid down from her back and put his arms around her neck, pressing his face against her body, holding her life into his. He could feel the blood pumping through her body, the air being sucked in through her nostrils. This great, beautiful animal breathing in the ocean, sky, and wind of her life and returning it to the earth as horse.

Nomad dropped his cutoffs and waded into the water. He walked until the water came to his waist and then he dived under a wave and swam out past the breakers. When he returned she was standing at the edge waiting for him. He had expected her to be gone, to have disappeared as suddenly as she had entered his life. And then, he felt his body change shape as another life moved through him with wings and a long, slim, snake-body. He saw an egret fly through his body. He wasn't certain if it had really happened, but he had felt her within him. Again, he had lost his skin, and he had been only space to the lives around him. He had become the egret and sky flying through the earth for food. Horse, egret, sky . . . he was no longer only human but all of those and he could only surrender to this destiny.

He rode back. He wanted to walk with her, to return as slowly as possible to where they had discovered each other, but she kept stopping until he finally jumped on her back. She walked and trotted, giving him the ease and gentleness with which he could relax into this emptiness that he felt. He rode back into the morning, moving slowly through this new life that he had become.

Again, he looked at his skin. It seemed even darker than it had been earlier and it smelled of wood smoke and sage. Whoever he had been before, he wasn't any more. His cabin and his former life had transcended themselves from his consciousness. He was going someplace else. He wanted to see high alpine meadows between mountain ranges blooming with camas and lupine; he wanted to be in an open valley where the air was so pure and clear a meadow lark's song could be heard for fifty miles. He wanted to feel the wildness of being alive, crazy, and drunk with passion as he chased eagles, wild horses, and full moons. He wanted to ride with this horse until they had married into each other. He wanted to go where there were no more fences, into the openness of the earth, to live, and be with the people who were calling him to them. He had felt the power of this great horse and he could only follow. Wherever he was to be taken with her, he was only the rider.

The Fat Mystic's Film Festival

(Dr. Dancing Arrow Meets
Don Coyote)

It was one of those mornings that tricks everything into a miracle. Spring in the mountains with the clouds rolling across the sky looking like a seventh chakra movie on its way to the Fat Mystic's Film Festival. Triple rainbows, eagles, blue herons, and a flock of blue Canadian geese were flooding the wild Idaho yonder, and the mountain peaks were challenging the heavens for supremacy. The lilacs were lethal, forming deep, lint-free pockets of pungent dizziness. The wild grasses, flowers, and the dark, rich earth were vibrating with iridescence from the morning dew. Everything alive was pushing to renew its life—shaking, pulsating, and eventually exploding toward the sun. It was all a well-laid plan of revolution, wild ecstasy, and outright obscenity.

Everyone and everything was in the parade to the festival except for Buddy Sunday, who had just arrived for work. All he could think about was that he had been grabbed by the balls until the last book of the Old Testament. Not only had he been busted, imprisoned, paroled, and farmed out to a government program entitled Euclid's Jockstrap, but somehow they (the illusive pronoun referring to those agencies that steal the souls from dreamers and drifters and recycle them into freeze-dried, onion-skin soup) had stolen his magic. Now, he was a reformed 'ate-to-fiver punching in on the Werewolf's time clock.

Buddy looked down at the ground as the sky was posing for a scenic view for the Audubon Centennial calendar. All of the many plants came to him. He knew them but he had forgotten their stories, secrets, and healing powers. Arrowleaf, balsamroot, sweet anise, Indian paintbrush, sego lily, wild onion, wild rose, horsemint, lupine, and yarrow. His job was to run over them with his backhoe, dig them up, and dump them into another hole. All previewed, inspected, and baptized by the high priests of Euclid's Jockstrap.

He rolled the backhoe over the drop zone and leaned back in the seat. He needed more time, reinforcements, something he could dream about to help him begin his work. He listened to a meadow lark, and then the answer, which to him sounded like a Zen Garden bugle call. "All right, all right, I'm going . . . take it easy . . . heh?" He couldn't think of anything else to do. The ground had already been staked out for a very boring prefab house; the fuel, hydraulic fluid, and the oil had already been checked, and the tires prekicked by his boss. "Nothin' more?" Buddy put the backhoe in gear and backed it up to the first bite. He lowered the loader and set the pods. "Perhaps . . . I should have a drink of water?" He started to jump down when he noticed that the door on the ten-by-fifteen shack they were going to replace was open and a pair of eyes was watching him. He could feel them staring him down. "Who is it?" he wondered to the mirrors of his sunglasses. "Another government inspector checkin' up to see that I ain't been playin' with myself?" Buddy waited, staring back at the black slit.

The door swung open and an Indian walked out. He was dressed in Levi's with creases so exact they could have been used for straight edges. His shirt was white cowboy with flowers embroidered on the collar, eagles flying over each breast pocket, and on the back the Cowboy Buddha was riding a black-eyed roan Appaloosa through a lightning storm in the Tibetan mountains. He had a blue scarf around his neck, and his hat was a high-crowned, pearl beaver with a slight crevasse on the ridge. His boots were mirrors to the morning sun, and he was holding a pair of white deerskin gloves. Buddy turned off the motor.

The Indian reached into the house and pulled out a bottle of beer. He pointed to the bottle and then to Buddy. Buddy raised a finger as a gesture of acceptance. The Indian sent his arm back into the shack and came back out with a six-pack. Buddy jumped off the backhoe.

"You must be Dr. Dancing Arrow," the Indian said to Buddy. "I had a dream about you. Let's have a drink."

Buddy looked at the Indian, head cocked, trying to figure out what he was talking about. "Dr. Dancing Arrow?"

"Yes, of course. My dream said you would be coming here and your name is Dr. Dancing Arrow. I was told to give you this bracelet." He handed Buddy a silver bracelet with a mother-of-pearl dragonfly inlaid in turquoise. Buddy held the bracelet in the sun, dive-bombing the dragonfly onto a beer bottle, not knowing what to say to the Indian.

"Go on . . . put it on. It's yours."

"Why?"

The Indian laughed and opened up two bottles of beer, giving one to Buddy. "You ask too many questions. Take the bracelet and wear it."

Buddy was confused but he put it on. "What does this mean?"

"Oh, shit! It means that I have given you a bracelet."

"But . . . why the dragonfly?"

"What would you like it to be . . . a backhoe?" The Indian clinked Buddy's bottle and drank the beer in long smooth swallows. He finished his beer and opened up two more as he leaned against the shack. "You're going to dig the hole?"

"Yup," Buddy said, finding more confidence with his job as the first beer hit the target.

"Good . . . that's damn good. We need a big hole here. Too many plants and flowers. And then we can have a big box with a full basement, wall to wall empty space. We'll put our horses in it. So do a good job. We've got good horses . . . O.K.?" He opened up the last two beers and handed Buddy the last of the six-pack. Buddy was still on his second beer. He drank it down as he accepted the third.

"What's yer name?" Buddy said, feeling more at ease with the Indian.

"Don Coyote," the Indian said, looking into his own reflection from Buddy's sunglasses.

"Don Coyote," Buddy repeated. "Nice name . . . sounds Indian," he said, laughing. The beer was making it much easier.

Don Coyote looked at Buddy, shaking his head. "You know about the coyote?"

"Sure. Kills sheep an' pisses off the ranchers. I always thought that since the ranchers can't control the coyotes they should raise them instead. Heard that if ya marinate a coyote in Coca-Cola it'll taste jus' like Peking Duck. Is that true?"

"Naw. Eagles taste like Peking Duck."

"Eagles?"

"Yeh . . . eagles."

"What do coyotes taste like?"

"Ranchers. But you've got to cook them a long time because they're always so stringy and tough. They never relax. You marinate them in diesel fuel and sugar beets. Nothin' like an old, weather-beaten, pussy-whipped rancher. But . . . you should never eat a coyote."

"Why?" Buddy was thinking how true it is. You really do learn something every day.

"Well, Doctor, coyote stole the fire from the Ohio Blue Tip Match Company and brought it to the Indians. The Indians used the fire to burn down the farmers' and ranchers' homes. So the coyote is sacred. Now, coyote works for the Indians killing the rancher's sheep since we can't kill the ranchers any more. We have a contract with them. When the ranchers go belly-up they move to Salt Lake City, Pocatello, or Australia. Coyote gets half the land and we get the rest. Fifty-fifty."

"All right. Sounds like a good deal to me," Buddy said, looking at his watch. "Hey . . . I've got to git goin' on this job. I've got two more lined up this week. It's m' ass if I don't finish this by tomorrow afternoon."

"Maybe it's your ass if you do," Coyote said, watching the label on the beer bottle. "Why don't you drive into town and buy some more beer? Maybe a couple of cases.

Let's have a party. We'll celebrate the beginning of the new house and we'll need some more beer. Lots of it. My truck is broken."

"Oh no! I can't do that."

"Start tomorrow. We'll celebrate today."

"Hey! Wait a minute! I'm on parole. If ah got caught I'd be back in the slam b'fore I could sober up."

"You go into town and while you're gone I'll dig the hole. I ran a backhoe during the war. Know all about them. Where's the transit? Got to keep everything on the level."

"Ah, sheeeet . . . Coyote."

"I could pick your nose with one of these monsters. I could snip dingleberries off a hummingbird's ass. You want straight walls? I'll give you straight walls. You want it shaped like a coffin? A coffin you'll have. No one will find out. Those government dudes don't come out here. They're 'fraid. The Indians out here are too wild and crazy . . . like me. If they start snooping around, we send in the coyote to steal their children, sheep, wives, and secret underwear. Harassment and subterfuge."

Buddy was drunk enough to be convinced. He had been on the wagon since his release from jail and three beers were like an avalanche on a ninety-pound Wyoming yogi. Buddy felt the bracelet on his arm. Don Coyote was watching him.

"The dragonfly is your magic, now. You'll need it, Doctor. That hoe over there sure ain't. Look at it. You've been tricked into thinking that machine is your teacher."

"Well then . . . what is?"

"Hmmmmm . . . let me think. Shit, maybe it is your teacher. Maybe it can teach me something. What do you think I have to learn, Doctor?"

"How to cook a backhoe so it tastes like buffalo?"

"That's it, Doc. You're right. We'll have to use some strong medicine to make it tender. What do you suggest?"

"How about dynamite powder 'n' camel piss?"

"Where could we find the camel piss?"

"Maybe coyote could steal some from the A-rabs."

"Coyote can do everything. I'll speak with him tonight. You stay with me and we'll speak to the coyote. You'll see." Coyote walked over to the backhoe and gave it a quantum study. "You know . . . I've never eaten buffalo. A full-blooded Shoshone and I've never eaten buffalo. I screwed a buffalo once but I've never sat down to the table with one. We should work on that." Coyote jumped up into the seat of the backhoe and started the motor. "Let me use your sunglasses, Doc. I must look like you . . . heh?"

Buddy walked over and handed Coyote his glasses. Coyote slipped them on and then flashed out a fifteen-megaton smile. "How do I look . . . Doc?"

"Like a pro, Coyote . . . like a pro."

Buddy was halfway to Sammy Jump's Buffalo Bar and Grill before he realized what he was doing. He eased down to fifteen miles an hour and rode the shoulder. His moon-craz'd half—Royal Ass Bandit, Heathen-Buddhist, the Ex-Trombone Kid, lover of swift whores and horses, and connoisseur of five-star rodeo queens—felt real good. But the other half, the Victorian woodchopper and Virgo Purissimo, was trying to throw a savior's lasso around Buddy's wayward side. Buddy tried to make peace, get them together, set up a blind date, but they wouldn't budge. Dualism and the Vendettas. "Hey, goddammit! The two of you settle down! I know this is crazy and I should be back there diggin' that fuckin' hole, but that goddam Indian Coyote's got me humpin' my fantasies 'gain. Okay . . . twenty minutes and we'll git back to work. S'that a deal? What? You want me to turn 'round and go back? And what 'bout you, Cock-of-the-Walk? Jus' as I thought . . . good. Well, this ain't gunna be some wild kundalini fandango, cowboy. We'll jus' have a beer . . . no more. Ah, sheeeeet, stop poutin' and sulkin'. If ya don't like the ride, find another one. No, I don't want to hear that story 'bout the grasshopper 'n' the ants again. You told it to me too many times already. It's boring. And you, you crazy sour-mash heathen, all you want to do is play, sing to the moon, get laid, and howl all night. Weed? No way, José. Now hold it down, both of you. Back off and leave me alone. I've got it all figured out." Buddy eased back onto the pavement.

Buddy pulled up in front of Sammy's Bar and Grill trying to look incognito. "Hmmmmm, no gov'ment cars but maybe they're traveling in disguise as pickups and hay thieves? Whew . . . three beers and I'm still looped. Well, let's git in there and see what happens." Buddy opened the door, slowly, and looked in. Two Church of the Last Chance Cowboys' missionaries were sitting at the bar; three tourists from California were drinking Hamms beer and eating buffalo burgers; and the town drunk had been taxidermied and stuffed in the corner. A beer mug full of cigars in one hand, the other hand was cupped for a handout. "Coast's clear," Buddy sideswiped. He looked over his shoulder and slipped in.

Sammy Jump, 1929 All-around Cowboy, part-time psychic, and full-time dirty old man, was behind the bar when Buddy walked in. "Back in the olden days," Sammy was telling the two missionaries, "I could bend silver spoons into turquoise bracelets jus' with my mind. But now, they jus' come out lookin' like bent spoons. Losing my powers . . . jus' ask my wife." He flashed a big smile so the two young men could see his teeth, which had been capped with turquoise. "Zuni. You can tell by their work. I met this Zuni dentist one night in Flagstaff at an inter-tribal dildo-carving festival. I gave him two thousand simoleons to cap my teeth. It took him three days, five bottles of Dickel, and two tanks of laughin' gas. I wanted to have inlay on every front tooth, but I could only 'ford two mountains and a water ouzel. I wanted to put Mount Rainier and the Grand Teton in there but we had to settle for mountains under ten thousand, and the smallest bird in the mouth." Sammy walked over to Buddy as the two missionaries fled clutching their Old and New Testaments of the Wild West.

"What'll it be?" Sammy asked, giving the counter a fast one-two with the bar towel.

"Twenty bucks' worth of beer. Don Coyote sent me."

Sammy laughed as he backed himself from the bar to bring Buddy better into focus. "You're a friend of his? And he wants his discount . . . huh?"

"Yup. Looks that way."

"Well, that old coyote saved my life one time, or claims he did, and he's never gonna let me ferget it. Always a discount. I was fishing one time over on the South Fork, gettin' a good share of rainbows, and the game warden came up behind me. I jumped into the river 'cuz I was fishin' out of season. I started shooting down river like a fart in a tailspin. Can't swim worth a damn downstream, if you know what I mean, and I thought I was a goner. Well, old Coyote was workin' iron on that new bridge jus' before the falls and he saw me yellin' and hootin' trying to make myself real noticeable. He jumped in. One-hundred-foot drop . . . straight down. He landed right on top of me. Dead-on. Knocked us both out. Cold-cocked. So we were both belly-up headin' fer the falls, see, and for some strange reason the current kicked us up onto a sand bar. He claims that if he hadn't of jumped I would have drowned or shot the falls. Don't know if I'll ever believe him, but he tried, and trying means a lot in my book. So I've always given him the ol' Sammy Jump Discount . . . twenty off the top. He's made me pay, by damn. That was twenty years ago."

Sammy was called into the kitchen. Buddy looked around the café-bar. There was a good feeling about the place. Simple and clean with no day-glo signs reciting proverbs about the right-to-serve, the bad times and the good, horses' asses, and cowboy chauvinism. No stuffed animals or plastic flowers. There were old and new photographs of Indians, a picture of Sammy when he was All-around Cowboy standing with three rodeo queens, and a large painting of the Cowboy Buddha riding a Brahma bull out the third eye of God.

"Here I am. Want some breakfast? Ma just blew an order. She made a cheese omelet instead of two fried eggs full-moon up. She asked me if you'd like this. On the house. She said you had a nice face. Honest. I told her I didn't think so . . . you look nervous. Anyway, here's the omelet. Eat it up . . . son. Best in the valley. Want some coffee?"

"Well . . . sure . . . why not?"

"That's the spirit. Take it when it comes cuz it don't come too often. You know, you remind me of an old friend. Hunting guide. He used to come in here all the time. Golden . . . Golden St. Augustine. Great man! Ever heard of 'im?"

"He's my uncle," Buddy said, pouring hot sauce over the omelet.

"Don't say. How about that? Hey, Mama, come on out

here! She's gunna be surprised. She was always sweet on him. I heard he's livin' with that Syringa Rose. Is that true?"

"I don't know. I ain't seen him fer a long time. I've been away . . . ah . . . school."

Molly came out from the kitchen wiping her hands on a towel. She was a very attractive woman riding early through the middle ages. White hair woven into braids; large blue eyes with a marathon's body. Breasts that looked like small tepees camped along a deep blue turquoise necklace. A Levi's-tight butt that translated the western migration into action. When she smiled everyone knew that the sun would never set inside her mountains, and she made it very plain to all of her admirers that she was still in love with Sammy. Her eyes revealed the hidden claws.

"Mama, this young man here, this good-lookin' cowboy, is Golden's nephew. You're right. You're always right."

Molly stuck out her hand. "Well, this is a surprise. I'm very happy to meet you. What's your name, son?"

"Buddy . . . Buddy Sunday."

Sammy was rubbing his palms together. "This calls for a drink. What should we have, Mama? Something stiff? Something to help the blood pressure, lumbago, piles, peegie-weegie, and hangnails? I know . . . Spud'odka . . . good ol' Idaho vodka with buffalo grass." Sammy caressed the vodka out of the freezer. "I keep it in here so it comes out like a blizzard. Goes down like a volcanic iceberg and then implodes like an ultrasonic orgasm. Oh . . . it's so good! Hey, let's have beer-backs as a bonus. To drown out the heat wave."

Molly took three beer glasses out from the cooler. "I never knew your parents, only Golden. Where you from?"

"Started out in Blackfoot but I left when I was sixteen."

"Parents still there?"

"No. My dad took off when I was a kid. Ran away with the bishop's wife. My mom moved to Hawaii after I left. She loves birds."

"Birds? Hey, did you hear that, Sammy? Why don't you bring out old Wiseass? We've got a parrot who loves limericks. She knows a whole passel of 'em." Sammy put the drinks on the bar and went back into their house, which was side-saddled to the bar and grill. He returned with the parrot perched on his head.

"Look at her, Buddy. Ain't she a beaut?"

"Say something for our new friend," Molly asked Wiseass.

The parrot kinked her head, didn't like that position, tried the other side . . . cock-eyed. "Squaaaak . . . Squaaaak."

"Oh, come on."

"Now don't be shy, sweetheart."

"Squaaak . . ."

"Maybe she needs to be wound up more. She's revolvin' in slow motion," Buddy said as he sipped his beer.

"Naw . . . she'll make it. Come on, Wiseass, do yer stuff." Sammy took her off his head and held her out on his arm. "I jus' washed my hair. Now listen to me, Wiseass. If ya don't purrform, I'm gunna have your ass cree-mated and put to rest in the chip dip. Parrot Supreme . . . the Sammy Jump Special. You'll be the talk of the valley. Now, git goin'!"

"Squaaak . . ."

"Come on."

"Squaaak . . . There once was a rose of a man,
        Who kept young virgins sealed in a can.
        When he would get horny,

He'd whip out his thorny,
And open them up with a Whang!
Squaaaak . . . squaaaak . . ."

Sammy cracked up and started banging the counter
with the beer mug, flashing his teeth into a Navajo sunrise. "Mama, I ain't never heard that one before. Did you
teach it to her?"

"Heavens no!" she said, blushing. "I've never heard it
either. She must be making them up . . . about you,
Sammy. The meter was off, I think, but we can work on
that. Oh . . . what a dirty mind you have my beautiful,
sweet Wiseass."

"Well I'll be a heart 'n' hand husband. That crazy bird.
Someday . . . it's chip dip for you, dip shit. Tellin' stories
'bout me like that."

"Listen," Buddy said to them. "I've got to git goin'. Ah
got a lot of work to do."

"Yeh . . . I bet, with four cases of beer. Here, let's
drink up." Buddy watched them as they threw down the
vodka. He picked up his drink and emptied it.

"Ahhhh . . . that's so good." Molly said, putting the
glasses in front of Sammy for another round. "Let's have
one more for the road."

"Where we goin', honey?"

"How about . . . you know."

"To bed? But what will we do with the place?"

"Yeh . . . maybe Buddy could watch things fer us.
How about it? Ever worked a bar 'n' grill b'fore?"

"Well . . . yeh. In Cheyenne. But I've got to git."

"Oh, hang on to yer hammer. Jus' help us out and you
can always have free food and drinks . . . anytime. We'll
be back in . . . how long, Mama?"

"Takes longer these days. A lot more dancing if you

know what I mean. Give us an hour, Buddy." They finished their drinks and started for the living room door.

"Hey . . . wait a minute!"

"Take it easy, cowboy. Don't worry about anything. Cook yerself a lunch-in. Have a few drinks. It's good fer ya . . . all organic. Be back soon. Ya gotta git it when you can or it might slip away from ya. Know what I mean, cowboy?" Sammy followed Molly through the door, clicking his heels and pulling the rip cord.

It was past noon when Molly and Sammy returned. The parrot was still perched on Sammy's head. Buddy wondered if they had made love with Wiseass hovered over them like a rodeo announcer. ". . . and now buckaroos and 'rinas, here is the 1929 World Champ-yun bareback, sex fiend . . . out of his shorts and into the saddle. . . ."

"Come back again, Buddy, anytime," they said to him. "Old Wiseass has a lot more pomes for ya."

"I'm sure." Buddy loaded the beer into his truck and went back in to pay Sammy. "No tricks now . . . I've got to jingle. See ya all later." Before Sammy closed the door, Buddy heard the parrot begin another limerick.

> "There once was a Cowboy Perverse,
> Whose magic was froze in reverse.
> To break from his jam,
> He went hunting for Lamb. . . ."

The door closed and Buddy didn't hear the last line.

As Buddy was driving back he kept thinking about the limerick, wondering about the last line. "Sheeeeet, stop it!" he told himself, "jus' git yer ass movin' down the road." Old Virgo was intolerable by this time and he had refused to ride in the cab. He was in the back sitting very straight-backed on the spare tire. His high-falutin' counterpart was over by the window singing songs about the good times, and all of the fun he was having. Buddy was worried. "If only Coyote has the hole dug . . . I'll be okay."

He turned off the highway and headed down the dirt road toward Coyote's cabin. He could see the shack along the side of a long stand of Lombardy poplars, but he couldn't see the backhoe. He goosed the motor and started looking for Coyote. Fifty feet from the turn he saw Coyote walk out of his house carrying a shovel. He walked over to where his new house would be and speared the shovel into the ground. Buddy couldn't see the backhoe, but there was a large hole and a mound of dirt. He stopped the truck in front of the old shack and jumped out.

"Coyote, ya sonofabitch! Where in the hell is my goddam backhoe?"

Coyote looked at him and smiled. "Dr. Dancing Arrow, take it easy. You're on Indian land. This ain't some dumb white man's land. Be respectful." He put the shovel in front of Buddy and gave it a little dance. "Would you like to help me finish burying your teacher?"

"What? You've got to be kidding! What . . . why you're out of yer fucking mind!" Buddy ran over to the hole and looked in. The backhoe had been covered with dirt except for a small part of the front loader. He dropped to his knees and looked up into the sky. There was nothing up there that could help him. Only mountains, sun, clouds, and space. "You conniving, scheming, sonofabitchin' boomerang. What didja do that fer? What am I gunna do now? Stealin' a man's backhoe is like stealin' his horse . . . don'ja know? I bet you had this all planned. You, Sammy, Molly, and that fucking parrot fartin' out limericks."

Coyote walked over to Buddy, squatting down beside him. "Nothing is ever planned. Some things are just put into motion. Old Sammy and Molly didn't know you were coming and it wasn't my fault you got caught into tending their business while they went off to screw."

"How did ya know that?" Buddy whipped back.

"Easy. That's what always happens. When you didn't return I figured you were stuck there. Every time that parrot starts mouthing off her limericks they get horny. I've been stuck there many times. But what the fuck . . . free food and drinks. Good people, too."

Buddy stood up slowly, dusted off his pants, and walked toward the river. His mind was being cross-circuited with anger and confusion. He didn't know what to do. He felt the bracelet on his arm, touched the dragonfly, and tried to understand what everything was supposed to mean. The synchronicity of events and why his life was changing so quickly for him. Why Coyote was calling him Dr. Dancing Arrow. He turned around and confronted Coyote. "How do ya think I'm gunna pay fer that piece of twenty-five-grand shit? I'm already on probation. I can't afford to fuck up."

Don Coyote eased himself out of the squat. He took off his hat, dusted the crown, and stuck it back on. "Doctor . . . it's easy. Everything is easy. Have you forgotten about the magic of white man's insurance. A no-good drunken Indian swiped your meal ticket, see, while you were having lunch. Everybody gets paid and you're off the hook. I'll be your new probation officer. See, I told you everything would work out. Besides, you can't afford not to fuck up. Here, help me finish the ceremony."

The shovel was put before Buddy once again. He

walked slowly toward it as if he were being pulled by
some strange power. Everything was jumping around
him, changing shapes, except for Coyote. He stood there
without a speck of dirt on his mirror-toed boots, smiling
and laughing and the sun was bouncing in miniature stars
from the sunglasses. Coyote turned around and picked up
the other shovel. The Cowboy Buddha was still riding
the Appaloosa but the sky was clear and there was the
beginnings of a magnificent sunset.

Buddy grabbed the shovel and slammed it into the pile
of dirt. He shook his head. He felt like jumping into the
hole to be buried along with his backhoe. Coyote was
busy shoveling in the dirt. Buddy scooped up a shovel of
dirt and threw it into the hole. Thumpff. Another one,
and then he got into the swing of it until he and Coyote
were matching shovels, swing for swing, and it suddenly
became a dance between them. They were throwing the
dirt into the hole, and the dust would billow up around
them, and the shovel handles became smooth and warm,
and Coyote was singing a song, and before Buddy realized it, they had filled up the hole.

The ground was as flat as it had been before. Coyote
went over to an old wooden box that was next to the
shack. It was full of coffee cans. He reached into the
cans, cupping seeds out of each can. "Seeds, Doctor.
Seeds of everything that grows along the river." He
spread them over the rich, dark, river-bottom earth, kicking the dirt over the seeds with the toes of his boots. "It
will rain tonight and in a week we'll have new life growing all over this spot. A very fine burial ground, don't you
think?" He walked back to where Buddy was standing.
"You can come and live with me. I've plenty of room."

Buddy was surprised. Another trick? He pointed to the
shack. "Thanks, Coyote, but it looks like it's too small fer

one let alone two." Coyote started to laugh. And then he began to jump up in the air, giggling and dancing around in front of Buddy. He stopped as quickly as he had started, pointing at the shack.

"I don't live there. I've got a room at the Cowboy Buddha Hotel." He stepped back, waiting for Buddy's reaction. Buddy looked hard into Coyote's face, deeper than the Pleistocene of his mask, looking for some origin of reason, the source of Coyote's five aces. Nothing . . . but the mirrors of the sunglasses. Buddy started to snicker, laughing within his confinement until he realized that everything he had created was the evolution of his own imagination. Good or bad it was his own breath. He began to hoot and holler, laugh and scream. He yanked off his hat and threw it into the air, stomping on it when it hit the ground. He ripped off his shirt and threw it into the trees. He pulled off his probation retreads and heaved them over the shack. He one-legged off his pants and beat them into the dirt with the shovel. He whipped the shovels around his head and shot them into an alfalfa field, kicking up two pairs of mating mallards. The noise echoed through the fields, bouncing off the trees, birds, and mountains. When he stopped he was covered with dirt and sweat, and he had the king's gift of the crazy-eye. He walked over to Don Coyote and leaned into the parabola of his smile. "Who does live there, Don Coyote?"

"I don't know," Coyote said, giving Buddy a full-house smile with everything wild.

Buddy looked up into the sky, sinking his feet into the soft dirt. A hawk was flying in a smooth circle caught in a thermal coming off the mountains. The afternoon clouds had disappeared and all he saw was blue into hawk into blue. He looked back at Coyote. "I surrender. I give up. Goddam, holy jumpin' Cowboy Buddha, Coyote, I give up."

Coyote leaned in close to Buddy, took off his hat, and started twirling it around on his finger. "How much beer did you buy, Doctor?"

"Four cases." Buddy had forgotten about the beer.

"Two apiece. That sounds about right." He walked over to Buddy's truck, climbed in on the driver's side, and started up the motor. "Let's take the beer down to the river and watch the birds. There are still some geese and ducks flying north, and maybe after it gets dark we'll sneak out into the night and find ourselves a nice, fat spring lamb. I haven't eaten today. I'll show you how to cook a lamb to perfection. How would you like it to taste . . . Doc?"

Buddy walked over to Coyote in low gear, easing his bare feet over the gravel, broken glass, and stickers. "How 'bout lamb?"

"You're on. For a while you had me fooled. I thought maybe you really weren't Dr. Dancing Arrow, but now I know you are. Sometimes my dreams trick me, sly devils. Even the old coyote can be tricked."

Buddy started to ask Coyote about Dr. Dancing Arrow, but stopped. He was too exhausted and he didn't care any more. It was a nice name, sounded Indian, sort of. He climbed in on the other side, popped open two beers, and handed one to Coyote. "Hey," he said as Coyote was driving down the road shifting and steering with one hand, "y'know that limerick that old Wiseass recites 'bout cowboy perverse?"

"How does it go?" Coyote asked.

Buddy pulled down the can of beer in one long swallow, threw it into the well, and leaned back against the seat with his feet on the dash.

> "There once was a Cowboy Perverse,
> Whose magic was froze in reverse.
> To break from his jam,
> He went hunting for Lamb. . . ."

Coyote finished the last line as he pulled up next to the river. ". . . Ol' Coyote has broken his curse."

Sun Trine the Gods

"He'll be here soon," Don Coyote said to Buddy Sunday as they were sitting in the Cowboy Buddha Hotel eating breakfast.

Buddy picked up a bottle of hot sauce, checked the temperature gauge, and poured a mean-looking parade of Mexican fire power over his omelet. "Who's gunna be here?"

"My son."

"Yer son?" Buddy mixed the question in with his eating, as he opened his mouth to air out the volcano that was being born inside his body. "Talk faster, Coyote, I need a cool breeze blowin' in from the islands of yer mind."

"Yes, my son," Coyote answered, ignoring Buddy's remarks.

"I didn't know ya had a son, Coyote. But there ain't many things I do know about ya. How old are ya anyway? At least two hunderd and twenty-five. Old, ancient, and wise . . . heh? And I'm jus' the Wind River Kid searchin' fer the truth."

"Well, Dr. Dancing Arrow, get your head out of your ass . . . you won't find it in there. Truth, Doctor, lives in cool places. Look at you. The only truth you're going to find this morning is a Mexican revolution flying right out of your mouth. Here . . . read this." Coyote took a newspaper clipping out of his wallet and gave it to Buddy.

Buddy took the clipping and began to read. "Hey! I heard about this man. Why?"

"He's been having the wrong kind of visions. I think we should pay him a visit."

"One hundred eagles shot down by one man! I can't even translate that story."

Coyote took the clipping and put it back into his wallet. "There is no translation. This man must be possessed by some kind of demon. He was only fined five C's. One hundred turkeys would cost twice that much. He should have been chopped up and fed to the Roto-Rooter man."

"At least pressed into oil of asshole. But what would ya do with it?"

"Somebody would probably use it to keep their pecker stiff. Look!" Coyote nodded toward the front door.

Buddy looked up as a dark-skinned man walked through the door. The stranger took off his sunglasses, studied the hotel, and then walked over to the counter and sat down. He had on sandals, Levi's, and East Indian white cotton shirt with embroidery around the collar and sleeves. Tibetan turquoise and coral were on his arms and neck, and a woven belt was laced through his belt loops. His long, black hair was tied neatly into a pony tail.

Syringa came out of the kitchen, stopped when she saw the young man. She watched him for a time that seemed to carry her through dreams, fantasies, a feeling of nights spent camped in the mountains, old photographs, and temples. Her immediate response was to smile for every cell in her body, and for all of her past lives as a woman who dreamed of a man who could touch without crushing, make love without the climax of a one-act play, give without asking. The smile was easy.

"Would you like a menu?" she asked, as she poured out a glass of spring water.

"No, thank you," the man replied. "Do you have any herbal teas?"

"Do you want to remain in your body or would you like to transcend? Your desire, our speciality."

The man looked around the room, studied his body, and pulled out a road map. "Am I back in Idaho? Or did I take the wrong turn and end up in Tibet?"

"Well, there are a few of us who would like to think that they are exactly the same. I even believe that there must be shitkickers in Tibet."

"If not, perhaps there are kickshitters."

Syringa laughed. "That's even better. The Khambas for sure. Well, let's see. I can give you just about any combination of herbal teas you can think of that grows within these borders."

"All right," the man said; "how about wood betony, gota kola, peppermint, lemon grass, and cloves. A modest breakfast tea. Are these within your borders?"

Syringa took a porcelain teapot out of the cupboard. "I don't believe in borders . . . only dimensions." She opened up another cupboard that revealed over a hundred jars of different herbs.

He watched her prepare the tea. "I just came from the

Coast. I brought some Chinese herbs with me. Perhaps you would like to have some?"

Syringa turned and smiled. "Yes, I would like to share the knowledge and experience with you. Will you be staying?"

"Well, I don't know exactly. I'll have to wait and see."

"That's him," Coyote said to Buddy.

"What? But he looked right at ya."

"Well, he doesn't know I'm his father."

Buddy looked over at Coyote, shook his head, and lowered his body down into the chair. His hat came down over his eyes. "Coyote, what tricks are ya up to now?"

"No tricks. You'll see. I was on a secret mission when he was conceived. It was my long-range coyote program. I knew that someday I would need him. He's been away for a long time. I sent for him but he doesn't know that either. I think it's time we met." Coyote stood up and walked over to his son. He spoke with him for a minute and then the two men returned to the table. "Dr. Dancing Arrow, I would like you to meet Nomad Spring." Buddy stood up and shook hands with Nomad. "Dr. D.A. still calls himself Buddy Sunday. He still doesn't believe that his real name is the Doctor." Nomad looked at Coyote, and then returned his eyes to Buddy. "Have you been to see your mother?"

Nomad sat down, but he didn't answer Coyote's question. There were so many things happening to him that he didn't understand. A collection of events that was beginning to gather within his life—strangers becoming friends within the pouring of a cup of tea. He was having subliminal flashes when he looked at Coyote as if he were finding an answer to an old question. He had been driving all night and he felt as if his life were floating outside of his body.

"I've known your mother for a long time," Coyote continued, "about forty years." Syringa brought the pot of tea over to the table and sat down. "Syringa," Coyote said, "this is a friend of mine . . . Nomad Spring. Nomad . . . this is Syringa Rose. I believe you used to know Syringa's two sons . . . Jonquil and Ranger."

Nomad smiled and placed his hand within Syringa's two hands. "I feel as if I've walked into a play that has been rehearsed by all of you for the last seven years."

"Well, Nomad," Syringa answered, "we've all been outside of our bodies for a long time, and now it must be the time to return. How long were you in Asia?"

"Four years, but I have been living on the California coast for the last three."

"Are you gunna stick 'round?" Buddy asked Nomad.

"I don't know."

"Well, why don't you stay with us? I would love to hear your stories about your travels," Syringa said to Nomad. "I don't think any of us has been east of Denver or west of Winnemucca."

"Well, it ain't the miles but the miles in between," Coyote said, kicking back on his chair. "I think Thoreau said that."

"I think I'm gunna throw up," Buddy remarked, as he tried to cut the chair out from under Coyote with his boot.

Coyote looked at Buddy, cocked one silent finger, and shot him right through his young, cowboy heart. "The only decent punishment for a smart-ass is a dead-ass hung to rest in eternal silence. Take 'im away and let the crows write folk songs about him." Buddy froze into a position of a gunned-down desperado: head down, tongue out, with one stiff leg quivering underneath the table. Coyote turned to Nomad as he cooled off his finger with a whiff, the sign of the Dead-eye. "I think you should stay with us." He put his hand on Nomad's shoulder. "I would like that."

Nomad looked at Syringa, Coyote, and smiled at Buddy. "Well, I know I'm suppose to be here for some reason. Is there room to pasture a horse?"

"We have stables, corrals, and a pasture behind the hotel covered with sweet grass, clover, and timothy," Syringa told Nomad. "Buddy has just finished putting up the first hay crop."

Buddy jumped up and began to clear off the table. "I'll take care of yer horse for ya, Nomad. An' then I'll fix up a room . . . the guest suite. How 'bout that?"

"Don't let the cayuse kick you into a funeral procession, wrangler," Coyote said to Buddy. "I'll be needin' ya for a secret mission soon."

Syringa touched Nomad's arm. "Pay 'em no mind."

Nomad wasn't. He was thinking about the horse, Black Rose, and the journey she was taking him on since the time she first appeared on the beach. "Sure, Buddy . . . she's gentle. I don't think you'll have any problems unloading her. She'll need some water."

"She'll be in good hands," Syringa told Nomad. "Horses are top guests with me. They'll always have the best rooms in the hotel. Animals first . . . humans whenever. That's our motto. I'll give you a hand, Buddy." Syringa and Buddy left and Nomad turned to look at Don Coyote. He looked into his eyes, studying their colors and the way they translated his vessel. There were thousands of stories of the coyote and ancient histories of his people. There was a profound understanding of his own fascination and love for the life that he was given, and for the peoples of the universe. There was laughter and serenity. A face that sees the world within its life as a thousand years; a face that has lived within the lives of trees, animals, birds, fish, and plants. Nomad had seen eyes like Coyote's among the mystics and yogis of India and Nepal. Eyes that knew and carried the sacred mystery within them. He studied Coyote's features: the high cheekbones, the smooth skin, the mouth that was always poised at the borders of laughter, the nose that had sniffed the winds through the migrations of survival. He saw the face that had gone beyond comedy and tragedy. A deep pooled lake folded within the layers of a million years; the four winds centered within the heart of the human.

"I feel as if I should know you, Coyote. I've seen you before. I saw you in a dream, and then a week ago, I saw you as I was riding Black Rose on the beach. I saw your face. It is a face that I feel has been living with me for a long time."

Coyote smiled. It was a deep, imploding smile that came from years of waiting for this moment. Twenty-eight years of waiting, studying, to prepare for the time when he could be ready to accept this man. His son. "Yes, I know you saw my face. I have been giving it to you for a long time. Not as me but as my vision. And now, I've asked you to come here."

Nomad didn't say anything as he continued to study Coyote's face. He poured out two cups of tea.

"It's time to know each other. Besides, I need your help. You see, Nomad . . . you are my son."

Nomad looked at Coyote, waiting for more information as to what he meant. Son? An earth son, a tribal son, a blood son. "Please forgive me, Coyote, but I don't know what you mean."

"Well, jus' to make it fast and clean, you're my blood son. No one told you."

Nomad sat in his chair, sipping the tea. Finally, he stood up and walked over to the bar mirror. He studied his face for a long time. He looked into his eyes, trying to reach beyond his features into his real life. He had spent many years trying to understand the spirit that rode within his body, and now he was given a question to ask that seemed so simple. He walked back to the table. "I believe you. I have felt for a long time that there was some other life in my body that I didn't understand. I could feel my mother, the female so strongly, but I could never feel my male as my father. Wow . . . it's almost too much for me right now. Things like this have been happening to me for quite a while." Nomad sat down in the chair. "Well, Don Coyote, I would like to know more. Why . . . ?"

Coyote was silent, thinking about all of the years he had lived with this secret, as it called through him like a silent mantra, waiting until he had learned how to pronounce the sound. And now it was ready to be released. "I've known your mother since I was ten. We were adopted by the same family. Cedar was six at the time. We were together for five years and then I took off and returned to my own people. I stayed with them for a short time, but I was restless. I wanted to see more of the world and so I wandered around the country for a long time. I rode the freights, boomed from job to job, lived in libraries, fought in the war, tried to go to college but at that time they weren't ready for the questions I had to ask. They were too jumpy and I was too fast. And so eventually, I arrived back where I began. Inside the coyote. When I did return to my adopted family I would always sneak in and visit your mother first. We would walk through the woods, or go to one of the lakes and spend part of the night together. For years, she was the only real friend I had. After Cedar was married, she and your old man found out they couldn't have kids. He was sterile but he wouldn't accept the responsibility. She wanted to adopt a couple of bangtails but your old man was too proud. He was blaming her for not being able to conceive. She rounded me up to find out what I thought she should do. I didn't need a Zen master to hit me over the head with a log from Mount Fuji. The coyote knew. Your mother is dark from your grandfather, old Juan Caverango, and your old man's got that dark Irish brood to him. Sheeeet, I figured a little more Indian blood wouldn't hurt any kid. Besides, I've always been in love with Cedar. She's a beautiful woman."

Nomad received the story as easily as a river would accept the division of its body by an island. It was a good story. Father? What does it mean, he thought, once the borders have been erased. The essence of life has always got to be what is alive. The generosity of being human. He poured the last of the tea into their cups. "Where did it happen, Coyote?"

"Your old man was buying land in Hawaii at the time. When he was gone your mother and I took some horses and rode up to a high lake on the Idaho side of the Bitterroots. I think you know the place. She used to take you there when you were a boy."

Nomad was trying to rerun his memory back twenty years to when he would go camping with his mother and sister. "The lake with the waterfall?"

"Yes, the waterfall with green eyes."

"I always had a feeling, Coyote, that someone else was there besides the three of us. You were always around when we were there for the summer?"

Coyote smiled. Half to Nomad's question and half to his memories of those summers. "Yes, but sometimes it was difficult. Having to always be the coyote. Sneaking in at dead-o-night when you kids were sleeping. I made you the bow and arrows that you found in the woods. Remember? And the moccasins that you wore were made by my sisters."

Nomad had his eyes closed, thinking about all of the treasures he thought he had found by himself. "Does my father know?"

"I don't think so. There was never any reason to tell him. He's never had the sense of affirmation. It wouldn't have worked. Earlier, you never looked Indian enough for him to be suspicious. But now, heh . . . ? You would have a hard time trying to take out the bishop's daughter."

"But why . . . ah . . . never mind, Coyote."

"Why didn't anyone ever tell you? Why didn't we ever get together? Once you ask those questions you move yourself into a forest where the trees, rocks, streams, and clouds all look the same. Now, you know they are all different because you have taken the time to know. Before, you would have only been confused."

"What about my sister? Are you her father, too?"

Coyote didn't answer. He looked as if he had gone somewhere else to be with a memory from a long time ago. The smile arrived as the answer. "Maybe someday we'll tell her. Right now she's too busy being a lawyer in your father's firm, raising horses and flying airplanes. She's gunna have a kid. Did you know that?"

"A baby? No, I didn't hear anything about it. Is this some more of your shenanigans, Coyote? Are you some kind of a stunt god who flies down and knocks up all of the beautiful women?"

Coyote leaned back in his chair and laughed. "Nomad,

such flattery. How nice it would be." He returned the chair to the table. "No. This is very strange with Virginia. She thinks God paid her a visit the night of the Yellowstone Earthquake."

"Hasn't anyone told her that God might not have genitals?"

"Not in her cosmology. God is a big, handsome, muscular buckaroo-hero who makes love like a crazy mustango with nothing on but a twenty-X powder blue Stetson and a pair of ballet slippers."

"Yes . . . and afterwards, she would still have her virginity."

"Of course. And her kid grows out of the haystack, nursing from the ancient Arabian mother. However, Syringa told me that Ranger is the father."

"Wow, they've been doing that trick for years. Looks like they finally pulled it off. She doesn't know where her kid is from, and she doesn't know you're her real old man. Coyote, do you think this is normal? I feel like I'm part of some ancient mythology and each millennium the characters become crazier and the stories juicier. Heroes, hardons, and flight . . . heh, Coyote?"

"Yin and yang, Nomad." Coyote picked up a spoon, turning it in front of Nomad. "Which side is the spoon and which side ain't? I think Einstein taught us that. And as I've always said about this life . . . Ein stein at a time . . . hey, Nomad?"

Nomad jumped up and ran across the room, pretending to catch a fly ball with his bare hands. "I got it, but the runner's stealing third." Nomad threw the ball at Coyote and then took off toward the table, sliding into home plate. Coyote snabbed the ball and laid it down just as Nomad slid through the ball and under the table.

"Safe!"

Nomad got up and dusted off his pants. "Good game, Pop, good game. Let's go out and see Black Rose, okay?"

"You've got a good arm, kid, good arm. Yeh, let's go out and see how old fiddle foot is doin'." Coyote put his arm around Nomad's shoulder and they walked out the back door to the training ring. "She's a beautiful animal. Were you surprised when she appeared?"

Nomad was just beginning to catch on to the ways of Don Coyote. He picked a blade of wheat grass and stuck it in his mouth, sucking the juice from the stem. Black Rose walked over to Nomad and put her head in his hands. Nomad put his face against her nose, breathing slowly within her breath. "She's a magnificent being, Coyote. I've never known such beauty. When she arrived I had no other choice but to be with her."

Coyote reached over and stroked Black Rose's neck. "I sent her to you. I needed you to return. You see, Nomad, she was your grandfather's horse."

Two

Later that afternoon, Nomad, Buddy, and Coyote had ridden horses to a high alpine lake on the west side of the White Cloud Mountains. There were flowers everywhere and the lake held the mountain peaks in a perfect reflection of their solitude. They had turned the horses loose to graze on the alpine grass. The three men were resting on the banks of the lake, talking, dreaming, and sleeping inside the conversations of each other. Coyote had just awakened from a short snooze, tuning his mind back into the bodies of his companions.

"In a few days we'll head over to Salmon. I think we

had better take your truck, Buddy, mine seems to have
sleeping sickness," Coyote said to them.

"It's always got something. I think it must have hypo-
chondriasis of the spirit. Or maybe it has a streak of conscience after doin' so many of yer tricks with ya."

Coyote looked up in the sky. "That hawk up there is
going to swoop down and steal away your brain. It's
behaving like a rabbit."

"Sheeeet . . ."

"What's this about?" Nomad asked them.

Coyote took out the newspaper clipping and gave it to
Nomad. He read the article and handed it back. "What
do you have in mind?"

"I've got it all worked out in my head. Strategy. It's
fail-proof, jus' like all my plans."

"Holy buffalo shit, Coyote, would ya please stop blowin' wind out of yer third-eye and git to the point."

Coyote looked over at Buddy. "You're feeling pretty
cocky now that you think you've got your magic back.
Beware of *hubris*, Doctor, beware of *hubris*."

"Hua! Alfred J. Hubris . . . discovered the Hubris
river."

"The gods, Dr. Dancing Arrow, the gods. They'll swoop
down here and steal away your magic. I won't be able to
stop them."

"You mean yer old sidekick, the Cowboy Buddha, and
I might jus' add . . . my secret god-hee-row!"

"Precisely, Doctor. He's everywhere. She is everywhere. The first time I met him I was camped over on the
Musselshell trying to bring back the buffalo. I had been
on a long fast and it had been raining for three days. I
was tired, soaked, and lonely. The Cowboy Buddha came
to me and we spent the night together. We made love.
Oh . . . how we made love."

"He or she?" Buddy asked as he picked up a stone and threw it into the lake.

Coyote pulled a stone out of the ground and threw it into the center of the rings Buddy's stone had made. "That night she was a woman. She can change back and forth. He-she . . . is a hermaphrodite."

"Did the buffalo return?"

"No. But we made love like the buffalo. I think that's what I was shooting for, anyway."

Nomad stretched out on the grass and looked up into the sky. A few clouds were gathering around the peaks. He took the air into his body, easily, thinking of each breath, correcting the passage until he felt that he had his breathing centered within the rhythms of the mountains and the breath of his own body. He closed his eyes as he felt the wind against his skin, pushing against his body's resistance. He began to concentrate on his body being without walls, stopping the erosion. To work within and not against. To become non-corporeal, the wind blowing through, vibrating inside the essence of each life-form, becoming everything until it is nothing . . . Is. The body begins to lift. He opened his eyes and looked over at Buddy and Coyote. "Transcendence," he said out loud, "it seems so easy."

Coyote stood up, walked over to his saddlebags and took out a pouch made from deerskin and covered with feathers and beads. He returned, giving the pouch to Buddy. "Here, Doctor . . . this is for you."

Buddy accepted the gift, carefully examining the pouch, studying the feathers, the design of the beadwork, touching every detail of the bag. He opened it up and slipped out a hand-carved bamboo flute. He rubbed his fingers over the instrument, fingering the holes, examining the intricate carvings in the wood. "It's beautiful, Coyote.

Thanks. I . . . I feel honored to have such a fine-lookin'
instrument. I hope that I can create music as handsome
as this flute." Buddy reached up and shook Coyote's
hand. "Thanks. . . ."

"You will. I know it," Coyote answered. "Besides, a
trombone is so vulgar. Can you imagine going into a temple and playing a trombone? Even though I heard that
you performed some of your finest pieces on your old
pawnshopper, I thought you could even do better with a
flute. Go ahead, see if you can play."

Buddy placed the flute under his lower lip, protruding
his upper lip over the mouth hole. He blew softly but
nothing happened. He looked over at Coyote and
Nomad. A weak smile and a forgiving wink. He tried
again and this time he was able to make a low, soft
sound, but when he tried to finger the stops the sound
disappeared. "I guess I'll jus' have to practice some."

"You'll make it. Soon you'll be able to play like the
wind blowing through the sweet grass and pines; like the
mountain canary calling her mate; like the buffalo lowing
to the heartbeat of the earth. The Cowboy Buddha told
me."

"Did he/she give ya this flute?"

"Yes, he has been helping me figure out this shindig for
the eagle killer. I need a flute whistler who can drop rainbows out of the sky like hailstones in August."

"Well, sheeet, it's been some time since my last great
concert, which, as I told ya, landed me right in the slam,
but I think that I can rise to the occasion."

"Good . . . that's good! And now for you, Nomad"—
Coyote sat down next to him—"your part in this ven-
detta's waltz is easy . . . real easy. The best part in the
show. All you have to do is sea-duce a beautiful woman."

Nomad, who had been celibate for the last year, looked at Coyote and laughed. "Oh . . . is that all?"

"Yup. Now listen. And, Doctor, I don't want any of your cracker-ass remarks. This man, who has been snuffing the eagles, lives over in the Pahsimeroi. His name is Jason Starbuck. Old New England whaling name, and he's running around a thousand head of beef, and he's leased out some land for a couple bands of woolies. Last week I drove over there and hired on as a ranch hand. I'll start next week . . . working from the inside. Exactly what the coyote does best. Buddy, when we get over there I want you to go up into the mountains and ride out a fast. Clean yourself out and learn how to play that tooter. It might take us a couple of weeks, maybe longer. But when the music comes out of you I want it to be so clear, inspirational, and filled with your vision that with the sound of B-flat a whole herd of white bufflers will come twitching out of the sky, prancing their asses off. This man is a tough hombre and I'll need all the help I can get. Now, I don't want you to get up there and get horny so that when it's time for the show all we get from your vision are naked women, orgies, big whangs, and titties for clouds. That's what put you in the calaboose before. Now . . . Nomad. You're our anchor man. Our safety valve. When we start breaking old Starbuck down, and he's a tough old grissel-heel'd pecker neck, we want him to get it from both barrels. I don't want any loopholes. This has got to be a very tight operation."

"All you want me to do is seduce his wife?" Nomad cut in, shaking his head, laughing into the ground.

"Exacto correcto . . . you win the prize! I've met her and she's neater than heck lookin'. Beautiful! Thirty-five years old and she ain't gettin' laid. The old fart can't get it up. Too much bronc riding destroys the little birds who fly into the cockaroo and make it sing."

"How do you know that . . . ?" Nomad asked.

"Oh, the coyote knows. You're the best-lookin' man this side of the Continental Drift and it's goin' to be as easy for you as running nude before an avalanche of liberated damsels. And the real kicker is that the ranch is in her name. He ain't got a plug nickel. She's got all the dough. He was just a rodeo pickup before he gave out the cowboy moves and got her looking at the stars instead of her pocketbook. But that was a long time ago. Well . . . whad'ya think?"

"I'm thinking that I'm back in the West."

"Well . . . climb aboard, it's gunna be a great ride."

"How am I susposed to meet this woman?" Nomad asked as he was taking off his sandals.

"I've got that figured out too," Coyote said, pointing to his head. "Smart cookie . . . jus' not too shabby. You're goin' to offer a yoga class at the community center and the first night I'm goin' to escort her in and sign her up. The rest is up to you."

Buddy started taking off his clothes. "Coyote, I think yer jus' horny. Why don't we go into town and pick up three young backpackers from some outdoor program. It'll be the best wilderness experience they'll ever git . . . all free."

"What if it doesn't work?" Nomad asked Coyote.

"I've thought of that too," Coyote replied as he was pulling off his boots.

"What . . . ?"

"I don't want to think about it," he answered as he was wildly throwing off his clothes. "Last one in has to drink pee water. Hua . . . get along old coyote. Get movin'."

Three

The second night of Nomad's return he and Buddy decided to sleep near the hot springs that were a quarter-mile above the hotel. Nomad had brought Black Rose with him and she was grazing in a small meadow just below their camp. The hot springs were a small, deep pool that came out of a cave that tunneled back into a large outcropping of granite for thirty feet. The entrance into the cave was just large enough to belly-swim through and then it opened up into a large cavern. It was like being inside a temple where every sound became a chant, every thought a prayer, evoking memories of life within life flying through a batholithic womb. When they emerged from the cave for the last time they walked down to a snow-fed stream to cool their bodies. They returned to their camp, their bodies already beginning to evaporate into the night.

After Nomad had rolled out his bed he walked down the hill to talk with Black Rose. He told her where he was and what they would be doing. He rubbed her body for a long time and told her that he would be away for two or three weeks, but that Syringa would be with her, looking after her needs. "She's like you, Black Rose, an ancient spirit of this earth. Someday perhaps, I'll have the wisdom that both of you have, and hopefully you'll be patient. Good night, great mountain flyer and swift dreamer . . . see you in the morning." He walked back up the hill feeling the cool winds of the summer night blowing against his body. He was alone and naked, walking through high grasses and flowers, the air perfumed

with pines and quaking aspens, and the closing mantra of
the owl.

Buddy was lying on top of his sleeping bag, looking up
at the stars. His body was already nodding into sleep; his
eyes floating with the life in the sky that asked so many
questions and returned endless mysteries. Nomad took a
blanket from his bed, folded it, and put it down above
Buddy's head. He sat down on the blanket and placed
Buddy's head in his lap. He began to massage his new
friend's temples as he took in a series of deep breaths
until he had released everything that he had experienced
during the day as the breath of the earth came into his
own being, his life. A body held onto this planet by his
own choices of gravity, accepting his new life in the
mountains, moving within his friends to accept them as
teachers and guides, challenging the changes that were
being offered to him. Opening, and bowing before the
destiny of his feet that walked the earth, and the wings
that flew his imagination.

Four

Syringa was sitting next to the flower garden behind the
hotel, listening to the night sounds as they arrived within
her consciousness, touching and caressing her imagination, calling to her freedom. She took off her sandals and
released the tie that held up her hair. She shook her head
and her hair fell against her neck and shoulders. She
began to rotate her neck, stretching the muscles to the
right, and after a short time she began the rotation to the
left. It was a warm night with only a soft wind blowing
down from the canyon. She felt a sound through the
earth, something moving toward her. She looked over and

saw Coyote standing ten feet away, waiting until she saw him so that he would not frighten her. When he saw that she knew he was there he walked over to her and sat down. She reached out with her hand and took his hand and held it, feeling his warmth, accepting his presence.

"It's such a beautiful night, Coyote."

"Yes . . . the wind is blowing like the breath of the deer sleeping in the meadow."

"I feel so childlike. The earth rocking my body, the stars telling me stories, and you, old man . . . my grandfather, father, lover, and teacher, watching me sleep."

Coyote leaned back and stretched out on the ground. "Ah . . . I think that Grandfather Coyote is tired. He might be asleep before the child has finished her prayers to the Great Spirit."

Syringa leaned over and kissed his eyelids. "Go to sleep, Coyote. There are dreams that are waiting for you. Tell them that you are coming."

"I'm almost there . . . I'm almost there."

Five

Nomad felt deeply attracted and moved toward Syringa—drawn to her as he had felt drawn to his teachers in India. She had a beauty that transcended her own physical body, a radiance that moved with her, surrounding her life. He wanted to be with her as soon as he was finished helping Coyote with his mission. He had not realized, before he left for India, that people like her were living so close to where he had grown up. But that was seven years ago, and at that time, he saw everything so differently. There were changes, a different kind of sensitivity was being created, and there was a softening that he hadn't known before. Like the hotel. When he had walked in the door yesterday morning he had expected to see trophies of dead animals, old guns, and traps, with the same old men hanging around the bar trying to hold onto a life and language that was slowly moving away from them. Now, there was no anger inside, and he didn't feel the violence. Everything in the hotel had been created by hand: the weavings, woodworking, the stained glass, the copper and brass lamps and fixtures, and the ceramic vases and dishes. Every craft had been used that demands patience, understanding of the self, and love. Humans shedding old skins to find their new life within the touch and smell of their ancient hands.

Nomad watched a shooting star move through the sky, and he looked over at Orion. Summer. Sun trine the gods. He looked down at Buddy's face . . . asleep. He felt good being with him, this Buddy Sunday Dr. Dancing Arrow, whose eyes danced and laughed like the hands of a singing weaver. He was always smiling and making jokes with Coyote, and Coyote always seemed to laugh at everything and everyone, even himself. It felt good to be with this man who said he was his father. It didn't matter. Coyote had called him and he could only bow before that power. The synchronicity of events. Everything eventually becomes everything when the mind opens to the destiny of all lives within life. A circle spinning through a dreamer's wind.

Silence. A thin curve of moon was moving behind the mountains. Another shooting star. He could see Black Rose's silhouette against the horizon. Nomad's body was becoming silent and calm. He pressed his finger tips against Buddy's eyes and gently rolled the tips over the lids. The moon disappeared. The night filled itself into its own body. He moved over to his sleeping bag and bowed to the night. Another shooting star.

Six

One week later Coyote and Nomad arrived at Buddy's camp. It was a high camp in the Lost River Range where two streams converge to form Doublesprings Creek. There were quaking aspens, pines, Douglas fir, beaver ponds, a bedding ground for deer, and below was a wide valley that was a pasture for antelope and wild horses. Buddy was sitting on a large rock overlooking the valley. He had been watching his truck as it rode along a dirt road, winding up through the lower hills until the road stopped. Nomad and Coyote jumped out of the truck, shouldered their packs, and started up the trail. Buddy picked up the flute that was at his side, held it gently to his mouth, and started to play. The sound was soft and warm, feeling like an old campfire burned down low. A haunting melody, calling from so many visitors of Buddy's fasting mind. He played from the streams, harmonizing with their own sound; and he took from the birdcalls, mimicking them, and then interlacing their music with other birds, blending them together with the voices of his ancestors.

Coyote stopped. "Listen to the whiz kid up there cooking on that whistle." He looked at the sky. "Can you see anything, Nomad?"

Nomad looked up. A redtail hawk was above them, held motionless by an upward punch of wind, flexing her wings to float above the draft. "Beauty, tranquillity. I see everything, Coyote. I can feel what Buddy is seeing with his flute."

"It's not strong enough, but it's coming." Coyote turned around and looked down into the valley. "Yes, he's going to do it. I can see it now. It's just what we'll need. He's come a long way from his old trombone days. Let's go. I'm anxious to see him."

Buddy had been listening to Nomad and Coyote's conversation. He laughed, pumped out ten push-ups with his mind, and when they were below the rock Buddy put his thoughts into an image, reaching down through all of his magic, calling on the Cowboy Buddha, and began to create around him a gathering of snow egrets, monarch butterflies, and rainbows. There were waterfalls cascading down flowered-covered walls. And within the mist of the iridescent water was Coyote's father, riding a black horse . . . running with a herd of antelope through a long open valley of buffalo grass and lupine.

When Coyote saw the vision he dropped to his knees and raised his head to the sky. "We're going to win, Nomad. Look at what the Doctor can do. Sheeeet . . . we're going to bring back the eagles."

That evening, after a sweat bath, the three visionteers were sitting around the campfire eating trout, wild carrots, and water cress. Buddy was taking the meat from the fish, sucking out the juice, and slowly chewing a little of the meat. It was the first food he had eaten in a week. He took the food into his body slowly to allow for the acceptance of the nourishment. To find the voice between his body and the breath of the fish and plants.

"It's going to be more difficult than I figured," Coyote said; "old Starbuck has been possessed."

"How do you mean . . . possessed?" Nomad asked, throwing a back bone into the fire.

Coyote was silent for a long time, thinking about what he wanted to say. How to tell them what he had experienced during the last week working for Starbuck. "There is another life living inside this man. A demon who is angry, pissed off at the eagles because they are such magnificent birds. He told me that the eagles have been working over his lambs. That's an old ruse, and really doesn't make sense. I didn't try to question him or let on that I knew about his past. He's very suspicious right now and pretty damn oily. He thinks everybody is a government spy. I think he trusts me okay. Probably thinks the government is too smart to send out an old, scalp-liftin' siwash. But I feel that Starbuck has been taken over by the demon Peesi-Painskwi."

"Who?" Buddy asked.

"Peesi-Painskwi! Didya fast yer ears off?"

"Sheeeet, sounds like a brand of shoe polish to me."

Coyote pretended that he didn't hear Buddy's comment. "Yes . . . Peesi-Painskwi. When everything was created, the animals, plants, birds, mountains, oceans, and fish, the Great Spirit had a few parts left over and so he made up Peesi-Painskwi. He had the legs of a gorilla, body of a kiwi bird, the head of an antelope, dolphin fins for arms. He was given the heart of an Alaskan mosquito, the brains of a magpie, and the genitals of a frog. At first, Peesi liked his body but then he discovered that he couldn't fly like the other birds, swim like the fish, and when he tried to run, well, it was the best clown act this side of the Winnemucca Stampede. It was funny and sad. He was the clown, the comedy and tragedy of everyone, but he had a disposition that was nastier than sour-owl shit. Old Peesi became angry at all of the other creatures, but he was especially jealous of the eagle, who could fly so magnificently above everyone else. He wanted to fly like that so no one could see his body. All of the other animals, fish, and birds made fun of him. Because he didn't have any real identity of his own he found out that he could invade the bodies of humans and make them kill the other creatures who had made fun of him. Peesi-Painskwi has taken over Starbuck's body. I've been having dreams about him. Peesi-Painskwi can't hide from the coyote."

"Seems like a dirty trick to make such a creature. Why would the Great Creator do such a thing?" Buddy asked Coyote.

"Well, no one really knows, but I think he got real tired from working so hard. He was probably popping speed and drinking wine. Got confused. Fucked up real bad. But then, how can we understand his long-range program? I used to think that all white people were evil, but now I only think that most of them are that way."

Buddy looked at his skin. "How do ya like my sun tan, Coyote?"

"It's not only the skin. Their brains are too big and their hearts too small . . . put together with spare parts like my old truck that never runs."

"Maybe Peesi's espionaged yer truck. Maybe he really has the heart of yer old pickup that only has two speeds. Mutter-sputter 'n' complain, and no way . . . José," Buddy told Coyote, throwing a piece of bark at him.

"What do you plan to do about Peesi-Painskwi?" Nomad interrupted the high-mountain squabble.

Coyote stood up. "I'll have the answer in the morning. I think that I should get some shut-eye. I don't want any fuck-ups. We'll get up at first light and have a good breakfast and then we'll find out what we must do." Coyote went off into the trees to make his bed. Buddy picked up a piece of wood, kicking the coals together with it before he dropped it into the fire.

"Your music is exquisite," Nomad said to Buddy. "I felt as if I was back in India. It made me feel as if you had transcended your own life . . . gone through your own memory into a dream that comes from so many other cultures."

"Yeh . . . it's the flute. It's inside. When I begin to play it seems that the flute has its own songs, and when I close my eyes I begin to see other visions and I play what I see. Somethin' happens. The flute an' the stories inside my mind become one sound translated through the spirit of that instrument." Buddy took the water jug and poured out two cups, handing one to Nomad. "What do ya think is goin' to happen when we have the showdown?"

Nomad was quiet. Watching the fire, thinking about all of the campfires he had been with in India and Nepal. The people he had met, their stories coming through their hands and eyes as they prepared their food and lived through their lives beside the fire. "Affirmation. I'm just building towards that one idea. Once, I met a Tibetan shaman who had devoted his life to the exorcising of demons. He was a master. He knew all of the sounds that were necessary to release the person from the demon. He had spent years in learning how to pronounce the sounds. And we . . . are only beginners except for Coyote. But as Coyote said . . . even the Creator fucked up."

A coyote was crying somewhere behind them. Buddy looked at Nomad. "Do ya think that's Don Coyote snorin'?"

"At least dreaming," Nomad answered.

"I hope he's callin' fer reinforcements."

Seven

Nomad had moved all of the furniture out of his hotel room in Salmon. His bed was a thin mattress on the floor. The walls were bare except for a photograph of a village in the Himalayas where he had lived with a Tibetan family for six months. Nomad was preparing a pot of tea on a one-burner camp stove. When the tea was steeped he poured out two glasses, giving one to Adah Ross. "I think you'll like this tea. It will make you very relaxed."

Adah Ross took the cup and held it close to her face, breathing in the fragrance. "What is it, Nomad?"

"It's from a plant that grows in the Himalayas. The plant sleeps during the day and is awake at night. It hunts the moon. Some mystics use it to induce dreams and visions, but we would have to drink a gallon before anything like that would happen. Perhaps another time. It will make us very peaceful. You'll see. When you begin to float away I'll give you a massage."

Adah Ross smiled, lowering her eyes into the cup of tea. "You make me feel so beautiful. I never knew my body held so many mysteries. I never knew that love-making could be so serene. All night long I think about you, wanting to be with you." She looked at Nomad, touching his arm. "I never knew a man could be like you."

Nomad didn't say anything, accepting in silence the compliment she had given him. He sipped his tea as he watched her face, studying her eyes. When she had arrived he had just finished his morning yoga. They had been together everyday for two weeks. She was the only student in his class and they decided to have their classes in his hotel room or by the river. It was an easy relationship for both of them, accepting the other's life, ready for the transformation that is created when two humans meet at the right time. They had made no plans. Each day was always the beginning. They never talked about the possibility of being separated. They were drinking from the same river.

"Adah Ross, would you like to have a child?"

"What?" Nomad's question kicked her out of the tea and back into the room. "I don't understand, Nomad. With you?"

"Yes, with me."

"But . . . we have only known each other for a short time. And . . . I'm married. I can hardly believe what you're saying. I think this tea is making you a little strange."

"There's something that I must tell you because I don't want to have any secrets between us. Mysteries . . . but no secrets." Nomad saddled-in closer to Adah Ross. He began by telling her about his four years in Asia, his cabin on the coast, his garden and trees, the three years he spent living alone, Black Rose, and how he had been lured by Coyote and the mare back to Stanley Basin. He explained to her about Coyote and Buddy, and how Coyote believed that her husband, Starbuck, had been possessed by the demon Peesi-Painskwi. Adah Ross was in love with Nomad. Loaded dice on a fast track. She ducked behind stage, rehearsing through the strange stories Nomad had told her, trying to interpret the ideas of Tibetan Doubtops, Buddy's Flute-a-Vision, Black Rose, the Great Creator's Bouillabaisse Fuck-up, the Cowboy Buddha, and the Dehorned Hotel.

"It's so hard to believe, Nomad. All of these things. This . . . this circus act of miracles just so Don Coyote can stop Starbuck from killing the eagles."

"No . . . not your husband but Peesi-Painskwi. If Starbuck will accept the fact that this demon has set up camp in his body, then it should be fairly simple. We just have to kick him out with a little Tibetan, Native American ju-ju. If he doesn't, then I guess they'll just have to square off and fight."

"Nomad . . . I don't know. I don't know if I believe any of this. But why . . . why did you ask me if I wanted to have your child?"

Nomad studied through his answer before he spoke. "I know, from the years I spent studying with my Tibetan Doubtop, that if Starbuck is killed his spirit will be free from the demon. But he'll have no place to go and he'll wander around forever until he finds a body that will accept him. With Starbuck's karma that could be a long time. I only want to make this offering. To give his spirit a chance to return to an earth-life. Yours and mine. If you don't want to keep the child, I'll take her or him. I can't offer you anything except my life, my beliefs, and my friends. I cannot be your husband as we think of that role in this culture. But I'll be with you and we can become teachers and lovers to each other as we have been in the last two weeks. Someday I would like to return to India and Nepal, and hopefully be able to live in Tibet. Perhaps you would want to be there also. The child would be cared for by my friends, Syringa, Golden, Buddy, Ranger, Coyote . . . growing up in a life that I could only envy a child to have. I know this all seems very strange, but it is what I know. It is what I would like to see happen. You have your own choices. You could tell Starbuck and perhaps he would listen to you. But from what you've told me about him he would probably try and beat you up. You don't have to have the child, of course, and that would not change my love for you. Or . . . we can begin right now."

Adah Ross stayed within range, hanging tough. "But, I don't want to have my husband hurt or killed. No matter how bad he is or what kind of a demon is in him."

"He won't be," said Nomad, "he'll be given another life, free from Peesi-Painskwi, free from killing eagles, horses, and all of the other animals and birds he has killed since the demon invaded his body. He'll learn about migration." Nomad took her hands, lacing their fingers. "Listen. There are so many things to give away on this journey to the spirit world, the first things we should learn to give away are our bodies."

"But . . . yes . . . yes, I believe that's true. But, what about the ranch. All of the cattle and the horses?"

"Coyote wants to have it turned into a preserve for buffalo, wild horses, and raptores."

"I'm suppose to give all of that up? My land, sell my herd, and have a baby, too?"

Nomad stood up, walked over to the sink, and poured out a glass of spring water. His black hair was loose, hanging down to his waist. Adah Ross watched him, studying his body, his long muscular legs and his narrow hips; his beautiful, serene face, which was so open and calm. She tried to see if he were joking, if he had made it all up. No. The signs were not there. She felt as if she were sitting within a forest listening to the songs of the flowing river, feeling so transparent against the blue of the morning sky. Knowing exactly where she would be in three million years.

Nomad returned with the water. He gave Adah Ross the glass. "It is water from the mountains. It's all I have to offer you as a ceremony to our relationship. It is clean and pure and it's what I have tried to have my life be. We will be together as long as our freedom with each other is stronger than it is apart. Hopefully, we will have a child and the child will be the spirit of our freedom, and we'll live where there is always beauty, without destroying, giving only love to our bodies and to the earth that is our parent. We will build a house somewhere in these mountains and it will be a temple to the earth. A temple to the sky and to the animals around us, and to our own lives. If we have any land that we cannot use for the growing of our food, or for the raising of the animals that we need, then we will give it to our friends who share the same values as we have. Or, we will return it to the earth. It is my acceptance of this life. It is my offering to you of my life. It is my love for our freedom."

Adah Ross held the glass up, as if she were talking through it to Nomad. "Nomad . . . I will drink this water with you, and I want to make love to you . . . now. But I will have to think about everything you have told me. I don't know. I feel so strongly about you, maybe too much. You are so clear, and you seem so right. Perhaps you are too strong. I don't know. I must have some time by myself. This is so crazy. It's so exciting and what you feel about the earth, people, and all of the creatures, I feel it also, but I've never known anyone who felt this way. I've only known men who want to possess everything they see and touch. They want to suffocate what they think they own. A strange way." Adah touched Nomad's arm. "Yes . . . I would like to have a child, with you. But I cannot promise that I will always be with you. I would like to learn how to live and be alone also. I would like to study and find a way where I could discover my own importance. I would like to feel that I am helping this earth and not destroying it. Yes . . . I would like to have a child. I could teach him, or her, to be strong and clear so that I could offer this human to this world as a sacrament of our love. A commitment of freedom for everything that lives. Please, Nomad, give me some time. I want to be able to feel deeply inside of me that this is right." She drank some of the water, smiling, as she gave the vessel back to Nomad.

Eight

Coyote and Starbuck had just finished herding fifty head of whiteface steers up to a higher pasture. Coyote had fallen behind Starbuck, sizing and making sure that it was Peesi-Painskwi who had jumped into Starbuck for the free ride. They were riding through sagebrush and quaking aspen when they kicked up three antelope who were grazing two hundred feet dead-on. Coyote reined up and stood in his stirrups to watch them. When Starbuck saw them he smoothed out his Winchester and mothered it tight within his shoulder and cheek. "Pow! Pow! Pow!" Jason shouted in make-believe. . . . "Got 'em, Coyote. Could have got all three . . . draggin' ass and eatin' dirt." Coyote eased his pinto over to Starbuck, and slid the rifle out of Starbuck's hands. "Let me show you how to shoot, Starbuck." He cradled the rifle, picking up the sights inside the head of the closest prong-horn . . . slowly sucking in the trigger along with his breath.

"Hey! Coyote . . . whatcha doing?"

"BaaWhooommm!" Coyote said softly as he watched the closest antelope drop to the ground.

"What the fuck!" Starbuck yelled as he rode up to the pinto. "What the hell's goin' on? You didn't fire that rifle but that first antelope dropped. I saw him. Who are you . . . anyway?"

Coyote swung the rifle on Jason. An easy pivot with one hand. "I think I've got the real trophy right here."

"Jesus H. Christ, Coyote! What the fuck ya doin'?"

Coyote spun the rifle in his hand and gave it back to Starbuck . . . butt first. "Must be one of those Australian boomerang smoke poles. Watch it, Jason. Someday you're gunna eat what you kill . . . real good."

"You do that one more time and you'll be down the road. I don't care how short of help I am. I'll run this fucking outfit myself."

Coyote heeled his horse and started to ride on ahead, but stopped. "I'll bet that was the first time you've ever had a gun stuck in your fat gut . . . huh? Makes you shiver jus' a little, doesn't it?"

"Fuckin' A . . ."

"For a second I thought you were an antelope. Are you sure about your old man? Maybe your mother had a little fling with Kwahaten? And then . . . sometimes your body looks like a dumpy old kiwi bird. Your legs are short and bow-legg'd like a gorilla's, and I'll bet your weenie is about the size of a frog's. Are you sure your mother didn't live in a zoo, mating with all the animals? You know, Starbuck, I keep gettin' this strange feeling that you're not really a man. Is that true?"

"Whereja git all that bullshit, Injun? I've got a good mind to string you up between those quakes and use you fer target practice."

Coyote looked up. A golden eagle was flying close to the cliff, building her flight from the heat off the rocks. "Look at her, Starbuck. My grandmother was an eagle." Starbuck was silent as he watched the eagle. Coyote watched Starbuck. "I heard you killed a bunch of them." Starbuck dropped his eyes onto Coyote. "You were only fined five C's. You should have been lashed to those rocks so the buzzards and crows could have a feast. Sheeeet . . . why punish them . . . heh?"

"Fuck off . . . Injun!"

"I bet you'd like to take a crack at that bird."

"Who are you . . . gov'ment spy? I had a feelin' you might be up to some trick."

"You're wrong. I'm no spy. I came here to find out why

you killed all those birds. They're my brothers and sisters. They're my religion. If I killed your brother, I would be strung up on the highest cross because I couldn't defend myself with your laws. If I even dared write something on the walls of your church building, I would be shot in the back, and it would be broadcast as a holy mass. I'm talking about religion. The earth . . . not real estate. But your people have written all over my church with your mines, freeways, dams, billboards, and cities. You've polluted the rivers, lakes, oceans, and air with your garbage. Where is the law, Starbuck? Where is the law of God? It doesn't exist for you. What would happen to me if I killed one hundred people? I know . . . you don't understand. It's not your law. I came here to help you, but now I realize that I can't. It's too late. You have been possessed by a demon. I know it now. Peesi-Painskwi is inside you."

"What? You're out of yer fuckin' mind, Coyote!"

"I know he's there. I've seen it before. This demon is jealous that he cannot fly like Kwinaa, and you will keep on destroying the eagles unless we can drive this monster out of you. It will take a long time, and it will be very painful. But we can do it, Starbuck. I know it."

"Coyote, I've had enough of yer Injun bullshit. Get out of here before I kill you." Starbuck grabbed his rifle and levered a shell into the chamber. "Get your red ass off this land or you'll be one dead asshole in moccasins."

Coyote rode up close to Starbuck. "Put that thing away, Jason. It's not you. It's the demon. Once we destroy him you'll be free."

"I'll be free when you're gone . . . Coyote!"

Coyote backed off. "Okay . . . Starbuck. Tomorrow morning I'm comin' to call Peesi-Painskwi out. I'm going to destroy him."

Starbuck squinted down the double barrel of his nose at Coyote, wishing to his itchin' finger that Coyote was armed. "Sheeeeet, you skinny, old eagle-fucker. Go work your G-string voodoo on some reservation. Ain't gunna take 'round here . . . see. Now git the fuck off my land and stay off . . . y'hear?"

Coyote stood up in his stirrups. "Peesi-Painskwi!" he shouted. "Tomorrow morning at first light, I'm going to call you out of Jason and Starbuck will be free. Peesi-Painskwi! Do you hear me? You, you cannot fly, or run, or swim. You are a demon and tomorrow you're going to die!" Coyote spun his horse around and rode off toward the mountains. As he came on the antelope, the animal jumped up and started running in front of Coyote and the pinto. Coyote started yipping and singing in a high, piercing voice, calling to the eagles in the cliffs.

Starbuck wanted to shoot Coyote, but his hands were shaking so much he couldn't get a bead on him. He reached into his saddlebag, took out a flask, and spun the top off with the heel of his hand. He took a long pull, looked back at Coyote, and then cranked down another. After the whisky began to soak up the adrenalin, Starbuck eased up on his own chomp and settled back down into the saddle. He looked once again to find Coyote but he had disappeared into the trees. "Okay . . . eagle-fucker. T'marrow we're gunna fin' one dead grandkid of an eagle. Adios . . . and fuckum all."

Nine

Buddy walked into the Owl Club and ordered a shot of tequila. It had been two weeks since he had seen Nomad and Coyote and he was tired of being alone. He figured that he could sneak into town and have a few drinks, slide out again, and old Coyote would never know. He took his drink to the back of the bar and sat down at a table in the corner where he could watch everyone. It felt good being with humans again. He had no idea what was going to happen during the showdown, but he knew that he had perfected his music to a place where he could create whatever Coyote needed. That morning, after he had practiced for three hours, a covey of mountain grouse had cartooned into camp, and he understood this over-ture as an offering for lunch. He picked up his flute and played a tune for them. He had been fasting for so long that he felt invisible, and when they came up to him it only took him a flash of the flute—quicker than a hungry mongoose after a voluptuous rattler—to have them col'-cocked and in the pot before he came to his senses. He dug up a fat bunch of yampa roots and stuck them in, and he added some wine that he had found near the base of Mount Borah. What was left over, he drank. By mid-morning, full-bellied, and dancing a strange variation of the Cowboy Minuet around the campfire, he decided that he needed to see some people, have a few drinks, and maybe, one or two ragtime quicksteps with the Salmon River Rodeo Queens.

By the time he had hiked down to the dirt road that wound through the valley into town he was sober, and he realized that it would take him all afternoon and most of the night to walk into town. He sat down on a flat rock and took the flute out of its case. He tried to think of the perfect ride into town: a chauffeured Rolls-Royce Phae-ton complete with bar, lady-in-waiting, and a Turkish bath; the Siberian Express with dancing Cossacks and Dostoevski reading quietly in the dining car; a stage-coach filled with fresh, young, pubescent virgins on its way to a famous hurdy-gurdy house being chased wildly through the valley by a band of avenging angels called the Boards-Up-Our-Ass Gang; a Venetian gondola with a Country and Western opera being performed in the bow; a hot-air balloon full of laughing kids and Chinese fire-eaters. Buddy couldn't make up his mind until he realized that what he really wanted was a Molly and Sammy Jump breakfast at the Buffalo Bar and Grill with a shot of Sammy's famous vodka for dessert. He stood up and played a few musical limericks that he knew Sammy and Molly would love to hear. Before he was finished he looked down the road and the Buffalo Bar and Grill was rolling toward him. It stopped in front of his rock; he opened the door and walked in.

Molly was behind the counter, Sammy was in the kitchen flashing his turquoise teeth, and Wiseass was perched on his head.

"Buddy . . . it's so good to see you. Where-ya all been?" Molly said as she canary'd her sweet ass around the counter to give Buddy a big hug. "Hey, Sammy . . . look who's here!" Sammy spun out, performed a little hard-shoe quickstep, and grabbed Buddy's hand, pumping it up and down. "Damn! It's good to see you Dr. Sunday . . . it's good to see you!"

"Listen, I haven't much time, so no more tricks . . . heh? I would like to have a big, fat-mama order of ham 'n' eggs, hash browns, toast, coffee an' a glass of milk 'bout this tall"—he held his hand right up to the eaves of his Stetson—"and a buffalo shot of Sammy's one-and-only Idaho Spud'odka."

"What's yer rush . . . son," Sammy said, writing the order down in mime with the invisible pencil dabbed on the end of his tongue for precision.

"I've gotta git into Salmon an' back to my camp 'fore sunrise."

"Oh . . . we understand. You're sneakin' 'round with that Coyote on one of his secret missions," Molly said as she poured out a cup of coffee.

"Yeh . . . sort of," Buddy replied as he sat down on a stool. "How's ol' smart-ass?"

"Not s' good. She's got one of those summer colds. Can't talk worth a damn."

"Good," Buddy said, "that's real good."

"All right," Sammy said. "Yer lookin' a mite thin so I'd better git a goin' on that order. But next time we want ya to stay with us fer a while. Old Wiseass has a whole new repertoire of pomes . . . all X-rated. Of course." Sammy walked back into the kitchen.

"How ya doin', Molly? Ya look tired."

"Oh . . . I'm okay, I guess. Well hell. No . . . I'm not. Tell me . . . before Sammy comes back. What do you know about open marriages?"

Buddy looked hard into Molly's face to see if she was talking turkey. "Well, I've heard some people talk 'bout it, but I don't know much. Why?"

"Well, Sammy has started talking about this open marriage business to me, and the way I got it figured out everyone gets to do what he damn well pleases. These young tunas come in here from California, Hawaii, and God-knows-where, and old Sammy starts flashing his teeth at them, quickstepping and reciting poetry. And old Wiseass gets all excited and blabbers off her limericks, thinking that she's going to be given a whole sack of trail-mix. Damn! Sammy's got them all buffaloed. Nineteen- and twenty-year-olds . . . maybe worse. Could be fifteen or sixteen. Kids. He had a fling with one of them last week, and he's got another one lined up for tonight. Now he's talking about having an open marriage. Looks to me like it's only open at one end and that's . . . you-know-where. Damn! We've been married for thirty-five years . . . seems like he would have more sense. Says that we should open up and have more experiences in our lives. What do you say, Buddy?"

Buddy ducked inside his thoughts, eyes rolling back and forth. "Molly . . . jus' as soon as I come back from this Coyote high ball I'll fix it up so as to scare the inlay right off Sammy's teeth. You'll have so many suitors and dates that he'll be in a perpetual spin jus' openin' the door fer 'em. An' . . . if you'd like, I'd be yer first date for this August Fools Fanny-dango."

"Oh . . . I don't know. I don't want to hurt him. But . . . yeh . . . it just might work. Maybe teach him a lesson or two."

"Sure it will. We'll git Ranger, Jonquil, Nomad, Coyote, and Golden. And if that won't convince him . . . well, I've got this magic flute right here. I'm sure I could conjure up a whole string of exotic lovers fer ya. It'll be the finest buffalo-blitz ever proformed."

"Heh . . . ha . . . sure. Now I'm beginning to understand about open marriages."

Sammy brought out the breakfast. Buddy jumped right onto it, elbows flying . . . cooing out lots of Mmmmmms and Ohhhhhs. However, before he could finish the food, Sammy tried to talk him into watching the place while they went into the back room for a late nooner. "Hey . . . no way. I've got to git going," he said as he backed out the door, tipping his hat. He bailed out just as the Buffalo Bar and Grill was pulling into Salmon.

Buddy flagged down the Owl Club waitress and ordered another shot of tequila. After it had arrived he pulled his hat down over his eyes, tilted back his chair, and hunted a dream about how he was going to conjure a ride back up the canyon, when he realized that the pair of boots standing on the floor was not the pair attached to his legs, but they were connected to the man who was standing over him flashing fire arrows and laser spears out of his eyes. Buddy eased back the chair to its four legs, lifted up his hat, and pulled out the chair next to him. "Have a seat, Don Coyote . . . ya look all tuckered out."

"What'nthehell are you doing in here?" Coyote whispered to Buddy. His voice sounded like an opera singer's after a three-hour aria at the Blackfoot rodeo grounds. "I should have you freeze-dried and stuffed into a vegetarian's cabbage roll."

"Well, sheeeeeet! What are you doin' here? Ya told us to stay out of the bars."

"I did. But that doesn't mean me. I'm the head honcho of this supernatural morality play. And . . . let me tell you, it's gonna be soon."

"Well, fuckahduck! It's 'bout time. I've had so many visions up on that mountain I could change my name fifty times and still have some left over for the adoption center. I've seen everything, Coyote. Demons, saints, three-legg'd third-base Hu-mans, renegade linguists from Moscow, a whole wad of eagle scatologists, eagles flyin' in formation over the Cowboy Buddha parade grounds, tap dancing buffalo pornographers, thirteen rainbows flying through the mind of a world champion frisbee player. Coyote . . . I've had it! Up to here! You're struttin' 'round the bars and Nomad is dancin' through the woods with Starbuck's old lady, and I'm stuck up there like a whimpy-peckered ol' hermit without any grub. I want to get goin'!"

"Listen! You get your boxcar ass back up to camp or you'll be having visions with your ass wrapped around your ears. And it won't be flying saucers that you'll be seeing but your own asshole . . . cowboy."

"Coyote . . . why don't ya go outside and diddle a leg of lamb with a hunk of ginger stuck up yer ass?"

Coyote looked at Buddy as a drunken heathen would look at the Gideon Bible in a four-dollar-a-night flea-ravaged motel. But he realized that he had better back off or he would blow the whole scenario. He walked over to the bar and ordered a shot of tequila for Buddy and a glass of beer for himself.

"Dr. Dancing Arrow . . . listen. Screw your head back onto its threads and pay attention."

Buddy gave him a halfhearted salute and moved his chair in closer to Coyote.

"It's tomorrow," Coyote said to him.

Buddy looked at the clock behind the bar. "No it ain't . . . it's still today."

Coyote snapped Buddy's hat from his head and pounded it onto the table. "I knew that I should have done this by myself. Fuck! I can't find Nomad. He's checked out of his hotel."

"Okay . . . Coyote. I'll git myself together. Tomorrow . . . the showdown?"

"Yes . . . at first light. We're going to call old Starbuck out, and I've got a feeling it's going to get real nasty. He and I went a coupla rounds today. I told him I knew about Peesi-Painskwi, but he wouldn't listen to me . . . ran me off his spread."

"Damn! I would have 'njoyed seein' ya runnin' off with yer bushy tail 'twix'd yer legs."

"Strategy, Doctor . . . strategy. I've got to get my gear together. We should take a sweat and be ready by dawn."

"Where's yer horse?"

"Over in the cemetery. Best grass in town. Now, do you think you're ready?"

"Don Coyote . . . don't worry. Whatever ya want, I've got. I'm the traveling supernatural, grand-prix, medicine show . . . complete with stampeding Arapaho virgins; an armada of eagles with laser talons; voracious turnip-eatin' wolves; Himalayan sun chanters, whirling medi-tators, rampaging rivers, tornadoes, and fer my finale, a . . . naw . . . you'll have to wait to see my best shot. But . . . I've got 'em all down."

"Good . . . that's good. I'm worried about Nomad, but I don't know where to look for him. Maybe he ran off with old Starbuck's wife?"

"Just remember, Papa Coyote, that Nomad could waltz through Hell, give the moon and the bird to the devil, an' get a standin' ovation. Don't worry 'bout him."

"Yeh . . . guess yer right. I'm getting carried away with this father business. We'd better get out of here. I don't want to be around if Starbuck shows up."

Buddy was feeling better and ready to begin. "Okay . . . let's go. Sorry 'bout bein' a smart-ass. A throwback from my old trombone days."

They stood up and started for the door. Buddy put his arm around Coyote's shoulder and gave him a hug. "Off to battle, Don Coyote . . . off to the crusades."

Ten

Four-thirty in the morning. Starbuck had been sitting up all night waiting for Adah Ross to come home. He wanted her to be with him so that he wouldn't feel so lost and alone. "In a way . . ." he thought, "I'm glad she's stayed away all night. Gives me a good excuse to be real mad. I'll git her. Damn! That goddam Injun's got me all spooked." During the night Starbuck had catnapped-dreams of throwing Adah Ross onto the bed and beating her until she begged him to forgive her. But he wouldn't give in. He wanted to hurt her and make her pay for everything that had gone wrong with his life. He walked over to the mirror and looked at himself. He looked hard, trying to find out if Coyote was really right about the demon. "Bullshit!" He looked deeper . . . "Bullshit! That goddam Injun's got some trick up his sleeve. Maybe's he's run off with Adah Ross. I'll bet she's with him right now." He walked over to the window and looked out. It was still dark. "Jesus . . . this is like some fuckin' Western . . . waitin' fer the redskins to attack." He opened the front door and walked out onto the porch. A gentle breeze was drifting down from the mountains. He could smell the alfalfa and sage. "Sometimes," he thought, "I really love it out here. It's so isolated and open, but now they're closing in on me. Damn! I won't be able to hunt any more. I wonder who ratted on me 'bout the eagles? Probably Adah Ross, or one of the hands b'fore I ran them off." He looked up in the sky, trying to remember how it felt when he was shooting the eagles. "It was better than anything else. Better than fuckin' or shootin' a grizzly." The morning star caught his attention and he watched it for a long time until he realized that it was beginning to be dawn. "Okay . . . Coyote. You slant-eyed moccasin fucker . . . I'm here! Waitin' for ya." He walked to the back of the house and looked around. He couldn't see anything. "Ah . . . that was all bullshit. Injun talk. The only one who's possessed is that Coyote." He turned around to check out his land. As far as he could see and then some. "Not bad fer bein' a down-'n'-out rodeo bum."

"What?" He turned around. "I thought I heard something. Mus' be gettin' spooked. No . . . there it is." It was a sound like a tune being played. He spun around, thinking that he would see something. But all he could see was the barn, the corral, and a few head of horses. He heard it again but this time he knew that it wasn't his imagination or the wind. It was some kind of instrument. The music was being played from somewhere close, but he couldn't pick up the source. He started walking back to the porch when he looked up to see a herd of wild horses coming off the hills galloping toward him. He stopped to watch them . . . amazed at what he was seeing. "But . . . what . . . how did they get through the fences?" He jumped up on the training-ring rails to get a better view. Fifty . . . maybe more, he counted, coming down through the alfalfa fields, heading for his house. They were coming right through the fences. "I've got to stop them . . . turn them around." He ran into the house, grabbed his rifle, and ran back outside. He fired into the herd but nothing happened. He shot at the lead mare, five rounds into her chest, but she didn't stop. They were only fifty yards away, and Starbuck ran back into the house and closed the door. He went over to his rifle cabinet and took out a box of ammo, sticking it into his back pocket. He pulled the drapes and looked out. Nothing. They were gone. He opened the door and cracked-out a look. Everything was silent. He walked out onto the porch and looked for tracks. "What the fuck is goin' on? Goddam you, Coyote . . . come on out here and show yer face!" He heard voices and the music started up again. A faint drumming, chanting, and the yipping cry of the coyote. Starbuck looked up on a curved bluff and saw a band of Indians. At first he thought they might go away like the horses, but they stayed on the hill. He stuck his hand into his mouth and bit the skin so hard that he broke through. They didn't leave. He ran back onto the porch and got down behind the railing, loaded his rifle, and waited. He could still hear the singing and the drumming, and then it stopped. The Indians began to fan out until they had new-mooned the house and then they began their charge. He had seen enough movies to know that he should wait until they were close enough so when he shot at them he wouldn't miss. He waited until they were within range, but when he tried to get a bead on them, they would slide down the sides of their horses and shoot at him from under their horses' necks. He fired at them, but like before, nothing happened. They were now riding around the house, screaming, yipping, screeching, and shouting; they were shooting fire arrows at the house, into the haystacks and barns, and leading the horses out of the corral. Starbuck had run out of cartridges, but when he stood up to sneak into the house they vanished through the dust their horses had kicked up.

He looked around. Again there were no tracks—not one arrow was stuck into the walls of the house. "Jesus H. Christ! What the goddam fuck is happening?" He walked out into the open field in front of his house. And then he heard the music again. It was a high note that soon became the screaming voice of an eagle. He fired at the bird but he missed. He levered another shell into the chamber, but before he could take aim the eagle was in a dive . . . head-on. The eagle swept over him and Starbuck felt a sharp pain in his legs. He dropped to one knee, clutched his leg, and kicked his head up to see where the eagle was flying. Two of them in a circle. He grabbed his rifle, which he had dropped to the ground, and fired at them. "Jesus . . . I can't hit them!" They dived at him, dropping down with their talons outstretched, ready to strike.

When they passed over him he felt another sharp sting in his chest. "They're not even comin' in that close, but I'm bleeding." He started to run for the house, but before he could jump onto the porch four eagles had strafed him. He fell to the ground. When he realized that he had not been carried off by the four eagles he saw that there were two more cuts on his body. His arms were bleeding, and there was a large gash on his forehead. When he tried to stand up he noticed that his body was beginning to change. Where he had been cut other shapes were growing out of the wounds. Feathers, fins, gorilla legs and feet. Slowly, his body changed into Peesi-Painskwi.

Coyote was up on the hill tucked inside a stand of aspen trees. He was wearing a breechclout; a coyote skin was over his head. The left side of his body was painted green, the other half blue. His face was painted yellow with a red mask. Eagle feathers were tied to his pinto, and a war club was attached to a piece of rawhide strapped to the horse's neck. "I knew it was Peesi-Painskwi," he said to the pinto. "Sure took a lot of fireworks to kick him out of Starbuck." He touched the pinto with his heels and they moved out of the trees.

"Peesi-Painskwi . . . get on your horse," Coyote shouted. "We're going to fight. I'm going to destroy you, and you'll never possess anyone again. You've been killing the eagles, buffalo, whales, and antelope since you were created. You'll never do it again. It is time for you to die!"

"Coyote . . . you sly, sneaky, evil-eyed half-of-a-wolf! You can't destroy me. I'm Peesi-Painskwi and I've been around forever and no one has ever been able to destroy me. I will continue to kill the birds, animals, and fish that I could never be. You have tried before and you've always failed. I'm too powerful for you. Even with all of your tricks you are only the coyote. I'm Peesi-Painskwi. When this is over I will find another body to live in, and you'll be chasing your tail in circles around your long nose."

"Get Starbuck's horse. I don't want to talk any more. You are too evil. The stench from your mouth is killing all of the birds, animals, and trees. The sight of you makes me want to cover my eyes because you are so ugly. The smell of your body is like the stink of rotting pigs. The sight of your toad's penis makes me laugh so hard that all of the mountains could fall into the valleys. Find a horse, or are you too frightened like the sheep who run and hide from the coyote?"

As Peesi-Painskwi began to walk toward the corral, Coyote rode past him and unhooked the gate so the buckskin could run out. Coyote had already put a bridle on the horse. He rode out into the open field where he had placed two war lances. He pulled one out of the ground and rode to the far side of the field. He turned around and faced the demon, who had just picked up the other lance. Peesi-Painskwi rode toward Coyote, stopped, rearing the horse and back-dancing to show off his riding skills. Coyote flank-kicked the pinto and started toward the monster, yipping and yelling, singing to his many powers to give him the strength and courage to win the battle over Peesi-Painskwi. The demon stayed, waiting for Coyote to come to him. As soon as Coyote was close, Peesi-Painskwi opened his mouth and released a flash flood of poisonous gas and smoke that rolled over Coyote, smothering his body with dark, yellowish-green crud. Coyote pulled the skin down over his face and rode to high ground. Buddy, sitting on a high rock above the bat-tlefield, began to play to the winds so they would come out and carry the breath of Peesi-Painskwi away. The trees heard the music and they began to move as the winds came from four directions, gathered up the smoke into a ball, and threw it out into space, where it was burned up by the sun.

Peesi-Painskwi was laughing and dancing with his horse, feeling confident that he had Coyote on the run. Coyote called to the monster to turn around and face him as he began to charge, dropping to the side of his pinto, protecting his body against any tricks that his enemy could throw at him. As Coyote passed Peesi, he threw his war lance at the demon, striking him in his belly, opening up a large wound. Peesi-Painskwi pushed out his stomach and released a river of scum that came from all of the polluted waters. The river of waste began to chase Coyote up the hill, covering the hoofs of the pinto, forcing the horse to stop. Coyote jumped off the stallion and grabbed the reins, pulling his mount to safety. Buddy was calling for help. He called to the herons and whooping cranes, the seagulls and the meadow larks. They flew down and drank the slime until they had filled up their stomachs, and then they flew over the monster and regurgitated the fluid over Peesi-Painskwi. He started to laugh and shout, yelling thanks to the birds. He opened up his mouth, catching the slime. What he drank healed his wound, which made him grow larger.

Buddy, still a little shaky from his drinking the night before, began to play as hard as he could. He created a spring that produced a gusher of white-man's whisky. He called on the crows and magpies to fly to the spring of rot-gut and drink the one-hundred-proof liquor. They drank until they were so big they could hardly fly and then they flew over Peesi and dropped the whisky over him. Again, he opened his mouth and caught every drop, swallowing gallons of the firewater, not wasting a drop.

Within seconds he was drunk. He began to shout and brag how great he was and how he could never be destroyed because he was so evil that no one was strong enough to kill him, even the Great Creator. He roared and bellowed so loudly that the clouds disappeared and the birds were blown out of their nests. He fell from his buckskin, got up, and began to jump up and down, shaking his fins at the sky, as he called for the eagles to come out of hiding so he could kill them. As Peesi-Painskwi was yelling at the eagles, Coyote came out of the field, riding down hard on the monster. Peesi was so busy bragging about himself, stomping and screeching at the birds to come down and fight, he did not see Coyote until he was right up on him. Coyote leaned over and dropped Peesi to the ground with a chop from his war club. He looked back and saw the monster drop, feet up and tongue out. Coyote jumped from his pinto, knife poised, ready to cut off the demon's head. Ten feet away from his enemy, Peesi-Painskwi jumped up, grabbed his lance, and threw it at Coyote. Coyote was taken by surprise, but Peesi was so drunk and dizzy from the whack on his head that when he threw the lance it turned sideways in midflight. Coyote was able to roll his body as the lance struck him on the side of the neck and head. But the blow was strong enough to knock Coyote off his feet.

Buddy was rapidly trying to figure out what he could do to help Coyote when he looked down the valley and saw a herd of mustangs coming from the canyon. He looked at his flute, wondering where the horses were coming from, when he realized that the herd was being led by Nomad and Black Rose.

Nomad watched his father fall to the ground. He called on Black Rose to reach into her magnificent body to find all of her strength so they could save Coyote from being killed by Peesi-Painskwi. Black Rose heard the voice and responded. She opened up her stride to the calling of her rider. Coyote looked up and saw Nomad just as the demon was coming after him with a club. Nomad reached down and grabbed Coyote's arm, swinging him onto Black Rose's back. The mustangs were right behind the black mare, but Peesi thought they were only an illusion like the herd that had ridden down on him earlier. He didn't even try to run away. He stood, facing the herd as it came down on him. One hundred wild horses rode over him; four hundred hoofs pounded his body until there was nothing left of Peesi-Painskwi but dust, which was picked up by the spirits of the slain eagles and carried to the mouth of the waterfall with green eyes.

Buddy came down from his rock, tired, smiling, but feeling sad that Starbuck had chosen to remain with Peesi-Painskwi until their destruction. He joined Coyote and Nomad, who were standing over the earth where they had last seen Peesi-Painskwi. Adah Ross came riding up on an apricot-roan Arabian stallion as she herded a small band of foals and yearlings into the corral. She dismounted, closed the gate, and joined the three men. Nomad took her hand and put his arm around her shoulders. "It's all over, Adah Ross. Peesi-Painskwi is gone."

"And Starbuck?" she said, looking over at her ranch house.

"He was destroyed," Coyote said, "when Peesi tore himself loose from Jason's body."

Adah knelt down on one knee, picked up some dirt, and sifted it through her fingers.

Coyote sat down beside her and touched her hand. "He's gone to the waterfall with green eyes, Adah Ross. This water will cleanse the spirit of Jason. Soon he will be ready to return . . . you'll see him in another form . . . free from the demon's power. The eagles will forgive us now . . . they too have been given new wings by the waterfall with green eyes."

Adah looked at Coyote, touched his face, and smiled. She took Nomad's and Buddy's hands as they sat down together—each taking a direction of the wind. Coyote took a pipe, filled it with Indian tobacco, lit it, and offered four whiffs of smoke to the four winds. After the winds had received their offering he passed the pipe to Nomad. When they had all smoked from the pipe they sat in silence, each offering their own prayers to the spirits who had guided them through this strange journey, accepting the powers and synchronicity that had brought them all together. Buddy took his flute and began to play. It was a quiet song, soft and gentle, a washing of their bodies. It was a song for Starbuck to help him on his journey, and it was a song to all of the guardians of the earth who had lived before them.

Coyote looked over at Adah Ross and Nomad. "It makes me happy that you are going to have a baby. Now, this man who has vanished from this earth through the waterfall into the sky will have a body to live in. It will be a beautiful child and we will all be He-she's parents. She-he will be as strong and noble as the trees on the mountains. The eagle will be its guardian, as the eagle is now the guardian of this piece of earth, which, now that she is free, only has to live with herself. She is free from the strange ways of people. Maybe, in a hundred or two hundred years, we will be ready to return when we have all learned how to be human." They took each other's hands as Coyote began to sing with Buddy's music.

This land, this small piece of earth, was free. It had

been given back to herself—to her own body to live, to grow, to heal, create her own destiny, and be with her own mysteries—always forgiving the trespassing of those who have not found the vision. A perfection that lives within the marriage of the dreamer.

The Wild Tibetan
Yonder

It was ten in the morning. Jonquil Rose was driving the road between Stanley and his cabin on Smiley Creek. He had been up all night in a twelve-hour poker game with the Boys at the Quick Draw Saloon, and he was looking forward to being alone. He finished the beer, crushed the can, threw it on the floor, and with one hand popped open another. The six-pack was now a one-pack, the rest had been his breakfast, side-ordered with a purple berry pie. He thumped his Stetson ten degrees to the north with his finger, leaned back in the seat, and poked his arm out the window. He had won two hundred dollars in the game and he was feeling good. When he came to the turnoff he eased up on the gas, slipped the gears into third, and made the turn. A gentle, hang-over slide toward home. The road wound up over a hill that was cov-

ered with sage, mule-ears, camas lily, and lodgepole pine.
The leaves were just beginning to turn. One week of two-
quilt temperatures had changed the whole chemistry of
the valley. The leaves on the aspens were flying their
colors with skiffs of new snow on the higher peaks. Jonquil stopped on top of the hill, leaned his arms on the
steering wheel as he looked down at his cabin. Smoke
was drifting out of the chimney, and parked in front of
the cabin was a stranger for a pickup. "What-the-hell
. . . ?" he said to the top of the beer can as he lowered
his hat down to a question mark. "Maybe Ranger's here
. . . got himself a new rig."

Jonquil stopped at the barn and unloaded twelve bales
of hay (collateral from Studley Wonder when Jonquil's
Diamond Ace-Kicker dropped Studley's empty house
over the bluff). "Hey, sweet Jimmi Maroon," he said to
his pickup, "when's yer ol' man gunna give ya a bath?
Well sheeeet, this way we jus' travel incognito as a dust
storm. But we know . . . heh, Jimmi. We know what's
lurkin' under the grime an' the grind of havin' a big
spread like this one here. Thirty-two rabbits and fourteen
heads of frozen cabbage. Now . . . that's a goddam
MEGAranch as I see it . . . or my name ain't Jonquil
Rose . . . jus' one more WALTZ king." Jonquil filled the
water trough as his Appaloosa, Mariposa Lily, came over
to him, sticking her head under his arm. "Hey . . . you
want some breakfast?" He went into the barn and returned with two flakes of hay. "That should do ya fer a
while. Who's here? Ranger? As soon as I git a little shut-
eye maybe we'll go fer a ride. Think yer up fer that? Yes
. . . no? Whatya think . . . you magnificent high-flyin'
spirit? Well, I'm goin' over to the house and see who
owns the mystery truck. See ya at the water hole . . . ol'
buffalo."

Jonquil went back into the barn, emptied a new sack of grain mix into a barrel, fed his rabbits, gave Hipshooter his two flakes, and walked over to the pickup. "Wooooooooweeee," he said as he eased off his hat and scratched his head. "Well . . . I'll be a seven-day heathen with hunner-dollar boots!" The pickup was a burnt umber, custom-design 924 Porsche pickup with a bed made from rosewood and piñon pine. He walked around the truck, whistled at the amazing places, sat in the driver's seat and ran through the gears, examined the motor, and walked around to the back to check out the bed. "Well, sheeeeeeeet! That bed is jus' 'bout big 'nuff fur two bales of hay and a spit shine. That kid's lost his touch. This rig's got too much class without any ass."

Jonquil opened the front door to the cabin. An easy entrance like . . . there jus' might be some hombre lurking behind that door. "Hey, Ranger! Who's the Frankenstein that bred that beast? That switchblade out there would prob'ly git bogged down in a wormhole." He looked around the front room but he couldn't see or hear his brother. "Hey . . . are ya ashamed? Hmmmmm . . . mus' be in the shitter." Jonquil turned around in the middle of the room. "Hey . . . what's goin' on . . . ?" His five-hundred-dollar saddle with an eagle on the horn, his antique Winchester, both missing in action for the last two years, were propped up on the back of the couch. "Well . . . I'll be a six-legg'd sourdough biscuit."

"You always were . . . and worse," Infinity Cactus said as she stepped out of the kitchen.

Jonquil stood ready-mixed to his boots as he began to feel like the polar cap after a six-month chinook. "Well . . . I'll . . . I'll . . . be . . . I . . . where . . ." He walked over to the door, yanked it open, looked at the pickup and then back at Infinity. "I shood have known. Damn! I shood have known. My god . . . yer . . ."

"Pregnant? Is that the mystery word the tip of your tongue can't find? Eight months and nine-tenths' worth of knocked up as a matter of fact." Infinity walked over to the table and pulled out a chair. "Up to your old tricks I see . . . staying out all night." Jonquil couldn't move. "Jonquil, will you stop slippin' your clutch and come over here. Sit down. I came here to see you . . . not to be looked at as if I was the main freak at the Virgins Forever Festival."

Jonquil stood his ground. "Damn! I've never seen anyone so knocked up. Ya look like one of those skinny-ass'd lodgepoles with a fifty-pound bear cub hangin' off the trunk. The Cowboy Buddha ain't up to some new trick, is he? Seems like I've been in this woodpile b'fore." He started looking around the cabin for something to drink.

"It's in the cabinet. I cleaned up some while I was waitin' for you. I wish this were a trick, Jonquil . . . this kid is wearin' blisters on my arch supports."

Jonquil found the bottle of Dickel's Deelux . . . Sour Mash Number 12 . . . SOUpreme. He took a long drink and sat down on a stool, still holding the bottle. "How long ya been here?"

"Three days. I've been over at your mom's. I came here last night. I was just about to leave. You look tired."

Jonquil took another swig. "Who's the old man?"

Infinity smiled. "Well, it's a good thing he's a three-day-ride away. You don't look very happy."

"Yer fuckin' A I'm unhappy. Sheeeeet . . . whaja 'spect?"

"Well, Jonquil, it's been over two years. What do you think I've been doing? Sightseeing on the Ganges?"

Jonquil was stung silent. There were no words inside

his cowboy heart that he would allow anyone of the opposite sex to hear, especially a stranger who at one time
had been his wife. An old cowboy ethic. At least when
sober.

Infinity stood up and walked over to Jonquil. "Listen
here, you flat-ass'd, stubborn, old army mule. I came here
to see you. I didn't come here to burn down your heart. I
can understand how you might feel, but, if you'd just get
your mind out of those tight cowboy Levi's of yours you
might be able to loosen up. I haven't returned to be with
you. Ho . . . I'm not that dumb. I would like to be
friends. Begin there and see what happens. I've still got a
soft spot in my heart for you . . . perhaps because I've
known you when you have pushed yourself beyond the
image that you like to display . . . as the rootin' tootin'
cowpoke rodeo boy wounded in action. You're more than
that and you know it. I didn't come back to move in on
you. So why don't you settle your chrome-plated ass
down, and let's begin by having some tea. An easy beginning. I've made a pot, or I could fix you some coffee."

Jonquil looked at Infinity. One quarter Apache, with
just about everything else thrown into the genetic
blender. She was sixteen when she showed up in the valley riding in on the back of a flatbed. She was twenty-six
when she ran off to Nepal. Jonquil had just come off the
rodeo circuit with a silver pin in his hip when he met her
at the Saturday night stomp. She moved in on him like a
hungry waif on a horn-of-plenty. They were married on
her seventeenth birthday. "Sit down, Infinity . . . I'll git
the tea fer ya." Jonquil walked into the kitchen, set a pan
of water on the stove, and poured out a cup of tea.

Infinity pulled the stool over to the kitchen door.
"Syringa wrote me a letter right after I got to Nepal. She
told me about your shoot-out with your pickup. I just

about died laughing. It was so funny. I've got the letter almost memorized. '. . . I don't care if you chain smoke, wear curlers to bed, or hate to buck hay . . . I love you. You can be anything you want to be, but for God's sake be here.' Was that it . . . Jonquil?"

Silence.

"That's not true any more?"

"Lay off . . . willya?"

"All that shouting to the moon, blowing a hole in the motor of your nineteen fifty-five Jimmy Maaa-roooon, and passing out right in the middle of town was just for show . . . to impress your friends? You didn't mean any of it?"

Jonquil poured the coffee grounds into the pot, and stepped out into the living room. "Yeh . . . I meant it . . . Infinity. I meant it. But that was two years ago. I ain't heard a word from ya in over a year. I've been here . . . alone, wonderin' 'bout ya . . . climbin' the walls b'cuzz I wanted ya to be here . . . jus' so I'd know ya were all right. I'm not mad any more. That went away ah long time ago. Though . . . I thought it was a low-down trick runnin' off with that smogsHOLE mountain climber. Leavin' me high an' dry suckin' wind. Now . . . ya show up here with a twenty-pounder hangin' off yer skinny little ass, an' I'm s'pose to throw up m'hat, shoot it full of holes, whip out the Flyin'-A Barbecue Shuffle, an' welcome ya back as if nuthin' happened? Sheeeeeeeeeeeet!"

Infinity smiled. It was what she wanted to hear . . . just like she had checked out the cabin to see if there was any evidence of other women. "You better pour some cold water over that coffee to settle the grounds."

Jonquil looked at her and shook his head. "Ya still ain't told me who the father is."

Infinity looked at him straight on . . . dead center, her

dark eyes radiating from her body, from where the life of her baby was living. She spoke from the center of their being. "A man from Tibet."

Jonquil felt the words. They meant nothing to him. A ten-thousand-mile translation lost in slow motion. He eased out the next question. "Where is this man from Tibet?"

"I'm not sure. He could be back in Tibet, Nepal, Kalimpong, or he could be in prison . . . or dead. He is a Khamba. His people have been fighting the Chinese for over twenty-five years. It is very much like the stories of the Native Americans in this country. I wanted to marry him so he would be able to leave, but I wasn't able to get a divorce in Nepal."

"Is he comin' over here?"

"Oh . . . I don't know. Hopefully, but there are so many politics involved. He has been fighting the Chinese since he was ten . . . always dreaming that someday they would drive the invaders out of Tibet. Perhaps, when that happens he will come over here. Like the Apache, the Khambas are some of the greatest fighters in the world. We are the same. We're friends. I love him . . . I always will. We spent a whole year together. Some of the things we did were very dangerous. Crossing the borders, smuggling in guns and ammunition, hiding in the mountains, being chased by the Chinese soldiers. Naturally we became very close. The Apache came out in me. Wah! It was so incredible . . . so exciting. And now . . . I'm going to have a Khamba-Apache freedom fighter. It's a beginning, and it's what I have to offer for what I believe in. For my people and his people."

Jonquil poured a cup of coffee, walked into the living room, and sat down. He took a sip, set the cup down, and smoothed out the coffee with a shot of whisky. Infinity moved the stool over to the table. "Namseling. That's his name. Namseling Tsering. He is an incredible human being. I've never known anyone so brave, strong, and sensitive. I felt as if it was a hundred years ago and I was living with the Apaches . . . fighting the whites for our land. He is the son of a very famous chieftain, and his mother's father was a Doubtop . . . a sage or wonder worker as they are called. The two of you would probably like each other very much."

"Ah sheeeeeeeeeeeet!"

"Well, dammit! You would, once you left your male pride out there in the barn with the rest of the horseshit. He would be your brother as he is mine. He is a bird lover like you. He has trained falcons, and raised and trained horses. Oh . . . how he can ride . . . all of them. The Khambas are the greatest horsemen in the world. The two of you would probably take off for the White Clouds and be gone for months." Infinity set her cup on the table, wrapping her arms around her belly.

Jonquil walked over to a chest of drawers, took out a pack of cigarettes, returned to his chair, lighting one before he sat down. He felt as if he were being swallowed up by a great wave of female ocean. He could neither move nor fight back. "Well . . . dammit, Infinity . . . I'm glad yer back. I can hardly believe any of this, it's so weird. I should be gettin' used to these heart-an'-gut twisters by now, but it's hard . . . damn hard. Brahma bulls, wild broncs, and five-day fandangos are nuthin' compared to what yer one-quarter Apache ass can do to me." Jonquil walked to the window and looked out. "But . . . I'm glad yer back . . . damn glad. What . . . ah . . . what are ya goin' to be doin' now?"

Infinity was rocking back and forth on the stool. "I thought I would stay with Syringa until the baby comes and then I want to move into the hotel. I bought the old Cowboy Hotel . . . guess you knew that . . . heh?"

"Yeh . . . I heard." Jonquil walked over to the door and looked at Infinity's pickup. "Where'd ya git all the dough?"

"Midnight raids in the Tibetan land."

"What in the hell does that mean?"

"Chinese silver, Jonquil, Chinese silver."

Jonquil could tell by looking at her that he wasn't going to find out anything more about her sudden jump into the green-back soup. "When's the kid due?"

Infinity was still holding onto her body, rocking. "Well, if what my body is telling me is true . . . any time . . . any time."

Jonquil stepped over to her and touched her shoulder. "What does that mean . . . any time?"

"Today, Jonquil. I think you'd better drive into town and find Syringa. Tell her that the contractions are about half an hour apart . . . but weak."

"Ah sheeeeet . . . really?"

"Now don't start racing your motor. Just do as I say. I'll drive over to the ranch and be there when Syringa arrives. It would be nice if you stayed. To help, offer a few prayers for a beautiful delivery and for the baby." Infinity went into the bedroom and returned with a small pack. "Drive carefully, and don't run your pickup into the river."

"Are ya sure ya don't want me to drive ya to the ranch?"

"Jonquil . . . get your cowboy ass moving down the road. I'll be all right." Infinity walked outside and carefully climbed into her pickup. She started the motor. Jonquil was running over to the barn. "Hey . . . cowboy!" she shouted, "bring back the best bottle of brandy in the hotel . . . heh?"

"Is that what yer pickup runs on?" he shouted as he was throwing the bales of hay back into the truck.

"That's right. Cognac and Chinese silver. What's the hay for . . . didn't you eat breakfast?"

"Ballast . . . m'lady . . . ballast."

"Oh, my God," Infinity said to her rearview mirror as she shot past Jonquil. "It's going to be one of those good days once again." On the back of her Porsche pickup Infinity had stuck on a bumper sticker that read, "Clap One Hand If You Love Buddha."

Two

Once Jonquil hit the paved road the speed signs flipped from fifty-five to the sign of Infinity. A cosmic gesture, no doubt, with all systems GREEN. The background music was a rhythmic four-four up-time as Jonquil punched his nitrous oxide, supercharged, nineteen fifty-five sweet waltzin' Jimmi Maroon with four on the floor and compound low into flying . . . high. Two reserve carbs moved in from a pit stop in Indy; one hundred cubes of Dee-troit pig iron left town and jumped into Rose's Ride; the Cowboy Buddha's legendary Gray Ghost of the Appaloosa came flying out of the mountains and dissolved into the shape of the pickup; two long skinny avalanches of Sun Valley snow jumped over from the Wood River Valley and ran up Jonquil's nose . . . On the House. Jonquil put on his one-way mirrored glasses, rolled on a pair of white, deerskin gloves, squared off his Stetson with the one-foot cantilevered eaves, unbuttoned his shirt down to the darkest center of the forest. And then, he went into a deep trance that only one-hundred-and-twenty-year-old Maserati yogis have ever been able to achieve. Once again, Jonquil Rose, Jus' One More Cowboy, had moved into action.

On his left were the Sawtooth Mountains; on his right the White Clouds; and riding drag were the Smokies and the Boulders. Zipping through the front windshield was the road that followed the Salmon River through the most beautiful valley this side of the Appaloosa Mantra. By the time Jonquil hit the old Sawtooth City turnoff the needle on the speed-on-meter was hanging ten off starboard; and by the time he passed Hell Roaring Creek, Johnny Donner, the notorious beef-humping sheriff, was drafting on Jonquil's ass calling in for reinforcements . . . thinking that Jonquil Rose had once again been given the Sign, and was out to shoot up the town.

"Woooooooooweeeeeee!" Jonquil shouted as he saw the sheriff in the mirror. "It's been a long, long time since my last good waltz." Jonquil flipped the bird to the sheriff, and then he realized that he had better watch the road because at one hundred and infinity a hard-nosed, self-righteous bumblebee could flip him end-over-end for fifty years through time which was just about all he had left riding on the books.

At the Redfish Lake turnoff he picked up the deputy, Slug Hornet, who had just come from the lake after spending the night with two Sweet-young-things from Wisdom, Montana. Jonquil gave Slug the high sign, which meant in Cowboy sign talk that somewhere beyond the dusty trail there was going to be one hellofa stampede, and the belly-to-belly races had already beegun.

Jonquil was closing in on the one crucial ninety-degree turn, and he knew that he would never be able to take

the downtown curve, so he took off through the sagebrush, which lifted him up onto the airstrip that was
floating like a desert mirage overlooking the town. He followed the runway to the end and then shot down an old
dirt road through the Airstreamer's Ghetto, slapping the
side of the truck with his hat. He flipped a one-eighty in
front of the Cowboy Buddha Hotel and landed royal-
flush-up with the trailer hitch shotgunned to the front
porch. The two sheriffs had missed the turn and they
were ten miles down the Salmon River, cooling their ra-
dials in the river and giving their mounts a good blow.

Jonquil bailed off his truck like a bulldogger onto a
four-second steer, hit the porch, and exploded through
the batwing doors. "Hey, Mama! Syringa!" he shouted.
"Where ya at? Infinity's havin' her kid!"

Syringa came running down the stairs. "Jonquil, what
are you shouting about? You damn near knocked this
hotel over with your pickup."

"Infinity . . . she's started her labor. Come on . . . let's
go!" Jonquil tried to grab his mother's hand and pull her
out the door.

Syringa shook her hand loose and went behind the bar.
She took out a bottle of Dickel's Sour Mash Whisky Number 12 and poured Jonquil a drink. "Here, drink up and
pull yourself together. Tell me what Infinity said."

Jonquil dropped the shot into his mouth without even
touching the rim. "Oh boy . . . that's good sippin'
whisky," he said as he put the glass in front of Syringa.
"She told me to find ya, and that her contradictions were
halfway apart . . . or sumthin' like that. An' that . . .
m'lady Rose, was jus' 'bout five minutes ago . . . includin'
jet lag."

Syringa filled the glass again. "Okay . . . don't worry.
She knows what to do. If need be she could have the kid

out in the Middle Fork with only grizzlies, water ouzels, and Indian paintbrush for attendants."

Ranger and Don Coyote came in the back door. "Hey . . . Rosebowl!" Coyote yelled to Jonquil, "what's goin' on? I jus' heard you broke your own speed record for doing the quick draw between here and yonder."

"Infinity's havin' her kid. Come on . . . you'd better come along." Jonquil looked over at his mother, who was setting up drinks for the crew.

"Sure . . . why not. The kid will probably need a birthday party. Let's have a toast for Infinity and her baby."

"Long live the Wild Tibetan Yonder," they all said as they shot the Dickel down for Infinity. Syringa grabbed a small rigging bag and headed for the door. "Oh, Jonquil, here . . . let me drive."

"Hey, Mom . . . you never drive over twenty-five. My ol' pickup won't even run at that speed."

"It will for me," she answered as she slid into the driver's seat. "Get in back, son. I don't want you up here telling me how to drive."

"Sheeeeet . . ." Jonquil said as he climbed up over the side. Adah Ross came running down from the hot springs, naked, carrying her clothes in both hands. She jumped on top of the cab, hanging her legs over the windshield. Syringa closed her eyes, thinking how nice it would have been to have had two lovely, sweet daughters who taught ballet and poetry at the community center.

"Hey . . . wait a minute," Jonquil yelled to his mother. "I fergot sumthin'." Jonquil jumped out of the truck and ran into the hotel.

"Where's Nomad and Buddy?" Coyote asked Adah Ross. "I thought they were with you."

"Oh . . . didn't they tell you? They took off early this morning for St. Kid."

"Dr. Dancing Arrow wants his trombone back so he

can return to Buddy Sunday. Hocus-pocus . . . am I right?" Coyote stated to Adah Ross.

"Yes . . . guess that's part of it. There's something else 'bout the sheriff, Jesse T. Rivers, running for governor."

"That's great!" Ranger said, laughing. "Buddy made it all up and now the sheriff will probably be our next governor. Damn . . . if this ain't the West."

"Every state needs a good law 'n' order man fer gov . . . Ranger Rose. Don't ya know nuthin' . . . kid?"

"How'd the doctor get Nomad roped into this dee-bubblization?" Coyote asked Adah Ross.

"Give ya three guesses . . . cowboy, and all three is gonna git ya a fat lip."

"Now . . . wait a minute, Adah Ross. Don't look at me like that. I didn't put him up to nuthin'. I didn't even know about it," Coyote said, standing up in the truck with his hands up.

"Ha . . ." Ranger said, "Nomad's goin' to put the cowboy mantra moves on Cody St. Kid. Seems like I'd heeerd that one b'fore?"

"Men!" Adah Ross said, as she spun around on top of the cab and faced the Sawtooths.

Jonquil returned with two bottles of cognac.

"What's that for?" Ranger asked his brother.

"Child support," Jonquil answered as he tossed the bottles to Coyote and Ranger.

Adah Ross looked down at the label on the cognac bottle. "Looks like French socialism to me."

Three

By the time the birth crew arrived at the ranch Jonquil's enthusiasm had collapsed. He was feeling like he had been demoted to assistant biscuit-shooter in charge of the road apples. Everyone was busy: Golden was in the bedroom with Infinity and Syringa; Coyote was in the kitchen preparing a large pot of soup; Ranger and Adah Ross were splitting wood. Jonquil walked around the house, picking up the treasures Infinity had brought back with her . . . looking at them and putting them back. He went into the bedroom, stood by the door, and leaned against the wall with his arms folded. Infinity was talking to Syringa and she didn't see him. He went back into the kitchen.

"Hey, Jonquil," Coyote said to him, "you know how to make bread?"

"Naw . . . I flunked out of Home Ec.," he said as he poured three fingers of cognac into a Mason jar. "Shouldn't someone be boilin' water?"

"What for?" Coyote answered. "That comes later when it's hot toddy time. Are you lookin' for something to do?"

Jonquil shook his head as he took off his hat and straightened the osprey feather in his band.

Coyote walked to the bedroom door. "Golden. Why don't you come in here and teach the cowboy how to make bread?"

Jonquil walked out the door. He went over to the corral and climbed the fence. All the horses were out in the pastures except for a Coeur d'Alêne blue Appaloosa stallion. "Hey . . . looks like me and you got sumthin' in common. 'Cept . . . you're probably gettin' more than me. How's it feel to be locked in with all those fillies and mares running wild in the fields? Tough huh? Makes ya kinda eat yer heart out. Maybe we shud high-tail it . . . go fer a ride. Cut loose 'n' see if we can find the ol' Cowboy Buddha. Heard Coyote say he'd seen him jus' the other day." Golden came over to Jonquil and climbed up next to him.

"It looks like it's going to be a while. Her contractions are still about the same. How ya feelin' . . . Jonquil?"

"Ahhh . . . I don't know. Out of place. Sort of like a shitheel at a good samaritan's t'do." Jonquil hadn't spent much time with Golden since he had moved onto the ranch. Syringa was always doing such strange things, and Golden had turned one of the barns into a weaving studio. Jonquil wasn't sure what kind of a relationship they had with each other. Shacked-up sidekicks was the feeling he had. Once, when he had asked Syringa about their relationship she gave him an answer that sounded like a Navajo translation of the *Pilgrim's Progress*.

"Jonquil. What would you like to be doing right now?"

"I would like to be in there with Infinity. Alone. I only saw her fer an hour b'fore she ran off to have her kid."

Golden was watching Jonquil . . . studying his face and watching his hands. "What about the kid? Does it bother you?"

"Well . . . yeh! Sure. Dammit! You're goddam right it does. I wanted to have one of those little buckos. Okay . . . I can take the fact that she didn't want to. But look at her now! She turns up in full bloom and I'm sittin' here feelin' like I've been pushed out into the rain with jus' an old, used rubber fer an umbrella."

"Well Jonquil, it looks like you've been caught in the cross fire. There's no place to go but inside. Into your body. Even then, you might run into an old enemy or two. Especially if you're not hearin' your own voice."

"Well sheeeet, Golden," Jonquil replied, "I'm hearin' voices all the time. The wind comin' off the mountains, the coyotes, the birds, the trees. I like what I do . . . dammit! Being a cowboy. It makes me feel real good. It makes me feel like I'm connected into this country, and I like bein' part of that myth. Bein' in the center of four winds hitting you right in the face at the same time. The earth, cattle, horses, and man. Four different creations all moving together to produce a legend. Damn! I like that. I don't want to become a soybean farmer. Even if everyone in the whole world became vegetarians I would still punch cattle. I'd still have my own herd. It's a good story and I like it. It's that simple. I like who I am even though I'm a little crazy at times. Sheeeeet . . . I like that too!"

"Well, I think that's some of the reasons she came back. She likes your craziness, but she sees a lot more than just that in you. This place is her home. And by damn, we can all come home. But . . . she needs to have her own life, something that belongs to her. Not your place, or Syringa's, but her own."

"Yeh . . . I think yer right. But . . . what the hell am I suppose to do?"

"Jonquil . . . it's taken me thirty years or more to learn how to live with a woman . . . even reach a place where I could gracefully bow before my own needs. It's working out because I'm not putting any demands on Syringa as to what I would like to see happen. Just accepting what is, what she is, and making my own life work for me. Somehow, we blend with each other. Acceptance. And being able to understand a kind of sexual, psychic economics that takes place between the female and male."

Jonquil didn't say anything for quite a while—thinking about what Golden had said. He was beginning to feel better about Golden. He never knew a man could be so tough, yet gentle.

"You know, Jonquil," Golden continued, "from the beginning the woman has always had to learn how to live with the man. Take It and the lumps too . . . without ever being able to leave. And now it's time, it has finally arrived, where the man must do the same. Infinity has found out who she is and perhaps she wasn't able to do that with you. But . . . she's back, economically independent, and I think that's great. It's up to you now . . . whether you want to try and work your life in with hers. We can't cut off her nose, or stamp a big fat A on her forehead. My father would have done that and he was a mean, onery, sonofabitch. Killed my mother jus' because he wanted to raise an army of field hands. Bred her like she was a cow . . . the bastard!"

Jonquil looked surprised. He had never heard a man talk about his father that way. "What was your mother like?"

"Ah . . . she was beautiful, Jonquil . . . just beautiful. Intelligent, sensitive, always wanting to read books, but never had the time. She'd daydream about other countries, traveling on ships, being an adventurer . . . explorer. But as soon as she would start talking about her dreams . . . Bam! . . . she was pregnant again. Legalized rape. That's what it was. After she died I cut out. Never went back. For years, I had this fantasy about going back and chopping off my old man's dong and stuffing it into his mouth. Shit . . . he was so mean and horny it would have grown back. It took me a long time just to feel good about my own body. About being a man. That's why I lived alone for so long . . . probably the reason why I was a guide. One day . . . I was down by the lake where I had my cabin. I looked into the water and I didn't see myself. I saw my mother in that reflection. She was smiling. It was so beautiful. I didn't dare move . . . thinking I would frighten her away. I heard something above me. I looked up and a trumpeter swan was flying over my head. When I looked back into the water my mother was gone. She must of known how angry I had been about my old man, and she came to tell me that she was finally happy. She was flying to all of the places where she had always wanted to go. I drank the water from the lake and stopped the battle. Ah . . . Jonquil, women. They can create in their minds and bodies what we have only been able to do with steel."

"How long you'd known my mother?"

"Oh . . . about twenty years I guess. She's changed my life too. She and that old grizzly bear. Three women, counting my mother."

"What's this story 'bout the grizzly?" Jonquil asked.

Golden put his hand on Jonquil's leg. "Oh . . . that's a long one, Jonquil. Someday, let's go for a ride and I'll tell you about her. I think we'd better get back in there and see how Infinity's doing."

Jonquil jumped down from the fence. "I'll take you up on that story . . . soon. I'm goin' to take One Singer out fer a ride. I'll be back. I jus' want to think . . . be alone."

"Good. I'll tell them. Everyone would be sad if you didn't come back. Especially Infinity. You know, you might think about working with me. I've got so many orders that I could weave my butt off for a year and still be in the hole. All those bank presidents and oil executives who used to be my hunting customers are now buying my tapestries. Damn! Never thought I'd see the day. I told them . . . if I ever caught them with a rifle I would shoot twenty holes through their after-shaved hides, have them stuffed, and hang their carcasses above their desks . . . ass out."

"Well . . . I don't know 'bout b'comin' a weaver. Cud I do it while riding a horse?"

"You're damn right you could . . . backwards if you want. Ranger has been working with me, and I'd sure like to see you join up. What a team we'd have. Weavers and

Dreamers. Don't forget . . . a good weaving is worth a thousand sheep. See you later . . . Jonquil."

Jonquil walked over to the tack shed, and Golden went back into the house. Syringa met him at the door. "How's Infinity doing?" Golden asked, putting his arm around her.

"All right. . . . She's just about the same. How's Jonquil?"

"He's sorting everything out, sulking a bit, but he'll be okay."

"What did you tell him?"

"I told him that if he didn't get his shit together I'd break both his legs and stick him in the barn as my weaver-slave."

"Golden . . . you didn't?"

"Naw. I jus' told him that we all loved him. Especially Infinity."

Four

As soon as Jonquil cleared the top pasture he gave One Singer the lead. "Okay . . . meeester, you've got it. Let's go." The stallion popped a three-sixty wheely, shot up the meadow before Jonquil had time to set his mind properly in the saddle. "Hey! . . . this ain't the sweepstakes. Jus' remember, widow maker, I bought a round-trip ticket." One Singer was so excited to be loose that he not only wanted to run, but he also thought it would be hot 'n' salty to crow hop, buck, snort, sunfish, and spin. The two of them covered a lot of territory, but it wasn't in any one direction. After the stallion finally quieted down, he still wasn't satisfied. He decided to see if Jonquil could handle the low branch trick as he set his ancient horse-gyro for the tree twenty feet in front of them. "Wait . . . hey . . . wait a second there. What'n-the-hell are ya . . . ?" They passed under the branch with Jonquil hanging onto the mane and saddle with his ass almost plowing up the ground. "All right . . . you wild ass'd broomtail . . . cut it out! Calm down! You're feelin' crazier than me . . . but you'd better remember that I'm s'pose to be the star of this back yard rodeo." One Singer took off for the end of the meadow one mile away. No stops . . . full throttle. The dance was over and it was time to get serious. Jonquil held on. "All right . . . go fer it! But jus' remember to stop when ya git to the granite wall." Jonquil tucked himself into One Singer's body and rode the express all the way into tomorrow and back again. At the end of the meadow One Singer slowed down to an easy, sliding trot. Jonquil looked like he had been playing pick-up-sticks in a wind tunnel. "Woooweeeee . . . One Singer. You're too good fer me. I've been havin' a desk job all summer, ridin' that old buckskin 'round." They stopped at a stream and Jonquil spun off. "Look at ya! Damn! Ya ain't even winded."

After One Singer had finished drinking they rode up onto a high ridge that lifted them into the White Clouds. On each side of the ridge was a watershed, and beyond the crest was a small lake at the edge of the tree line. On the far side of the lake a high wall of granite hawk-nosed out over the water. It had been a diving platform for Jonquil and Ranger when they were kids. He walked One Singer down the ridge to the lake and staked him out by the edge of the water. "Jus' in case ya dee-cide to go visit the ladies. Now . . . if ya git colic from eatin' too much green grass I'm gunna kick yer ass right back to the B.C.B. . . . Bee-fore the Cowboy Buddha . . . and that was bee-fore there was horses. You'd be only a dream. Got it?"

Jonquil climbed up to the ledge. The granite was warm from the afternoon sun, a smooth, even heat that felt like it came from the center of the earth. He took off his clothes, lying down on the rocks and scooting his body out over the ledge. The old-timers said the lake was bottomless. There was another story that told how this cavity, before it had been filled with water, was the entrance for the Native-American migration. Somewhere inside the lake there were hot springs that kept the surface water warm enough for an enjoyable swim . . . even in the fall. Syringa had told her sons that the water came from the Himalayas in Tibet.

Jonquil looked into the water. Layers of blues that descended through time until he felt as if he were seeing into the Pleistocene, or going through into the troposphere. It was all there—the cowboy and the Buddha—everything into everything. He stood up and dived into the water. It was a smooth, graceful dive and it felt to him as if the water was moving away as he chased the surface into eternity. When he finally caught the water he pushed down into it as far as he could swim. He wanted to lose the feelings that had been with him all day. He wanted to be released from the suction of his own body that kept him wingless without mythology. And he wanted to descend so far that he would swim through his own imagination and return as a legend within the pride of his own wake. As he realized that he could go no farther he arched his body upward and slowly kicked to the light. When he finally reached the surface he felt as if he had been inside the cavern of water for hours, days—swimming inside a life that he felt had at one time been his home and his enemy. He filled his lungs with air, blowing out, filling . . . releasing. Then he turned on his back and began to float—concentrating on his body as a strange ship within an ocean that was limitless—accepting the eternal curve.

When he returned to the ledge he discovered a man sitting on the rock. He was dark with black hair in long braids. He looked as if he had been traveling for a long time through an ancient trade route. The man stood up as Jonquil approached him. They were exactly the same height and build. They looked into each other's face—seconds without dimension. "My name is Namseling," the man said.

Jonquil felt as if he were being drawn through this man. As if the man were empty, pulling him through his shell. Jonquil sat down and the man sat down in front of him. "What is this?" Jonquil said. "Namseling?"

"It is as easy as you want it to be. Yes . . . I am that man."

Jonquil touched the rock below him and then he returned his eyes to the stranger. "I don't understand. Is this some kind of trick?"

"No. It isn't a trick. Unfortunately, I am not that talented for such things. Touch me. I'm real just like you are real."

Jonquil reached over and felt Namseling's hands. "How could this be?"

"Look at me, Jonquil Rose. Look at my body, my face, and go beyond the external features. Look deeper. What do you see?"

Jonquil did as he was told, trying to look through him so he could perhaps understand what was going on. "I don't know. I only see you."

"Close your eyes, Jonquil, and take my hands. Feel who I am. Only feel."

Jonquil took Namseling's hands and closed his eyes. He could feel their hands pulsating and tingling together. He could feel the warmth of Namseling's hands and a passage of human understanding that seemed to melt between them. "I feel both of us at the same time. I can't tell us apart," he said with his eyes closed.

"Now, Jonquil, open your eyes and look at me."

Jonquil did as he was told. He looked at Namseling—through his eyes—and he saw his own face.

"What do you see now?"

"I see myself through you."

"And beyond that . . . deeper?"

"You. I see you past me . . . farther on. . . ."

"And again . . . ?"

"I see me . . . again."

"Yes. Isn't it amazing, Jonquil? Do you know why you see all these things?"

"Sheeeeet . . ." Jonquil said quietly. "Of course not."

"Because we are of the same mind. We have only taken different outside forms. You see, Jonquil . . . we are twins. We have the same father."

"What?" Jonquil questioned as he tried to move his hands away, but Namseling held onto them.

"No . . . don't jump away. Yes, we are exactly the same person, and if we could move ourselves through time we would eventually become the same. But, unfortunately, our bodies are so bound to this dimension. But our spirits and our minds can travel through so many more dimensions. It is very simple and once you understand you will be amazed. It is like those flowers right there, coming out of the rocks. They have the same father."

Jonquil looked over at the flowers. "Air, sunlight, rain . . . pollen. Is that what ya mean by father?"

"Exactly . . . see how simple it is?"

"Sure . . . when yer talkin' 'bout flowers."

Namseling was silent, looking into Jonquil's face. It was like looking into a mirror after being away from your reflection for many years. "How old are you, Jonquil?"

"Thirty-one . . . las' June."

"I too. And what day were you born?"

"Fifteenth . . ."

"That is my birthdate."

"Sheeeet . . . there mus' be thousands of men with the same date. So what?"

"Perhaps," Namseling answered, "but I don't know about them. It is possible, but then we do not share the same woman."

"Ah ha. Now I git it. You're here because of Infinity."

"Oh no. I think you are here with me because of Infinity. Look around you. What do you see?"

Jonquil looked around. "I see mountains, the lake, clouds, trees . . . rocks. . . ."

"Are you certain?"

"Hell yes. I ain't blind," Jonquil answered, thinking that Namseling was trying to whipsaw him with doped cards. "I jus' rode up here a short time ago."

"What happened when you dived into the lake?" Namseling asked.

Jonquil didn't say anything. Thinking. He began to look around. Everything seemed the same but then he couldn't see One Singer, and his clothes were gone.

"Is it possible, Jonquil, that you could be in Tibet?"

"Hell . . . I don't know. I've never been there."

"Yes, you have. You have lived here in Tibet before, and I have lived in Idaho."

Again, Jonquil was silenced by Namseling's answers. Everything seemed to be coming from a strange language that held no time inside its mind, but somehow made sense inside Jonquil's spirit. "And so . . . who is our old man? I was always curious . . . Syringa never seemed to really know."

"I told you . . . the same man."

"Ten thousand miles apart? Mus' be some stud."

"Yes . . . isn't it wonderful?"

"How'd you know all this shit?" Jonquil asked . . . looking around to see if One Singer had broken his picket pin.

"Fortunately for me, I live in a land where this is all so easy to understand. And where you live, this kind of understanding is just beginning to unfold. My people have known all of this for centuries, but then, there are so many other mysteries that we are just beginning to comprehend. You have to understand about time . . . both in the physical and mystical studies. Your mother has always known this. She must be a very special being. And from what Infinity has told me, the Native-Americans have this power. And now, you know it. See . . . it is so easy like I said. And soon, we will be a father."

Jonquil gave Namseling the quick-eye.

"Oh . . . I'm so happy for all of us, and especially for our baby. But I can see I have lost you again."

"Yer darn tootin' you've lost me. I feel like I'm in the middle of a snow-blinder with no chains on my brain."

"Tell me, Jonquil . . . that feather you wear in your hat. Is it an osprey feather?"

"Ya . . . sure."

"When was it given to you by the osprey?"

"Well . . . hell. I can't ree-member. Last year sometime."

"Think back carefully, Jonquil. How did it happen?"

Jonquil started running the circumstances through his

head. "Well . . . it was bee-fore Christmas. I'd been out skiin' and I decided to take a little snooze. It was a clear sunny day. I put my parka on the ground and while I was dozin' I had a dream 'bout Infinity."

"And what were you doing in this dream?"

"Well . . . ah . . . we . . . ahhh sheeeeet, Namseling . . . we were makin' sweet love. So what?"

Namseling clapped his hands together. "Yes . . . that is when it happened?"

"What happened?" Jonquil said . . . one eye zeroed in on Namseling.

"The baby was conceived."

"Oh . . . big deal. Ya got the piece of tail and I got the feather."

"Ho . . . I think we both got the piece of tail . . . as you say. Don't you believe your dreams?"

"Well, dammit! I know I didn't shoot-off ten thousand miles. I ain't that good."

"Well, Jonquil . . . how do you explain the feather?"

"Hell . . . I don't know. Old osprey flew over and let out a big fart, and knocked the feather loose. Sheeeet . . . how would I know?"

"Jonquil . . . you have such a strange sense of humor. But it is good to be silly. I think when the baby is born you will discover that it will look like you and me . . . and Infinity, of course. I believe at the moment she conceived she could have been dreaming about you."

"Namseling . . . you'd make a good diplomat . . . or at least a good corn-binder salesman out in farmers' daughters country. You'd talk the pants off any sweet young thing. No wonder Infinity fell fer ya. Here . . . look at us, holding hands."

"Yes . . . isn't it nice that we can have the time to be able to talk . . . just be alone and feel close with each other. But . . . I must go. Someday, I would like to return to your country . . . this Idaho. Perhaps you could teach me how to be a cowboy."

"Sure . . . anytime, Namseling. Ain't nuthin' to it. But you've got to like the smell of horseshit, sweat, 'n' sagebrush all kinda stuck in together. After while . . . gits in yer blood. And you've got to be able to ee-luci-date with a silver tongue. Slur yer words together and don't deescribe anything like it should be. Jus' make up a whole passel of new words if ya can't find the ones yer lookin' fer. Like snarky fer bein' well dressed, 'n' chaffonsified. Ya go like this after ya've had ee-nuff grub at the dinner table. No thank yee, ma'am . . . my capacity has been completely chaffonsified. . . . See how it goes? Ya kinda try and make yer own palaver jus' a shade off frum the next cowboy . . . so they know ya got some class. Jus' like ridin'. And when ya dance, see . . . you've gotta stick yer ass out in the room so yer body ain't touchin' the whoa-man's . . . but yer cheek-ta-cheek upstairs. I cud teach ya a few ropin' tricks . . . like ridin' into the bar on yer bes' Sunday-go-ta-meetin' hoss and lassoin' the beer right out of yer bes' friend's grip. Or . . . if he's dancin' real sweetheart like with his favorite cow bunny ya jus' drop a hooley-ann over her bosom an' ride out of town with nuthin' on but a big grin on yer chops. An' . . . these days ya gotta larn how ta drink a fifth of good sippin' whisky and drop a coupla hits of El-S-Dee jus' fer a goooood Saturday night. Hell . . . ain't nuthin' much ta bein' a cowboy these days. There's onlee a few of us who's still doin' it the old way. Mos' of 'em are doin' it with pickups, airplanes, computers, Countree 'n' Western bands, 'n' mov-ee contracts. But . . . ain't nuthin' much ta bein' a cowboy. I love it. Ain't nuthin' better. What's

yer hosses like over there? Or here . . . Ah, sheeeet . . .
whatever country I'm in."

"Ah . . . Jonquil, we have magnificent horses! Horses
that can run at full gallop in the high mountains for
twenty or thirty miles. They have incredible stamina. My
people have been riding horses for over three thousand
years. We have horses like the one you are riding."

"Yeh . . . ? I thought the Nez Percé bred 'em."

"You see . . . they are in the same dream as my people.
They carried the dream with them and after they had
been given the horse again they created the Appaloosa.
See . . . how simple everything is, Jonquil? But we must
go. The baby will be coming soon and we must run down
the mountain . . . to the woman. We can always go up,
Jonquil, but we need her to bring us down. Home. Well,
my brother, I know now that you will be a good father
for the baby. Infinity was worried, but now I know that
everything is all right. Let us meditate and pray together.
Touch each other and be friends." Namseling took Jonquil's hands and held them inside his. Jonquil closed his
eyes but they kept popping open . . . watching Namseling. Finally they closed by themselves and he felt his
body float through the hands of his brother as their spirits
joined together—finding the one heartbeat that is within
all life—listening to the songs of the flowing river. It was
so easy, as Namseling said.

When Jonquil opened his eyes, he saw that Namseling
was watching him. "Ah . . . there you are. I want to give
you this necklace. I would like for you to wear it so that
you will always know that we are the same. This was
given to me by my grandfather, who was a very wise and
magical man. He was a Doubtop." Namseling put the
necklace around Jonquil's neck.

"Well . . . thanks s'much, Namseling. It's real beautiful. I'd like to give you something too. But . . . as ya can see, I'm as naked as the day I was bucked out of the chute."

"It is not necessary, Jonquil. You can give me something later . . . when we meet again. I know you'll be a good father to the child. That is the most precious gift I could have. Come, let us return to our homes." Namseling stood up, still holding onto Jonquil's hand. Jonquil put his arm around Namseling as they dived into the water. They disappeared into the lake that goes on forever. And, as the old story is told, is fed by the snows from the Himalayan mountains.

Five

When Jonquil emerged from the lake he swam over to the bank and lay down on the grass by One Singer. His head was just below One Singer's body as he looked into the sky, giving his mind into the multidimensions of blue —a healing, silent symphony of infinite calmness. "Ahhh, One Singer, it's so beautiful here. These mountains. I don't think I could ever leave." He rolled his head back so he could look at the Appaloosa. He watched the stallion for a long time—studying his body, his markings, his conformation—feeling the incredible life that was living within the body called Appaloosa.

"Aaaaa-paaah-luuuuuuuuuu-saaaahh. Aaaaaaa-paaaaah-hhh-luuuuuuuuuuuu-saaaaaaaaahhhhhhhh, Aaaaaaaaaa-pa-aaaaaahhhhhhhh - luuuuuuuuuuuuuuuuu - saaaaaaaahhhhh-hhh," Jonquil chanted as he carried the sound within the music of the wind blowing through the trees. "Aaaaaaaa-paaaaaaaaaahhhhhhh - luuuuuuuuuuu - saaaaaaaaaaaahhhhh-hhhhhh." One Singer put his nose into Jonquil's face. Jonquil put his arms around the stallion's head as he closed his eyes, feeling their breath as they were married together by the arrival of their two bodies inside the sound of the Appaloosa mantra. "Aaaaaaa-paaahhh-luuuuuuuuuuu-saa-aaaahhhhhhhhhhhh." One Singer finally gave Jonquil a nudge with his nose. "Hey . . . that tickles. What's the matter, high flyer? Don't ya like this mush 'n' sop?" Jonquil jumped up and vaulted onto One Singer's back, wrapping his arms around the horse's neck. "I'll make a deal with ya. One more jump into the lake and then we'll do some of the finest ridin' in the West. We'll do some tricks we ain't never done b'fore. We might even discover some that no one has ever done b'fore. So ya jus' start thinkin' 'bout all the concentration we're gunna need jus' comin' off the mountain . . . goin' home."

Jonquil slid off the stallion and ran up the rocks to the ledge and without stopping he jumped into the air, twisting, spinning, kicking, and making strange faces. He kept doing these airborne acrobatics over and over again, and with each jump he threw himself farther and farther out into the lake; and with each performance he became crazier and stranger as he traveled through the air into the lake. Just before his last performance he found an empty bottle and lid by an old campsite. He washed it in the stream and took it up on the ledge. His dive into the water began with a swan, and then he tucked his body into a one-and-one-half spin, entering the lake as an arrow shot from many years away. The two forms moved into each other, equally balanced, each shape accepting the other until the arrow was lost through the ultimate female. He pushed through the water as far as he could penetrate. When he had reached his depth-limit, he took the lid off and filled the bottle. He returned to the surface. When he was dressed he put the saddle, bags, and bridle back on One Singer. "We'll jus' stick these boots right here in these bags. Won't be needin' 'em . . . right, swift dreamer? Now listen . . . As soon as we hit the meadow, I want you to take the left lead, and we're gunna stay in an easy canter. Okay? Now, I'm gunna put this strap 'cross the saddle and hook it over to the front riggin' rings . . . jus' enuf room fer my feet. I've been told that a gelding is the best hoss fer this kind of ridin', but I figure I couldn't pre-form worth a damn if I was gelded. So we'll jus' see how we do . . . heh? Damn! Showin' off fer the ladies is what it's all 'bout . . . hey, mountain dancer? This is jus' gunna be like makin' love fer the first time. Ya never know what's gunna happen. All right! Now . . . let's see who the best horsemen in the world are . . . heh?"

Six

Infinity, resting between contractions, looked up through the large windows and saw Jonquil riding down through the meadow on One Singer. Jonquil spun sideways on the saddle and executed what is called a Free Lazy-back—laying his body across the saddle at ninety degrees to the stallion. He stayed in that position for about ten yards and then he grabbed the horn and the back of the saddle, flipping himself over backward until his feet touched the ground. Then he pushed off, pulling himself back into the saddle. "Syringa . . ." Infinity called softly, "is that your son out there?" Syringa turned around just in time to see Jonquil lying over the neck of One Singer, turning his body and swinging onto the ground, kicking himself back onto the horse.

"I think he could be the reason you fled
. . . look at him ride. Got his father in him f(

Ranger looked over at his mother. "Who is

"Well, son . . . I'm not sure. But how h
. . . how he could ride. Look at him . . . h
arabesque."

Ranger stepped over to the window to watch his
brother. "I'll be damned! I never knew the Arabs and the
Basques ever made it together."

Infinity dropped her head onto the pillow and looked
up at the high, log ceiling. "Oh, God . . . please forgive
me for having such strange friends. Please don't take it
out on the kid. Jus' give her or him a chance to be a normal Apache-Khamba-Cowboy. Sure would be appreci-
ated . . . God."

Coyote went over and sat down by Infinity. "I think
your cowboy is coming home. My . . . this is better than
a rodeo."

"Coyote . . . since when did you ever watch a rodeo
while having a kid?"

Coyote looked down at Infinity—his black eyes dancing. "Never . . . but perhaps it is time to learn. What
should I do?"

"Go outside and get knocked up. . . . Ohhhhh."
Infinity stuck her knuckles into her mouth. "Ohhhh . . . I
think this freedom fighter is trying to ride out on a mes-
teño."

During Infinity's next contraction, Jonquil was per-
forming the Fender Drag by holding onto the stirrup and
the saddle's fender with his feet and legs, leaning backward, and picking flowers as he swung his body two feet
above the ground.

"I think he wants to steal our show. . . ." Infinity said

s..e was trying to take a deep breath. "Look at him . . . ohhhh . . . damn!"

"Do you want me to close the curtains?" Adah Ross asked Infinity.

"No . . . of course not. In a few more seconds the kid can watch too."

Jonquil was standing on top of the saddle in the Cossack Stance as One Singer entered the lower pasture. "Now easy . . . jus' easy, ol' boy. Ride right up there next to the house . . . right in front of that big window. One more trick and we'll land right in the middle of this Tibetan dream." Jonquil eased his feet out of the strap. As One Singer passed the window Jonquil flipped over backward in a full spin, landing on his feet right in front of the window. He took off his hat, still holding the flowers, and bowed before the window just as the baby was being born.

Ranger was looking over at Infinity and then back to Jonquil. "Hey . . . I don't know where to look. This is the best two-ring circus I've been to in a long time. Look at Jonquil . . . he's got more smoke than a wet fire. Oh . . . look . . . it's a girl! Hey . . . Jonquil . . . Jonquil . . . it's a girl!" Ranger was pounding on the glass trying to tell Jonquil that Infinity had given birth to a girl. "Oh . . . holy Buddha bananas . . . look who's comin' now," he said. "It's Buddy and Nomad ridin' on the top of an old truck. It must be Cody St. Kid. Look! Look at that! Buddy has got his old trombone back. Well . . . I'll be a hoolihanin' fool dogger clown. This is wilder than a Wild East-Meets-West show."

Golden opened the french doors so Infinity and her daughter could watch the arrival of Nomad, Buddy, and Cody St. Kid. Buddy was blowing a parade of bubbles filled with singers, chanters, dancers, and birth prayers for Infinity and the new baby. He also had blown a series of bubbles that were the animals, birds, and fish that had, at one time, been made extinct by the sticky valves of the human flying machine. The bubbles circled the cabin, floated into the trees, and out into the fields and pastures. Some of them made camp at the hot springs to wait for the celebration.

"Hey . . . Ranger Rose!" Buddy shouted from the top of Cody's old truck. "I got one fer ya."

Ranger ran outside to wait for the bubble. "Think ya can do it . . . Buddy?"

"Sheeeeet. . . ."

"Spin her out then and I'll take it from there."

Buddy knew that he had to give this one lots of try and a lot more heart. He wasn't sure that Virginia really wanted to come out of seclusion where she was waiting for another lucrative consummation from God. He went through his warm-ups and slide twirls, and then he let it fly out into the mountain sky blue. There was a Bach organ recital, lightning bolts, a multitude of celebrating hosannas and hallelujahs, flooding rivers, Greek orgies, chariot races, sinners trying to knock out one hundred push-ups, and two stoned-out gate attendants trying to figure out how many heads could dance on top of a roach clip and still call themselves angels. And then . . . the voice of God: "Virginia . . . Virginia Spring!"

"Yes God . . . I've been waiting for you. Where have you been since Yellowstone?"

"Busy . . . real busy with all these interplanetary conferences I've been having. And then, there are all of these women who won't be satisfied unless I perform the deed. Like you. Whew . . . I need some help, Virginia."

"Oh, God . . . I'd be more than happy to help you."

"Good . . . that's good, Virginia. I've hired on some assistants and the one I've picked out for you lives in Stanley Basin. You used to know him. I want you to go to him and make him happy. Real happy."

"You mean Ranger? Ranger Rose?"

"Yes . . . that's him. Good man . . . real good man. That's why I've got him on my team. Take care of him, Virginia, and when your time comes I'll make sure that you are right up here leading the cosmic cheerleading team. *Adios*, Virginia . . . *adios*."

"Goodbye, God. I'll make Ranger happy. I promise."

When the bubble finally descended there she was. Virginia Spring, Sweetheart of the West. She was riding a tapioca palomino, and holding on behind her was her one-year-old son . . . Kid Yellowstone.

"Holy sheeeet," Ranger shouted as he ran out into the field. "Is it true . . . Buddy? Will they disappear?"

Buddy punched Nomad on the arm. "What do ya think . . . partnah? Yer the reality versus illusion expert."

Nomad studied the bubble for a few seconds. "I thought we'd already decided this a long time ago. Everything is Everything."

"Well, Ranger . . . there ya go. Virginia and yer kid. You've finally got 'em."

"Whooooopeeeeee. . . ." Ranger whipped his hat into the air and ran over to the bubble and jumped onto the back of the palomino.

Coyote walked up to Buddy. "Well, Doctor . . ."

"Hey, Coyote . . . you ancient, old, granite shiver. How's Infinity?"

"She had the kid. Come on in. I see you've managed to finagle your trombone back. How'd it go?"

"Easy, Coyote . . . easy. Once Nomad set up the diversion. Damn! No one should be that good-lookin'."

Coyote flashed a like-father-like-son smile . . . shining

onto the backs of the mountains. "What happened to the town?"

"Vamoosed. Nuthin' left but the old Cody St. Kid. The straightforward and upright citizens of St. Kid, Idaho were makin' a rerun of the West. Jesse T. Rivers became the mayor; the Messiah Brothers became the sheriff and deputy; they'd killed all the bufflers; and they were gettin' ready to round up the Indians and ship them to Mexico along with Arco's atomic waste."

"You erased them?"

"Jus' one bubble. Clean. Right back to a desert. Not even a coyote was left. Sorry 'bout that."

"No compassion, Dr. Dancing Arrow?"

Buddy relaxed into the question—trying to thin out the weeds in the broad, alfalfa pastures of ontology and moral philosophy. "Compression?"

"I said compassion."

"Oh . . . did I blow it?"

"Yeh . . . some blow job, I'd say. Clean. Real clean. At least you could of left a few coyotes and an old building as a landmark. You're more deadly than a neutron bomb."

"As good as God . . . maybe."

Coyote shot over the weird-eye. "Yeh . . . maybe. How's Cody doin'?"

"She didn't miss a beat. Stepped right out of the old woodwork as if nothin' had happened. Amazing. She jumped into her ol' truck an' took off fer Stanley hangin' on to Nomad's eyes. I had to jump onto the bumper else I'd been left behind. Some son ya got there . . . Pop. Sri Casanova . . . swift lover and high roller."

"Well, Doctor . . . as I've always told you . . . it's good to have a giant around when you need one." Coyote put his arm around Buddy. "Come on . . . God, let's go see the new kid."

When Jonquil was finished taking care of One Singer he went into the house and sat down next to Infinity and her baby. Infinity was sitting up on the bed and the baby was sucking on her breast. Infinity took Jonquil's hand. She saw the necklace. Silver, turquoise, and coral woven through the mind of earth, sky, and water of Namseling's people. A story about a sacred journey to where the two worlds meet within the mountains of the flowing river. "How ya doin'?" Jonquil asked.

"Fine . . . you big show-off. All of you. Never in my wildest dreams did I think I would be having my baby inside a Cowboy Buddha Fandango. It was wonderful! But look at her . . . isn't she beautiful?"

Jonquil took the baby. "Hey . . . she looks like you. How'd that happen?"

Infinity looked at her daughter. "Coyote said she looked like him."

"Yeh . . . don't he wish." Jonquil touched Infinity's arm. "Hey . . . ya know, I'm glad yer back. That goes fer the kid too. Yer the best thing my eyes have settled down on in a long time. Infinity Cactus . . . jus' one more beautiful one-quarter Apache whoaman.'"

Infinity put her hand on Jonquil's face. A touch of acceptance. Everyone had finally settled down within the living room. Buddy was playing the flute; Nomad and Adah Ross were sitting next to the hearth; Virginia and Ranger were by the bed next to Syringa. Kid Yellowstone was jumping on Syringa's back, chomping into his grandmother for the first time; Cody and Golden had just discovered that they were siblings; and Coyote was singing a welcoming song to everybody in the room. Jonquil gave the bottle of water to Don Coyote and told him where it had come from.

Coyote said a prayer to the water and then he passed

the jar to Infinity. She put a drop of the lake water on her baby's forehead, took a drink, and passed it to Jonquil. The vessel made its journey around the gathering of thirteen friends, and was returned to Coyote. He drank the last swallow of water and then he placed the bottle in the middle of the circle. He took Infinity's hand on his left, and Syringa's hand on his right. Everyone joined hands until the circle was completed. Coyote looked at everyone and smiled into their eyes, singing to their own mysteries.

"Tomorrow," Coyote began, "we will have a celebration with all of our friends who have come for this important occasion. We will sing and dance, tell great stories, eat lots of good food, and drink wine as we toast to the new life of this beautiful baby girl. It will be a day that will be remembered for a long time. Now, I would like to have our own private celebration. A ceremony of silence. A time of meditation to say our prayers to the Great Spirit, to all of the animals, birds, and fish who live around and with us, and to ourselves and each other. And I would like for us to offer a prayer to a very important place on this earth. It is a place where our hearts and bodies have been able to live within our own dreams of being human. This place . . . this old dwelling that has become the vessel for our sacred journey. The Cowboy Buddha Hotel . . . where we have lived and where we will continue to live as long as we are able to tell the stories of the Cowboy Buddha, and listen to the songs from the flowing river."

Coyote removed the lid from the jar. "Infinity said to me that until this baby is old enough to choose her own name she would like her to be called Appaloosa Rose." The room echoed back the name as everyone in the circle smiled at Infinity and her child. "This name is the sound of the migration that has completed its circle and now lives within all of us. It is the breath of the horse that has carried us inside the migration of the Cowboy Buddha, and it is the flower that grows whenever we walk within beauty. It is the voice of the lake that has no end where the Cowboy Buddha rides between mountains. Appaloosa Rose. She is within all of us. She is our daughter." Coyote pointed to the empty jar. "Our prayers will be gathered and distilled inside this bottle that Jonquil carried from his pilgrimage to the lake. When it is time for this child to choose her own name this vessel will be given to her. These prayers will become the guides for her spirit and the voices for her dreams. But, for now . . . this daughter of our vision will be called Appaloosa Rose." Coyote bowed his head. The hands within the circle tightened, the prayers began to fill the room as everyone moved out alone into the silence.